Glimmer

By
Rayna Noire

Chapter One

England 1915

Asnap of a tree branch signaled Meara wasn't alone. Her breath caught and swelled her belly as she waited. A tiny thrill danced across her skin, leaving the hairs on her arms upright. Mother Superior strictly forbade the sisters from entering the woods. She called it *going into the world,* and they'd renounced the world when they entered the convent walls. The rule was for the sisters, not her, an orphaned child who by chance had been born within these same walls.

A speckled fawn stepped into the sun-dappled clearing, allowing Meara's breath to escape in a whoosh. A deer, a baby, which meant the mother wouldn't be far behind. The doe stepped out from the brush, giving the girl leaning against the tree a speculative glance before foraging the mosses and delicate wildflowers. If she stayed still, the skittish forest inhabitants would ignore or possibly accept her. It meant a great deal that they accepted her in an offhand way.

Birdsong accompanied the play and the chuckle of the nearby creek. The area around the convent walls drew her. Here, she felt at home. It certainly felt more right than walking in straight lines with the sisters chanting somber words to an unseen male deity who demanded constant homage in the form of prayers six times a day. Her hand covered her mouth, hoping she hadn't said such a thing aloud. Even thinking it was a sin, but speaking it would result in excommunication and horrible punishment.

Anytime she'd made the mistake of complaining about the endless monotony of convent life, Sister Phillip reminded her that her mother died a painful death in childbirth due to her sins. A few sisters whispered "bastard, changeling, dark whelp" within her hearing. Perhaps, they needed to point out she was different, as if she couldn't have figured that out herself.

Outside the walls, she'd slip off her shoes feeling the cool spongy moss under her feet. It tickled, but more importantly, it lived and touched her. The lack of physical touch within the cloistered walls intensified her yearning for something to touch her, even if the touch was passive as she trod upon it.

The tiniest shift of light motes moved through the air, forming and reforming, tumbling through the air. The grass beside her pushed down as if to something landing beside her. Although her eyes did not convey such information, she knew something was there, just as she knew her mother did not die from any great sin. Dozens of Hogstead village women died in childbirth as Sister Gabriella explained when she found Meara crying in the garden shed after another verbal attack on her parentage.

Warmness crept over her body, a comforting peace that some-how came from the unseen presence beside her. To speak of it would destroy it. Even Sister Gabriella, who was bolder than the other sisters—since she took an angel's name as opposed to a saint's—wouldn't understand.

The lengthening shadows indicated the vanishing afternoon. Soon the bells would toll for the three o'clock service, and her absence would be obvious. She stood, brushing the leaves off her plain brown tunic before giving a head bob to the area where she'd been sitting.

"Good day to you."

Even though no words rode the air, she felt a response, one of respect and care. Her measured footsteps allowed her to move past the wildlife without sending it fleeing. Once she cleared the woods, she grabbed the hem of her tunic with one hand and clutched her shoes in the other. Meara's loping sprint carried her across the open green space. Her most ardent prayers happened outside the walls, as she mentally bargained with God to allow her to slip back in unnoticed once again.

The high convent walls kept out intruders, according to Sister Bartholomew. Of course, it made her wonder why intruders would want in. A large locked gate was the only entrance and even then, the visitors came no deeper than the foyer where the Mother Superior greeted them. The temptations of the world did not overcome her, as it might a lesser sister.

A horseless carriage chugged, snorted, and belched noxious smoke as it trembled on the narrow convent road. The black vehicle had shiny sides, roof, and a glass shield at the front to provide protection from the rain.

Meara forgot about her tardiness as she stood in the shadow of the trees and watched the vehicle lumber closer. The convent only possessed a dog cart and a mule for transport. With the need of them being so seldom, Amos, the mule, grew more cantankerous forgetting his real purpose.

Even more curious than the vehicle were the two individuals riding in it. They both possessed beards, which would make them men. Not counting the various saint statues scattered across the grounds and inside the sanctuary, it was her first glimpse of an actual male. The beards were the only thing the saints and men had in common. As much as she wanted to see what happened next, she knew time was a priority.

Staying in the forest's shadow, she dashed for the bolt hole. The tiny opening came about from overzealous vines pulling the bricks apart in the gardens. A large blackberry bush hid the opening. Since her job included picking the berries, no one else had any reason to be near the hole. Would any of the sisters be tempted to squeeze through for a look at the world they left behind? They might not be as interested since they voluntarily left it.

A quick glance assured her no one observed her outside the walls as she wiggled through the tight break. The tunic caught on a brick and tore. *Oh no*, she only had one. The tear would be noticeable and would invite questions. A moment of indecision had her half in the hole and half out.

Sister Gabriella's voice called, "Do hurry. Mother Superior is asking for you."

Her left hand smoothed down her tunic and pulled it off the evil brick that had snagged it. What was more surprising? That Gabriella knew she snuck out on a regular basis or that Mother Superior requested her attendance? The fact Mother Superior asked for her could relate to her outside visits. An image of her gate into the natural world slamming shut played in her head.

Inside the cloistered walls, running was forbidden, along with talking in a loud voice. It didn't matter now since she had no desire to do either. A sense of foreboding pressed down on her shoulders. Her already sedate pace slowed more. A desire to escape back to the forest glen tugged at her. Back underneath the trees, she had felt safe and welcomed. Years of obedience kept her feet moving forward despite her desire to do otherwise.

The sisters kept her out of Christian charity. They fed, clothed, and even educated her, a luxury for many of her gender. All she ever read were the scriptures, but even those were limited to her for fear she might tear or soil the delicate pages. Sister Gabriella once spoke of a wonderful place called a *library*, full of books, but it existed outside of the walls. What would it be like to read into the late evening hours? The possibility distracted her a little from the upcoming meeting. No books would be allowed or the extravagant use of lamp fuel.

Once she'd picked up a shiny scrap of metal on her unsupervised walks outside. The scrap was smaller than her fist. When she held it up to her face, she could see one eye staring back at her and the bridge of her nose. It fascinated her since the sisters were not permitted to look at their own reflections. To do so would cause the sin of vanity. No mirrors existed anywhere. Meara had never seen her face, except for that one wide, unblinking eye.

The scrap metal would have caused trouble if found in her tiny cell of a room, but it had vanished mysteriously. She suspected Sister Gabriella. The woman gently guided her, more with actions than words. There were no very young nuns in the convent. Sister Gabriella was closer to her age than any other sister was, although she had no clue of the kind nun's age, only that her face was unlined and her eyes lively. Often, she felt the youngest sister was her only friend.

A large door with an arch at the top separated her from Mother Superior and whatever edict she would issue. Someone as low as she never received too much of the good Mother's time. When she did, it was never good. The last time she'd entered the hallowed room was because of whistling. Her poor efforts were to mimic the birds, even call them to her side. Someone heard her whistling while gardening and reported it. After doing a three-day indulgence that included crawling to the chapel, which made her knees bloody, she never whistled again inside the convent walls.

Mother Superior believed whistling was associated with the sins of vanity and pride. After all, it drew attention to oneself. Her eyes narrowed as she searched her memory for any recent whistling. None that she could recall.

Her raised fist hesitated before knocking the prescribed three knocks of medium force. The door swung open before she had mentally prepared herself for the ordeal. No matter what the infraction levied against her, she couldn't show any emotion. Any tears, pleadings, or remonstrations fell under the sins of pride and falsehood.

The tall robed figure of Mother Superior filled most of the doorway, but the sliver of a pant leg of a seated man drew her eyes more than the frowning matron did.

"Mary, you are late."

The name always grated, giving her a mental jar strong enough to bring her back to the current situation. Her gaze dropped to the floor. "Sorry, Mother. I came as soon as Sister Gabriella told me." She sucked in her bottom lip, wondering if Gabriella had been searching long. It was not her intention to transfer blame to the kind sister.

Mother Superior snorted her disbelief, but rather than say anything else, she stepped aside and gestured for her to enter.

Meara's shoe stuck to the stone floor, akin to stepping in spilt honey. Both men stood and turned curious gazes her way. Her eyes traveled over them both, memorizing their features and their strange clothes. Later, when she was alone in her cell, she'd reexamine it.

A flash of white teeth showed in one man's beard. A smile. She recognized it without being told, although smiles were rare inside the walls. It was a sign of frivolity, a lightheartedness that did not become a bride of Christ.

Even though the sisters accepted that their God took male form, they seldom spoke of the male gender at all. This other sex could roam free outside the walls without worrying about falling prey to the temptations of the world.

"Make haste, Mary." Mother Superior slapped her hands together, which bespoke her irritation.

Meara shook off her initial fear and strode into the room, stopping short past the door. The smiling man's expression changed as he sent a sharp look at the Mother Superior.

"You told me her name was Meara."

Her heart leapt. Outside of Sister Gabriella whispering her name when she asked for details about her birth, she'd never ever heard another person say it. Mentally, she called herself *Meara* in an effort not to lose that slender thread that connected her to her mother.

The woman swung around so fast her black veil fluttered from the motion. Even though she couldn't see her expression, Meara knew it would be stern enough to cause trembling in the most stalwart of the sisters. The man did not seem intimidated. *Strange.*

"Meara is a heathen name. Even though her mother chose to name her Meara, I chose the name of Mary to inspire the child who came from a sinful union."

A low growl emanated from the man's throat. The other man placed a hand on his shoulder while speaking loud enough for her to hear. "Careful, Simon, don't be doing something you might regret."

He shook off the man's hand before addressing Mother Superior. "Meara is my mother's name, a good Celtic name my sister chose to keep in the family. It means the sea. As for my sister, you slander her good name. She was married to one of your kinsmen, an English-man." He spat the last word as if it were poison and needed to be out of his mouth. "Meara, come closer." He gestured to a nearby chair.

She regarded it the same way she did the large cat she'd encoun-tered in the woods. It was an unknown and possibly dangerous creature. Once she reached the wooden chair, she slid into it since her legs had turned weak.

"Could you give us a few moments alone?" He directed the re-quest to Mother Superior.

"Certainly not. I have the girl's welfare to consider. Whatever you have to say can be said in front of me."

The man called Simon mumbled some unfamiliar words. They were enough to make the abbess gasp in consternation, which made them very powerful words indeed. She wished she knew them. The other man touched his companion. "Remember where we are. This isn't a public house."

"Sorry, Meara." He nodded at her and smiled again. The simple lifting of the lips caused his face to light up. Even his eyes sparkled. He studied her as if she were an unusual bug. "You have the look of my sister, Sorcha, when she was younger. Doesn't she, Angus?"

The other man gave her a contemplative look before replying,

"She does indeed."

"My mother's name is Sorcha. I never heard it before," Meara told him.

This somehow angered Simon, who threw another accusing glance at Mother Superior, who huffed, making no verbal reply.

He reached for her hand, clasping it in his large, masculine one. Warmth flowed between their hands along with a sense of connection she'd never felt before. "You are," she tried to shape the word she wanted, but it eluded her since all talk of families were forbidden. That was the past. "Family?"

Mother Superior moved faster than Meara had ever witnessed and pulled their hands apart. "No touching is permitted."

Her hand felt suddenly alone after the brief touch. Worse, she'd lost the connection, the only time she felt a sense of belonging, outside of the forest. Mother Superior spoke truly. Touching was never permitted except in dire circumstances, such as healing or catching a sister who might be falling. Even then, if the sister was only falling a little distance, helping could disrupt a divine lesson. Many a sister had tripped on the uneven stones and tumbled headfirst to the hard floor.

Simon's lips pulled down in a forbidding frown as he glanced back at the older woman. Meara watched with interest, not only because she'd never witnessed such a display of emotions, but she also never seen anyone go up against whatever pronouncement Mother Superior made. Inside the convent walls, she served as a direct extension of the patriarchal deity they bound themselves to, which meant this god had to be a stern, unforgiving figure who hated laughter and frivolity. The men, what did they have faith in?

Simon turned to face her, his former smile returning. "I can't believe I finally found you. Sorcha wrote me that I'd be an uncle years ago." He looked past Meara's shoulder as he took a long, unsteady breath.

Angus stood and dropped his hand on his friend's shoulder and squeezed. He nodded his head at Meara. "It's hard on your uncle. Travel is never that easy between countries, but now the war and the various navies crowding the sea made it a diabolical trip, fer sure. Simon never gave up on Sorcha. We came on the university's coin to join a team heading for Egypt."

"Egypt." She repeated the word, remembering it from the scriptures. A noise caused her to look back in the direction of Mother Superior, who'd managed to shuffle closer while Angus spoke.

Simon transferred his gaze from the wall to her. He threw a dark look at the hovering nun, daring her to say anything. "Forgive my behavior, it's just that…" He paused, gulping loudly. "I always assumed Sorcha lived. My sister, your mother, could be a stubborn one. She gave her love freely and strongly. On the other hand, no one could hold a grudge like her."

Angus leaned in to add, "Sorcha was known to be a right grudge holder of Galway County. People did not cross her."

"That, she was," Simon agreed. "My sister did everything with passion. I remember when she met your father, who was visiting his people nearby. She marched home all smiles and told me she intended to marry Fulmen."

"Fulmen." She said the name slowly, sounding it out. Even though she'd never heard her mother's name, having an actual father's name made her beginning more tangible. She wasn't a changeling, a gypsy's git, or any of the other unflattering terms whispered about her.

"Aye, I asked her what type of name was Fulmen."

Meara wondered too, although the only male names she knew belonged to the saints.

"Ah, Sorcha put both hands on her hips and proudly announced the name was Druidic."

A feminine gasp emphasized Mother Superior's location.

Simon continued with a sad smile. "She told me it meant lightning. He stole her heart just that fast. Sorcha, proud as the day is long, threw her flaming hair over her shoulder and declared she'd have no man but him. I should have realized she meant what she said."

"What happened?" The love story of her parents fascinated her, the first love she'd ever heard of due to the sisters never mentioning their past. As green as she was, she knew if a woman had a great love, she wouldn't become a sister, or if she did, her love must have perished.

"Da forbade the union."

Before he could continue, Mother Superior harrumphed her way into the conversation. "Well, he should. No good would come from hooking up with a heathen."

Simon threw her another ominous look that had her sliding back a few steps. "My da, your grandda, was a great one for the church, although he attended the services only on the high holidays. In his grief over my mother's death, he turned bitter and hard. The only thing that mattered to him was family. All he saw in your father was an Englishman who would steal his daughter away, one of the last living remnants of his beloved Colleen."

Meara knew the couple must have continued to see each other or she wouldn't be here. "Did they run away together?"

"I figure they must have. One day she was at home, the next day not. Over a year later, a letter came from Beacon, Wales. Sorcha told me how happy she was and that she was expecting a babe any day. My first impulse was to find a freighter heading that way, but I couldn't leave."

"Why?" The question popped out of her mouth before she fully thought it through. She'd worked hard to correct the habit. Especially since her saying what she thought was a sign of uncontrolled spirit. Her shoulders hunched for the expected lash she'd receive, but it didn't come, neither did the verbal reprimand.

"When Sorcha left, me da took to his bed. Some say it was his heart, which I know to be true. It was broken. My Da lingered on death's doorstep for many years. In the intervening time, I met my wife, Erin. She helped care for Da and even urged me to seek out Sorcha, which is what I did."

Meara squirmed in the hard chair wanting to ask what had taken him so long, but she'd already had one outburst. Instead, she asked with her eyes full of pleading, hoping for more details.

Angus answered instead. He leaned forward, resting his large hands on his knees. "This isn't Simon's first trip. The first one took place about six years after your Grandda died. He went down to the Brecon area, but mouths were tight, and none mentioned Sorcha by name."

Simon shook his head. "If only I had taken more interest in Fulmen. I didn't even know his last name. As extraordinary as the name sounds, there were more than a handful of Fulmens in the place, but none was Sorcha's Fulmen. I did offer to pay people for information. Even though they were Celts as much as I, they told me nothing. Colleen was expecting our own babe so I returned to Galway. The next trip was two years later with the same result. It was as if Sorcha and Fulmen vanished from the earth. I made up cards with my name, contact information, and passed them out. This year I received a letter for my efforts."

"What did it say?" Meara pressed her hands together in a prayer-like position against her heart, forgetting her vow to forgo any future outbursts.

"The sender refused to give his name on the grounds his own relatives took part in a dastardly act. Fuelman's cousin died without any children and left prime farmland to Fulmen. It was a big holding sought after by many. Along with it came the house and outbuildings, some of the best in the area. A few offered to buy the land from Fulmen, but offered an insultingly low bid. Fulmen intended to stay on the farm until Sorcha delivered, maybe indefinitely. The writer didn't know. All he knew was his da and uncle were worked up about it. The squatter wasn't welcome there. The writer claimed he was only a child at the time and overheard talk when they thought he was asleep."

As much as she wanted to hear about her parents, this tale was not going the way she wished. It didn't seem like her parents had a fair life the fleeting time they were together. Her mother had abandoned her family for love and apparently stepped into a desperate mess in England.

Simon stopped talking and glanced back at Angus, who cut his eyes in Meara's direction.

"Go on. I want to know," she urged, knowing they had reached a difficult point in the retelling.

Her uncle cleared his throat. "To put it plain, they meant only to scare Fulmen off the land, but he was determined to protect you and your mother. Your father's death may have been accidental, but the results were the same. Your mother fled the scene, apparently walking for days until she came across the convent where she had you."

The brutal ending didn't surprise her, but waves of sadness buffeted her. She'd hoped her mother had lived a happy life until the time she died. Unfortunately, that hadn't been the case. Instead, she'd had a slim escape after witnessing her husband struck down. A sigh escaped her. "Poor Sorcha. Poor Fulmen. What happened to the farm?"

Angus raised his eyebrows. "Now, that sounds like something a Cleary might ask." At Meara's surprised look, he explained. "You're a Cleary. It's the family name of both Sorcha and Simon. It means *clerk*, which suits since the Clearys always know the bottom line."

Simon's hand covered his face. He brought it down slowly and gazed at Meara with eyes that reminded her of the eye she had seen in the tiny reflective fragment she'd found.

"Aye, that's a good question. I expect those who cut down Fulmen now sit on the land."

A rush of outrage filled her, causing her to shake. What justice was there in her father's inheritance taken by the same greedy villagers who killed him and caused her mother's horrible run across the countryside? "That's wrong."

"I agree. My concern wasn't about land, but about my own blood, which you are. I came for you to take you back to your family. My son, Ronan, is a few years younger than you are. You have a cousin, Brigid, who may be your age or a few months older. You have a family waiting for you in Galway. I have work to do for the university, but I'll come for you when I'm done. It will be less than a month."

A home, a family, someone near her age. Her heart swelled with joy making Meara wonder if it could burst out of her chest. "I'll be ready." Truer words she'd never uttered.

Simon held up his hand, signaling the interview was over. She stood and looked at Mother Superior who made a slashing movement with her arm, which meant she should leave. Meara hurried to do so, knowing she'd already broken several rules with her unruly tongue. If she could escape while Simon planned her trip, perhaps she'd escape punishment.

She stood for a moment outside the door, listening for the sound of her uncle's voice.

"I'd like to see Sorcha's grave."

Her mother had a grave on the grounds? This was news to her. Looking both ways to be sure she wouldn't be seen, she rested her ear on the door to hear better.

Mother Superior's strident voice conjured up a mental picture of the angel barring Adam and Eve from paradise. She would have made an excellent avenging angel with righteous certainty filling each word. "Your sister was not buried on sacred ground."

"Why the hell not? She was as good a Christian as you are. I suspect better."

"Now, Simon, calm down. Don't go forgetting where you are at."

She recognized Angus's voice and the fact he was trying to placate her uncle. Obviously, she wasn't the only one in the family who had difficulty holding their words.

"Sir, remember we had no way of knowing the identity of a dirty, battered woman. She collapsed on the doorstep, like a stray mongrel ready to whelp."

"I thank you not to refer to my sister as a dog."

Meara wished she could see the tableau taking place on the other side of the door. It was as much emotion as she'd ever heard in the Mother Superior.

"I will speak plainly. We tended to your sister. Brought your niece into the world and cared for her these last sixteen years, for which you owe us. A hearty contribution to the convent would be in order. If we had known she was a Druidic git, we would not have raised her."

The indrawn breath had to be her uncle or possibly Angus, maybe both. The sisters would have let her die due to her father being a Druid. She didn't even know what a Druid was. Maybe Sister Gabriella did.

"I'll be back in two weeks or more. I expect my niece to be ready to leave. No doubt, you'll be anxious to get her off your hands."

The words signaled the end of the conversation, which sent her rushing down the hallway. There had to be something she could busy herself with to appear as if she hadn't been eavesdropping.

Chapter Two

SISTER THOMAS STEPPED into Meara's path from the side hallway. In her rush to get back to her cell, she hadn't anticipated anyone in the usually empty passage. Even though Meara checked her speed, she made solid contact with the rotund nun.

The nun kept her feet, although she grunted something under her breath. Meara didn't fare as well and tumbled backwards. Even though she hadn't heard Sister Thomas clearly, she was sure she used one of the same words her Uncle Simon had uttered earlier.

The idea interested her. "My pardon, Sister Thomas." She pushed to her feet and brushed the dust from her tunic.

"All is forgiven, little sister." A look of amusement flickered across Sister Thomas's face before she schooled it back into a somber expression.

The sisters came from outside the walls. Only she had been born in the convent. Sister Thomas was a recent addition. Sister Gabriella referred to her as a rich, devout widow, which explained her girth. The fodder at the nunnery included plain bread, cooked vegetables, and the occasional stew, which resulted in an involuntary weight loss among most of the postulants.

A forbidden thought popped into her mind. Any talk about the secular world or even a sister's past was against the rules. It was never a hardship for her since her entire past inside the convent walls was not only uninteresting, but was known. She had no secrets, except for her forays into the woods.

Those weren't even as clandestine as she previously thought. An image of Sister Gabriella standing by the berry bush pitching her voice into the hole proved at least one person knew. Even knowing about her activities, the kind sister never prevented her from visiting her natural sanctuary. Still, if she were going into the unknown in a few short weeks, shouldn't she have knowledge of it?

"Sister Thomas?" She glanced down the hall both ways as she spoke. No one. It was relatively safe unless Sister Thomas felt the need to report. A few of the older sisters had borne witness against Sister Thomas for humming a popular ballad, which meant she might not be so quick to tattle, unless she wanted to prove how she conformed to standards. Meara's lips tightened as she considered the consequences of asking about the world outside. At best, her punishment would last little more than two weeks.

"What is it, little sister?" The woman angled her head and waited.

The term *little sister* annoyed her since she hadn't taken the veil. Still, Sister Thomas was learning her way around and probably didn't know her name yet. Having a name was a step up from one of the other convents Sister Gabriella told her of that didn't allow names, forbidding them as a form of vanity.

Another furtive glance revealed no one headed their way. She took a step closer to the nun. "A relative has come to take me away. Before I leave, it would benefit me to know what waits outside the walls."

The woman's habit moved as she took a deep breath and exhaled. "Well, my girl, life outside the walls would be different for you than me."

The words didn't make sense. "Why would it be any different? It's the same world no matter who steps into it."

Sister Thomas snorted something that would have merited a report if the right ears were in listening range. "Oh no, you're wrong there. It's the reason I came here. A woman like me, old, past her prime, won't attract too many loving glances. Any I do will only be for my money."

"What about children?" Meara always assumed if her mother had lived that they would have had a happy life together. At least now she could add a father to the faded fantasy life.

"I would have stayed if my son had lived, especially if I had grandchildren to dote on. I left and took all the wealth my husband left me and bequeathed it to the Church. I did that deliberately to prevent my husband's shiftless brother, Birney, from grabbing it all. I knew once the church got their hands on it no lawyer stood a chance."

Untrustworthy brothers, greed, deceit. She made it sound like Cain and Abel. "What did you mean it would be different for me?"

"Ah." The woman inhaled deeply again before letting loose a noisy sigh. "You're young, pretty, and your innocence shows, which will attract the men, both young and old, good and bad. I hope you have some male relative to look out for you."

"I do," she answered somberly.

"Good. He won't let any oily sort court you." Sister Thomas wove her fingers together over her stomach and bobbed her head, as if agreeing with herself.

"What is court? Why would a man want to court me?" The word puzzled her. She'd only heard it used to refer to the place between the gardens and nunnery as a courtyard.

This time, Sister Thomas swiveled her head to check out the passageways before speaking. "I'd heard you were born here, but truly you know nothing. You've must have read in the scriptures that men take wives and have children."

"Yes, I know." It seemed so obvious it puzzled her as to why the woman would even explain it. "What does that have to do with anything?"

"Hmm." Sister Thomas hesitated and shuffled her feet. "I'm not the person to speak to you about this. You should have a female relative."

"You know I have none!" Her voice grew loud in her agitation. The last thing she needed was to attract attention to Sister Thomas, who didn't have the option of leaving. She lowered her voice to a whisper. "Tell me."

The woman worked her jaw back and forth before speaking. "There are several good things outside the convent. I forgot about this as I ran to the nunnery to shelter me from Birney's machinations. There are roses, delicious food, and laughter. The memory of them haunts me. Well, there used to be, a year or so ago. Right now, there's a war happening."

The word hit Meara comparable to the concentric circles a small pebble makes when thrown into a pond. Her basic education mentioned wars with the central theme that those representing God triumphed, but not without sacrifice and bloodshed on both sides. A chill ran up her arms. No one had ever mentioned a war, although conversational topics were limited. "A war?"

"Yes. The Germans have huge flying machines called *zeppelins* that drop bombs from the sky. If you ever see," she stopped speaking to make an egg shape in the air, "one of these, run the opposite way it came."

"Zeppelin." She repeated the word, thinking it sounded like a sky-born monster.

The sound of footsteps had them both looking to the left hallway. Without speaking, they gave each other a quick nod and hurried off on their separate ways. Meara slipped into her cell to repair her tunic with the needle and thread she'd hid under her simple corn-shuck mattress. This wasn't her first tear.

If anyone found the needle in her room, she'd be charged with theft. Sister Peter still had a small stub of a candle when she had asked for a new one. Someone told on her, and she'd been forced to wear a sign with *Glutton* written on it. The discipline made no sense to Meara. If the woman waited until her candle was gone, she'd be in the dark. Perhaps her thoughts meant she wouldn't make an appropriate sister gliding through the halls with folded hands and a serene expression.

Meara knew she belonged out among the trees, open sky, and the elusive natural spirits. It energized her even if there were a large object traversing the skies and promising death. It had to be better than creeping around in the dark halls where every turn promised another horrific artistic image of a tortured man on a cross that somehow her sins of today had put there several hundred years ago.

There had to be more than trying to earn her way into heaven, which from what she heard, wasn't that much different from the convent. If only she could taste some of the rich food Sister Thomas spoke about. Her uncle might take her unusual places, maybe far away from where the zeppelins cruised the skies. Even though it frightened her a little, a sense of anticipation was slowly building. Less than a month was not long, when she considered how many years she'd spent keeping her voice low and her mind reasonably controlled.

THE FULL MOON hung low in the sky spilling silvery light across the cobblestone courtyard. The time after vespers was supposed to be a time of personal meditation before lights out. Each nun retired to her cell and spent it in solitary contemplation. To Meara it felt like an endless torture of quiet kneeling. Supposedly, she should be considering the various sufferings of the saints, but the hard stone floor under her knees distracted her. The oppressive silence often felt like no one lived inside the walls, that somehow all the sisters had transformed into stone statues. It made her the only live individual. The possibility caused her breath to catch in her chest. A nightingale's clear song allowed the tightness to ease. Life existed outside the walls. While most of the creatures had gone to sleep, a few came out at night. Perhaps, she should, too.

The idea tantalized her while she wrestled with the temptation.

What would be out in the woods at night? This was England, which meant no tigers or lions stalked the forest. Sister Michael claimed the walls were to protect them. Bears and wolves were what she initially assumed the sisters needed protection from, but she'd found footprints of neither.

A red fox with a liquid gait and a glorious tail was the only four-legged predator she'd sighted in the woods. The mice would roam the woodland floors while the owls patrolled the skies looking for tasty rodents. Night calling birds and bullfrogs created an evening chorus. For once, she'd like to be in the middle of it.

Meara stood at the door listening. Was there any other sister about, breaking curfew? When it was time to sleep, one nun rang a bell signaling the change from contemplation to a sanctified slumber. Without a watch, it was hard to know how long she had. Her ear rested on her door, feeling the wood against her face. Her fingers spread across the worn lumber.

It was time. No one walked the halls. Without her shoes, she should be able to slip into the courtyard without a sound. Her dark tunic helped her to fade into the night. Her bright hair, confined in a tight braid, would be the only thing to draw attention.

The red flame color of her hair often drew comments that it was the color of hell-fire and she should hide it under a headdress. The new nuns wore a headdress that was more of a scarf, showing a few inches of hair at the forehead. Even the scarf frightened her. Once she wrapped one around her hair, she'd be the same as everyone else. Who she was when she was in the woods would no longer exist.

She found a surprising supporter in the Mother Superior who didn't seem anxious for her to take the veil. The woman sensed Meara didn't conform as well as she should. It shouldn't surprise anyone she'd sneak out.

The door hinges groaned as she pushed it open. Her heart skipped a beat as she waited. Surely, someone would call out and ask what she was about? *Nothing.* Then the bell rang, sending its shrill peal throughout the convent. All candles or lanterns would be out, which would make it perfect to move about unseen, especially since the bell ringer had to sleep close to the belfry, which was at the other end of the building.

The absence of light should have made it hard to navigate the passageways, but it didn't. She'd walked them endlessly ever since she had her own cell. Her bare feet moved across the smooth stones, recognizing the cracked one, signaling she was close to the turn. Another fifteen feet and she'd be in the courtyard. A footstep sounded, freezing her in place. She flattened herself against the wall and held her breath. Whoever it was carried no candle. Only a whisper of a breeze notated the passing.

Her heart raced as she continued to hold her breath, waiting for whomever it was to be far enough away before she dared to release it. The slight clunk of the exterior door closing signaled she could breathe once more. Her breath gusted out in a noisy rush. Still, she waited. Who else had decided to go out for the night? The better question was *why*.

After counting to one hundred in her head, Meara moved silently, her ears alert for any sounds out of the ordinary. She hadn't expected someone else to take advantage of a full moon and a summer night. Outside in the courtyard, the fountain splashed, and an owl hooted beyond the walls. A tiny skittering sound had her peering at her feet in time to see a tiny rodent scurry by with something in its mouth. The convent cat dropped down from the wall to follow.

Go little mouse, run. Meara found she had more in common with the mouse than she did with the cat. Her bare foot came down on a thorn of some sort. A deep inhale managed to hold in her yelp. Bending slightly, she rubbed her thumb over her foot until she found the offending item. A woman's laughter drifted over the wall. Meara stood in her half-crouched position, straining her ears.

Who knew the night was alive with so much activity? A man's

deep voice muttered something, and then came the sound of movement through the brush surrounding the walls. The feminine giggle sounded again. Puzzled, she picked the thorn out, proceeded toward the hole, and clambered through it, considering what she'd heard.

Who could it be? Couldn't be a sister. She was almost sure they'd forgotten how to laugh. Often, she wondered if she knew how. Would it be something she did once she ventured out into the world, especially with a war going on?

The soft moss gave away under her feet, indicating she was close to her favorite spot. The trees looked different in the darkness, almost malevolent. How could her own little piece of nature ever hurt her? Something brushed her cheek with a gossamer touch. Ahead, a light bounced and weaved through the branches. Other lights dipped and swayed through the air, dancing, joining the initial glimmer. Meara watched transfixed, wondering if what she saw was play or joy.

Her experience with *play* was limited to a caustic scolding when she had bumped an inkwell, scattering the dark liquid everywhere. The sister who served as her teacher had informed her, "To quit playing." If accidentally hitting an inkwell with her elbow was playing, she'd seriously doubted anyone wanted to do it, especially when it came with a scolding.

Her eyes focused on the lights as her feet followed them deeper into the woods. If only she could get close enough, then she could join in the dance. The urge propelled her forward despite a sensation of being watched that caused the hairs on her arm to stand up.

Meara glanced back the way she had come, realizing nothing looked familiar. How far had she wandered from the path? The rustle of movement and the snapping of nearby sticks sped up her heartbeat. A week ago, she'd panicked thinking someone had followed her, only to have a deer wander into the clearing, but this time two large shadows grew out of a nearby underbrush. *People.* She hadn't expected this. Could they see her? One gestured in her direction and said something in a guttural language she couldn't comprehend. The other answered in the same tongue. The time it took her to realize the men were after her, one had slipped behind her and grabbed her arm, pinning it painfully behind her back.

He spoke, as his companion reached out for her hair. *"Kriegsbeu-te"*

Meara twisted, knowing at an instinctual level she needed to get away from these strangers. The man holding her captive laughed, then muttered something before releasing her arm. She stumbled away recognizing an opportunity. A quick glance back showed the two of them being attacked by the bobbing lights. An occasional yelp assured her the attack was painful. They must be some type of glowing bees.

One hovered in front of her. *Follow me.* The musical voice sounded in her head. Besides the strangers behind her, there was no one else here. Certainly, no one with a voice as clear and bell-like that it reminded her of a raindrop or dew glistening on a flower. Somehow, this bobbing light placed the voice inside her own head. Her impulsive foray into the woods had landed her into a situation she didn't know how to handle. The shimmering light blinked, indicating a need to hurry.

Show me. She placed the thought in her head, hoping the light understood. It moved forward about a foot and then stopped. It was waiting for her. Meara followed, doing her best to ignore the sharp sticks under her feet and the occasional oozing mud between her toes. At least she hoped it was mud.

The tiny creature grew brighter, illuminating the path so the rocks and other pointed objects could be avoided. Her attention wavered between the mysterious creature and watching the ground. Every sound in the woods, even the familiar ones, froze her blood. It could be them, the strangers who'd grabbed her.

For a brief, terrifying moment, she felt the hard buttons of her captor's shirt press into her skin. Their meaningless words reminded her of a dog growling before it attacked. The bitter stink of sweat clung to them. Even now it coated her own skin. Had they left their mark on her or was it her own fear she smelled?

"Keep going, not much farther."

The voice sounded in her head. It couldn't be hers since it sounded calm and certain; two things she wasn't.

Exhaustion pulled at every limb, making her go slower and slower. Each step felt as if she were wading in the courtyard fountain, with the knee length water weighting every move. *Must follow the light.*

Each step forward became an individual battle with the ground exerting a siren call to rest and her muscles longing to answer it by lying down on the welcoming earth. No, you must not yet. Not safe.

The not safe comment gave her an extra boost of energy to enliven her lagging steps. Her body moved more as a matter of momentum than actual thought. Maybe the convent was right to build a wall to keep evil out.

A flash of light and a thundering boom sounded to her left. Meara threw herself on the ground certain the world was coming to an end as so was often foretold, which put her in a quandary. She wasn't ready for heaven and didn't like the alternative.

The light buzzed about her head and called out in a bell-like voice. "*Get up, now.*"

It must be the voice of an angel, so clear and pure.

A light laughter floated on the breeze, out of place in the frightful night. Tiny pinpricks of light resembled low hanging stars, glistening in the darkness. Their appearance, rather than alarming, reassured her.

Get up, Meara, we promised Fulmen we'd look after his own. It's been hard with you walled away.

The light knew her father. Impossible, since she had only heard his name today. She pushed to her knees and glanced to her left where bright flames lit up the landscape. A fire was always a threat, especially in the forest with dried underbrush and leaves.

The lights swarmed around her, peppering her body with soft touches. Strength flowed into her as panic faded. These small guardians were here as a legacy from her father. She stood, blinked twice, accepting that otherworldly creatures were serving as her own private sentinels.

The hiss and growl of hungry fire moved toward her left flank, worrying her, but at the same time, a serenity settled around her like a cloak. It had to be a borrowed cloak, because she'd never felt this way before. Her shoulders went back and chin up. She was the daughter of Sorcha and Fulmen, which meant something. No longer was she a child without a history or family. Her father must have had been extraordinary to be able to communicate with these light beings.

The fire no longer worried her with the certainty it would not touch her appearing in her mind, along with the knowledge she could never return to her old way of life. Her deliberate decision to answer the call of the night had sealed her fate. Did the nun who slipped out before her have her life irrevocably changed, too?

A break in the woods appeared as the first rays of dawn touched the green circle. A few wildflowers decorated the area. *"You're safe now. Rest."*

Meara collapsed on the cool grass, intending only to rest, but not sleep. Her eyes closed as her breath slowed, sending her into a deep slumber where a vision came to her.

A bearded man stood staring at her. His cobalt blue eyes twinkled as his teeth flashed white in his beard with a smile.

"My Dear Meara, it does my heart good to gaze on you finally."

Even in her lucid dreaming state, she knew she was seeing her father. Her heart recognized him and jumped at the warmth of his voice.

"This is not the way I wanted to greet you. Still, I see the evilness of the human heart still roams the land unchecked. Your mother and I

wanted to share with you the wonders of nature, the generous spirits of the earth that would guide you on your way. Modern people have forgotten everything natural has energy and a spirit."

The man nodded at her as if he expected a response.

"I believe, Father." She liked the way the word father sounded in her mouth. It felt right.

"As well you should since the faeries saved you this very night. On the whole, they've withdrawn from human contact."

Faeries? She hadn't ever heard the word before. "What are faeries?"

"It saddens my heart that my own child would ask such a question. It all depends on who you talk to. In Ireland, some believe them to be the original inhabitants of the isle. They are a gentle, nature-loving race. They went to the woods and the earth to live in peace.

"As a Druid, I honor every living creature, plant, and animal. Many believe the faeries inhabit these things. I'm not certain. I do know the faeries existed before people and will outlive them, too. If you honor nature and its inhabitants, then you honor the faeries."

Had she honored nature? She always enjoyed her time in the woods. She had no desire to chase or hunt the woodland creatures. Back at the convent, she helped with the garden and the berry picking, but was that enough?

"It's a start." Her father nodded his head. *"You'll learn how to do more as you go. Right now, you're so much more attuned to the natural world than any of the sisters in the convent. As for them, do not worry. They're victims of men's inherent greed for power and land."*

Something balled up in her throat, making it hard to ask, but she had to. "What do you mean?"

"Ah, it pains me to tell you that almost all you knew were wiped out by an errant bomb. Even now a fire rages through the convent, burning everything in its path."

"Sister Gabriella?" *The thought of the kind sister dead upset her more than any of the others. While she regretted their loss, they had never tried to form any relationships with her. The idea of friendship might indicate a reliance on others as opposed to a deity.*

"Her desire to see an old love saved her. Snuck out even before you did."

"Thank God," she murmured to herself.

"I, too, am glad she is safe. You might be better off thanking Eros or Venus since love pulled her away from the convent."

"Why did I leave?" It was a puzzle to herself, since she had never left at night before.

"That's easy. I called you. On this side, I can see things that have happened, are happening, and will happen. I knew the convent wasn't safe. Even though Simon thinks he's suddenly found you, I was the one guiding the actions that led him to you.

"Unfortunately, the man never seems to rush, even though I warned him about the need to retrieve you via a dream like this. He felt a few weeks was enough time. No wonder Sorcha was so impatient with her brother."

Her father existed in another dimension watching over her and protecting her. The thought comforted her. *"Will you be able to talk to me from now on? Teach me things I need to know."*

A somber expression smoothed out the man's ready smile. *"That would be my fondest dream. The veil between the worlds is thick. Only at certain times does it become thin enough for communication. At Samhain..."* He hesitated, maybe seeing her uncomprehending expression. *"That would be the day before All Saints Day."*

Oh, that she remembered. It was one of the few times the deceased sisters' names were ever mentioned.

"Often at midnight, a transition time. Sometimes in the liminal period right before dawn or full night. My will is only so strong. I've had much help to reach you. Even now, I have more work to do to guarantee your safety."

His image shimmered and became semi-transparent, allowing the trees to shine behind him. Meara blinked, trying to hold the man in focus. Her father, dressed in a faded work shirt and pants held up one hand, and then vanished.

A bird trilled nearby. The sound woke her.

The early sun filtered through the trees, touching her with its warmth. A hare watched her while its whiskers quivered. Meara pushed up into a semi-reclining position and regarded the smooth grassy expanse ringed with wildflowers.

How did she get here? Had she sleepwalked? What was real and what was just a dream? Meara pushed to her knees and stood. Using her hand as a sun shield for her eyes, she slowly turned in a circle. To the south, a large plume of dark smoke rose in the sky indicating a fierce burning fire.

No, it wasn't a dream.

Chapter Three

T HE EVERYTHING SHE knew felt strangely distant as if she'd entered another plane or dimension and was watching from the outside. Her fast flight the night before seemed weeks ago. Surely, not everything was gone. Her hand pressed against her chest as she considered the chickens they kept for eggs, the milk cow, even the old mule. Who'd care for them?

No doubts lingered about the sisters, despite a long dead man offering the information via a dream. She had encountered the foreigners in the woods. The memory made her inhale sharply. Holding her breath, she gazed carefully around her. The sunlit circle remained peaceful without any dangerous figures lurking on the perimeter. No one interrupted the songbirds celebrating the dawn.

The helpful lights, that her father called faeries, were gone. Although a person shouldn't be able to see a light in the daytime, she still knew they were gone. When they were close by, there was an awareness, a tingling of sorts. When she'd sat under her favorite tree in the woods, she often felt as if something brushed her cheek.

The aroma of roses floated on the air even when there were no roses nearby. There had been a solitary rose bush in the convent courtyard. A villager had brought it as homage to Mother Mary, but eventually it had died. Still, she remembered the exquisite scent of the pink buds. Although she knew no roses grew in the forest, she accepted the aroma as a memory.

Without overthinking it, she stood and gazed in the direction of the woods. The smoke signaled where the convent rested or what was left of it. Her abused feet throbbed with every step. At least the daylight provided illumination to guide her. She stepped on every moss covered rock or smooth grass expanse, but there was not enough to insure a pain free path.

The overpowering odor of burnt wood, along with something less familiar, assaulted her nose as she drew closer to her former home. The combined clamor of shouting along with the chickens frantic clucking hurried her steps. Someone survived.

Whoever it was, she'd help. Nurse them back to health, which would make them grateful. Instead of being some oddity that lived on the charity of the sisters, she'd matter. The sudden need to help any of the suffering sisters had her darting through the wood with the refrain *I'll matter* echoed in her head. In her haste, she failed to notice the large branch across the path and ended up tripping and landing with a hard jolt. The fall knocked the breath out of her.

A pair of small, worn work boots appeared at the edge of her vision. "Take my hand."

Meara's eyes traveled up to the outstretched hand attached to a sturdy woman with kind eyes encased inside a time-blessed face. She took the hand, trying to rise on her own as much as possible. The elderly woman would probably topple if she pulled too hard. Since she had no experience with the outside world, she chose to address the woman as she would a sister.

"My thanks. I need to hurry to the convent and help."

The woman held onto her hand and didn't let go as she expected. Meara gave a small tug, but the woman held on with a steely determination.

"You'd do well not to go. Right now, the villagers are busy *helping* themselves."

The woman emphasized the word *helping*, as if it should be meaningful to her. If they were helping, then there'd be no reason for any gratitude directed her way. Meara gave another strong tug, but the woman miraculously held on.

"Be still," the woman hissed and pointed to a tumbled down section of the convent wall. A young woman attired in a dress and kerchief carried a protesting rooster under her arm as she stepped over what was left of the wall. Two young children followed her, a boy clutching a hen and the girl cradling the basket used for gathering eggs.

"They're stealing the chickens!" She couldn't believe it. People would casually stroll in and take what wasn't theirs. If she yelled, they'd realize their sin and drop the chickens. "Stop!"

The woman clamped a dirty hand over Meara's mouth. "Hush. You'll end up getting yourself killed."

Killed. Why? Nothing made sense anymore, not egg-shaped balloons raining death from the sky, her uncle's promise to take her away, strangers in the woods, faeries guiding her through the night, and her deceased father talking to her in a dream. She wanted it all to disappear and have things go back to the way they used to be.

"Doesn't matter what you want." The woman hissed the words near her ear as Meara watched a man hide two full bags behind the berry bush.

It all seemed surreal, rather like when Sister Thomas told her about the zeppelins. Poor Sister Thomas. Maybe this was what she meant, that the world would be different for her.

The hand pressed harder against Meara's mouth. "Will you be quiet if I take my hand away?"

She nodded, since she couldn't talk. The grip on her mouth loosened, and then the hand fell away. It would be the last time she'd underestimate the strength of a little old lady.

The woman shook her head. "Not as old as you might think. I prefer to think of myself as weathered. Name's Eleanor."

"Meara." She glanced at the woman, then back at the villagers looting her former home. "Why?"

"It's not right. I agree. Although, it's wartime and people tend to go a little bit crazy due to fear. Most had little to start with, but even staples such as bread, sugar, and meat go to the troops. Whatever is left is very dear. Whatever a person can raise, hunt, or scavenge is free."

Eleanor angled her head to the convent. "Many were against a Catholic Nunnery here. You'd think they were Puritans with the teeth gnashing that went on and talk about the excesses of the Catholic Church insisting on gold candlesticks when plain cast iron would suffice. Your Mother Superior didn't make any friends with her arrogant ways, either."

Mother Superior would answer that her purpose wasn't to make friends, but to do God's will. Of course, it was never clear on how a bunch of women living together and attending endless services was beneficial to anyone. On an instinctive level, Meara had known better than to ask.

"They're stealing. That's a sin."

Eleanor sighed. "I can see how you might see it that way. The woman who took the chickens. Her man is away in the war. Even though the government is supposed to send her his pay, she hasn't seen any. Don't be too hard on Clarice. She's just trying to feed her children. In her eyes, if there are no sisters, then there's no need for the chickens to go to waste."

The man with the bags reappeared with two more bags that he stuffed behind the bush with the other two.

Eleanor continued explaining. "Clarice had to hurry before Gus took everything. The man is probably getting all the altar finery."

While the Holy Rosary was not a rich convent, they did have elaborate altar vessels and candlesticks. "That's sacrilegious. The man could burn in hell."

"Oh, it's possible," Eleanor concurred. "I doubt it worries Gus, him not being a Catholic and all."

Not being a Catholic? The idea stumped her. Obviously, her father wasn't a Catholic. Mother Superior would have left her out in the cold to starve if she had known. She said so clearly enough. "Is not being Catholic a terrible thing?"

Eleanor gave her a measuring look. "You're a strange one. Even though I'd take you to be close to marrying age, you appear unaware of basic human nature. As for not being Catholic being bad, well it depends on whom you talk to. It matters not to me. Now the villagers," she motioned to the people still scavenging the convent for whatever they could get, "most of them are Anglicans, which makes their actions more rational."

True, she knew nothing of the outside world, but she couldn't see how their behavior made sense. "Why? How can ignoring the dead, perhaps those dying, be rational?"

"Aye, I agree." She arched her eyebrows before continuing. "Some woman came out of the woods years ago and dropped her child here. Heard she died in childbirth. Was that your mother?"

It never occurred to her that those outside the wall knew of her existence. Although the image of her mother stumbling out of the woods, giving birth, and then dying wasn't any more flattering that Mother Superior's description of her inauspicious beginnings. The label "some woman" diminished her unknown parent.

"Her name was Sorcha." She wanted to dignify her mother with a name at least.

"Sorcha. Sounds Irish to me."

Meara kept silent. The villagers probably felt the same way about the Irish as they did about the nuns. The image of the sisters lying stiff in their narrow beds caused an abrupt shudder.

"You come home with me. We'll find something for you to wear. You can be my cousin who has come to help me. We could say you fled the city due to the war." Eleanor pointed to another path leading away from the convent.

Even though she had no love for her drab tunic, she didn't understand the need to change. "I'll admit to it being dirty from my run through the woods, but why change clothes? I could wash mine."

Eleanor walked for a few steps, looked back over her shoulder, then gestured for her to hurry. A finger to pursed lips meant now was not the time for explanations. The path turned and twisted back into the woods where the shadows enveloped the two of them. This unknown stretch of woods could harbor wolves, bears, and other fanged creatures looking for soft flesh to feast on. She shuddered at the prospect. Hadn't the night brought enough terrors?

Eleanor stopped, glanced back at her, and raised an eyebrow. "Bears and wolves are extinct in England. People killed them all." After delivering the pronouncement, the woman kept walking, setting a rapid pace.

The ability to answer her questions before she even uttered them unnerved Meara. Yet, she never questioned the validity of Eleanor's statements because they felt right. Meara had to half-jog to keep up. People obviously did not confine their murderous ways to one another, but wiped out wildlife, too. Was she truly a part of the treacherous race that killed to suit its own purposes?

The stories her uncle related about her father described a romantic figure who wooed her mother. Of course, those who wanted his land murdered him. This outside world was a place where people killed or were killed, not the wonderful world that Sister Thomas described.

A small cottage with a thatched roof came into view. A raw timber fence enclosed the cottage and the small kitchen garden behind it.

"Home sweet home." Eleanor gestured to the neat little house. "I'll make you a cup of tea, and then we'll see what I can fix up to suit you."

The offer of tea surprised Meara. Only Mother Superior and a few elder nuns merited the luxury. She remembered the tea service in Mother Superior's office, which must have meant guests received tea.

Eleanor scooped up an oversized tabby cat waiting at the door. The woman cuddled the cat making nonsensical noises, then angled her head and swung it in the direction of the open door. "Come in." She leaned over to place the cat back on the ground. "Oscar's mousing days are far behind him. He relies on me to provide his dinner."

At the convent, they'd turn out a cat who no longer could mouse. She'd seen it happen more than once.

Inside the cottage, a huge stone fireplace took up a quarter of the wall. Herbs dried, hanging upside down from the wide ceiling beams. A bouquet of wildflower blossoms graced the plain wood table. Pictures decorated the mantle.

The photos served as a lure drawing her to the mantle, where black and white images of people with their arms wrapped around one another, smiling or laughing rested. It was easy to see they enjoyed being together. Meara picked up one with a tall boy, large dog, and a young girl who resembled Eleanor. "Is the girl you?"

"Goodness, no. It's my daughter Lucille. The photo was taken a good twelve years ago. My husband's people brought in a photographer for the reunion. He took several photographs at a great expense. I thought it was a waste of money at the time. Little did I know I'd lose my family to the cholera epidemic. At least, I have the photos."

Meara gently replaced the precious memento on the mantle. "The boy was your son?"

"Thomas," Eleanor answered as she filled the kettle. "The dog was Rex. The poor animal was inconsolable after Thomas died. So was I, which is why I moved here to start over away from all I'd known."

Tough story, probably tougher than hers. It was hard to miss parents she never knew. The lack of any family relationship bothered her more. Every sister had a family, a history, even if she never spoke of it. Interactions from the outside took the form of an occasional letter or a childhood memory.

Technically, relationships were unacceptable within the convent. Mother Superior believed it split a person's focus from her true mission. It didn't stop covert relationships from developing, though. She'd seen the signs from certain sisters always walking together to services, from shared looks, an occasional head nod, or prolonged conversation.

Eleanor lit a match to the wood already stacked in the potbelly stove and set the kettle on to boil. She kept her back to Meara, making her wonder if she were crying. While strong emotion was discouraged among the sisters, Meara's eyes filled, close to brimming over. Silent tears for the right reason were permissible. They included tears resulting from an epiphany of humanity's truly depraved state or a miraculous sighting of Mother Mary or any of the other saints. Meara suspected that the glassy-eyed look she spotted occasionally among the other sisters might not be the result of a transcendent experience.

"All you sure all the sisters are gone?"

Sister Andrew taught her to read. Sister James seldom spoke, but often worked companionably beside her in the garden. They couldn't all be gone.

Eleanor looked up from the tea tray she was preparing. "We have a volunteer fire unit that showed up first. It's only five men, but their wives also came to nurse if needed. They weren't needed, not really."

The woman's reply hinted at the worst, but managed to say nothing at the same time. The strangeness of the night, exhaustion, and frustration crowded into her, making her voice sound shrill in her own ears. "Are any alive?"

"Not now." Eleanor placed round flat cakes on a small saucer, not looking up from her task.

Talk about being ambiguous. The statement hinted that some might have lived during the time she slept in the woods. "Who?"

"Sister Thaddaeus." Eleanor glanced back at her before turning to attend the steaming kettle.

The older nun had never been one of her favorite people, especially since she had always been fond of predicting horrible scenarios, including rivers turning to blood and eternal darkness. The information delivered in her hoarse, croaking voice made it even more ominous. Sister Gabriella hinted that the woman could have lost her wits, but strangely, Mother Superior treated the woman with respect as if she did have a gift of prophecy.

If she had a gift, why hadn't she seen the destruction of the convent? Still, the thought of the elderly woman gasping out her last breath in such frightening conditions made her cringe. "Did she say anything before she died?"

Eleanor poured the steaming water into each cup before answering. "She said enough, which is why I showed up to find you." The tray made a thud as her hostess settled it on the table and motioned for Meara to join her.

Whatever Sister Thaddaeus's final words had been, resulted in Eleanor seeking her out. Her walk slowed as she pondered the significance. The steaming cup and plate of cinnamon laced goodies reminded her she hadn't eaten since the night before. Her stomach rumbled on cue.

Eleanor who had been seated, jumped up, turning back to the stove. "I should get you some real food, instead of biscuits. Fry you an egg."

"No, this is wonderful. I've never had tea and…" she hesitated before repeating the unfamiliar word, "…biscuits. It's fine."

"Not have biscuits! That would be a *real* sin." Eleanor's overloud tone merited a judgmental glare from the cat before he resettled back down to sleep.

"No, never." Meara agreed, staring at the plate waiting for grace and permission to eat.

Eleanor slid into her chair and reached for a biscuit. "Go ahead, girl. Eat up. My biscuits are good. I use woodruff since sugar is so dear with the war on."

No longer able to withstand the temptation, she reached for one.

The confection felt light in her hand. As she drew it up to her nose, she inhaled. "Sister Thaddaeus used to sprinkle woodruff around the convent, declaring it kept out witches. Mother Superior allowed it because it did eliminate insects."

The memory made her wonder about the sister's last words. She bit into the cookie without the benefit of grace, wondering if it would turn into ash. Sister Andrew explained when she asked why they prayed that it was to sanctify food, and without the prayers, it would be ash in their mouths.

The sweet treat melted in her mouth, tantalizing her taste buds with a myriad of flavors. Some she could identify, but others she couldn't. The butter, eggs, and flour she recognized. It was gone before she knew it.

"Eat more." Eleanor nudged the plate closer to her.

Meara didn't need encouragement. She gobbled down three more biscuits, not even stopping to speak. This must be what Sister Thomas meant by rich food. Sadness returned at the thought of the helpful woman left to die in the fire. Her shoulders drooped as her jaws stopped chewing. *Poor Sister Thomas.*

"Wouldn't worry about that one." Her hostess reached for her own cookie before speaking again. "More than a few women took the fire as an opportunity to escape an avocation that didn't suit. Didn't mention it before as a way of protecting their privacy. They have enough determination to start new lives under different names."

The thought of Gabriella and Sister Thomas starting new lives outside the convent walls eased her sorrow some. The horror of the other women dying in the fire remained. Ironically, the heat and hungry flames they hoped to avoid ended up as their death.

Eleanor reached for the pot and poured herself more tea. "Most died in their sleep from smoke inhalation, never waking."

"I'm glad they didn't suffer."

"At least not in death, as they did in life." The woman gave a sage nod as she lifted the cup to her lips.

Another cryptic statement just like the one she made about the doom predicting nun. "What did Sister Thaddaeus say before she died?"

"Ah yes, that." Eleanor put down her cup and rubbed the bridge of her nose. "Wanted you to get some food inside of you before mentioning the toxin she spewed with her last dying breath. She claimed the fire was the wrath of God punishing them for taking in the Druid whelp."

Mother Superior was looser lipped than she would have thought. "If that were the case, why didn't the convent burn down years ago?"

"People want to fix blame. Somehow, it gives them a feeling of control, especially if they aren't fixing the blame to themselves."

Blame, she'd enough of that to last her lifetime. The last thing she wanted was the nuns' deaths on her head. "I can see why you waited to tell me. Will the villagers believe it?"

"You'd think they wouldn't. Hard to say with emotions running high. Could be just the thing to paint a target on your back. That's why I suggested you pose as my cousin. Drink your tea. It will make you feel better."

The warm tea slid across her tongue, bringing with it momentary comfort. True, she had wanted to escape the confines of the convent, but not like this. "My Uncle Simon is coming back for me in a couple weeks."

Eleanor picked up a cookie and held it aloft. "I guess we'll have to wait and see."

Chapter Four

MEARA PULLED THE print dress over her head. It sagged on her despite Eleanor's quick tailoring. The pink flowers strewn across the cotton fabric intrigued her. "I've not seen flowers on any clothes before."

Eleanor answered around the straight pins in her mouth. "It's a relatively new thing. Before, all the designs had to be sewn or woven into the fabric, which made it heavy. This dress was my sister-in-law's. It came from France and was quite the rage.

The lightweight fabric fluttered from her fingers to rest against her legs. It was a change from the heavy durable tunic. She started to ask why the sister-in-law didn't want the attractive garment anymore, but she stopped herself. With all the death in Eleanor's family, there was a good chance the sister-in-law numbered among the dead. No need to pry. If she did, she'd realize she was wearing a dead woman's clothes. Not something she wanted to taint the gossamer feel of the material against her skin.

"I like the dress." Meara twirled, causing the dress to bell out and flutter against her ankles.

Eleanor pulled the pins out of her mouth and placed them on the table. "Much better than that drab garment you wanted to wash." The skin around her eyes crinkled as she circled, inspecting her handiwork.

Realizing she was the object of inspection, Meara stopped swishing the full skirt and stood still. What did the woman see? Outside of glimpsing a wide eye in a shiny shard, she'd never seen herself.

Any comments on her appearance, such as dirt on her nose, or a dab of gravy on her chin, came from the other sisters.

"Hmm," Eleanor murmured to herself. "It's big on you. Not too surprised since you're a skinny stick of a girl. They must not have fed you much at the nunnery."

She ate, every day, every meal. Nothing was ever as tasty as the biscuits Eleanor served her though. "I ate, but the food was simple fare and not a great deal of it. None of us wanted to commit the sin of gluttony."

The woman grumbled something too low for comprehension. "You don't have to take me in. I know it's a hardship and all."

Eleanor had her open hand resting against her furrowed brow. Her hand dropped; she shook her head and shot Meara a confused look. "Now that I made the effort to find you, why would I turn you out?"

Her shoulders went up in a shrug. Plain speaking was not something she was accustomed to. What type of answer would be best? Unfortunately, since the topic had never occurred before she had none to choose from. Instead, her eyes traveled over the needlepoint pillows on the two overstuffed chairs angled toward the fire. A series of pegs along one wall held various garments. Blue, green, even clear bottles crowded shelves. On the far wall sat a framed oval that reflected the rest of the room. Forgetting the original question, she pointed to the oval.

"Is that a mirror?"

A short nod preceded Eleanor's verbal confirmation. "It is. Have you never seen one?"

Her feet moved as if on their own volition, anxious to see the mysterious object. "Oh no, a mirror would encourage the sin of vanity."

Eleanor's snort reminded her of Sylvester the pig. The hog had provided them with sustenance through the cold months one winter in the form of stews, soups, and the occasional *rasher* or *streaky* with their midday meal. She had found it hard to eat anything associated with her porcine friend. Not to eat would equal the sin of waste and ingratitude. In the end, she forced herself to swallow it while mentally thanking the pig for his shared bounty even though he had no choice in the matter.

"Go take a gander at yourself." Her hostess threw open window shutters, allowing sunlight to flood the dark corner. "Most of the sisters would have had no fears of committing the sin of vanity even if a mirror had existed in the place."

Though the desire was strong to look, her feet slowed. What if she was hideous? Gabriella once told her when she taught her to plait her hair that many would envy its bright color. Still, other sisters whispered it was a sign of her mother's sin. Nuns had to give up their hair as they pledged themselves to the religious lifestyle.

Even Sister Thomas had her head shaved when she entered the convent. The act symbolized putting aside what the world considered important. Her hair must have called controversy simply because she had some. Although she couldn't be sure if the other nuns had hair since no one was ever out of habit.

Eleanor, sensing her hesitation, came up behind her and gently pushed. "Go ahead. You've nothing to fear. Just a little dirt from your stay in the woods."

It was an important thing, to see her face in its entirety. Her feet, legs, hands, and body she could view as she dressed for the day. Her face would be somehow more personal, more hers. Uncle Simon remarked that she looked very much like her mother. The possibility of seeing her mother's image compelled her forward.

Her fingers reached out to touch the cold smooth surface as she stared at the pale stranger with the flaming red hair. Tendrils sprung free like spring flowers breaking through the frosty ground. Her dirt encrusted fingers brushed the hair from her face. Freckles danced across the bridge of her nose while large green eyes stared back at her.

"So, what do you think?" Eleanor's visage joined hers in the mirror.

The first time of viewing her own face was rather overwhelming. It was like meeting a stranger. Her lips parted on an exhale, exposing the strong teeth which she took for granted. "I'm not sure. My uncle said I look like my mother."

Her eyes strayed to Eleanor's pleasant, but wrinkled, countenance. Her finger drifted across her forehead and down her cheeks. "Why is my skin so smooth?"

The woman's husky laugh betrayed her amusement. "You're young. Haven't you ever met anyone who was young?"

It was hard to know what was young and what wasn't. She'd heard another sister explaining Gabriella's refusal to take a saint's name was the result of her youth. It wasn't enough that she took an angel's name. She went the extra step and feminized it. "Sister Gabriella, but even her skin wasn't as smooth as mine."

"Ah, it's hard for me to imagine a child growing up with no other children to play with." Eleanor's smile sagged a little as she pawed through a sewing basket.

Meara didn't want her rescuer to think badly of her. She stared into her own green eyes, wondering if the sensation would be similar if her mother had lived. "Oh, I never played."

"Such a shame. I imagine you had no contact with the villagers, either."

"No, I didn't. Mother Superior handled all outside matters. After all, she was strong enough to resist temptation while some of the other sisters may have been tempted."

"Ha. Little more than propaganda, if you ask me." Before she could inquire what the word meant, Eleanor wrinkled her nose. "It's not right. Not natural."

Her lips tried to pronounce the unknown word. It began with a *P*, something about a *prop*. Maybe it had something to do with proper. Everything inside the walls had been the same every day. No new experiences or words until the arrival of Sister Thomas and her Uncle Simon. Now everything rushed at her at once, with the helpful lights and voices guiding her through the woods. Strangers grabbing her and speaking in an unknown language. All the sensations coming at once overwhelmed her.

Meara caught the word natural. That one she knew. A sense of being on firm ground came with the certainty. Often the sisters had her repeat her catechism, which included the word *natural.* She assumed it meant being born in sin.

Her shoulders went back as she turned to face Eleanor, ready to quote what she'd memorized in a strong clear voice. When she recited or sang was one of the few times she felt approval. "Man's natural nature is a sinful, depraved one, which is why we must suffer."

Instead of acting pleased with her statement, Eleanor clucked her tongue. "Goodness, what a load of drivel." She motioned for Meara to come closer.

"What's drivel?" The words were out before Meara could even think twice. Asking questions was impertinent. Sister Thaddaeus often reminded her if God wanted her to know something, then she eventually would. Usually, she received a long stare that served to remind her not to ask. On occasions when no one else was around, Sister Gabriella and Sister Thomas did answer her.

One eyebrow went up as Eleanor shook her head. "Never heard that word, eh? It means to talk foolishly. When someone speaks drivel, the words have no value."

Her eyes enlarged as she stared at the woman who had rescued her. Could she be the devil? She'd been warned that he took many different forms.

"Goodness, you're looking at me as if I just sprouted horns." Eleanor rubbed her hand across her face. "Let me see if I can explain better." She inhaled, and then paused. "I know you were taught to memorize lines of religious doctrine because that's what you do in a convent. You've accepted all this without experiencing life on your own. People are not inherently bad."

This went against everything she'd been taught. "What about the man we saw stealing from the convent?"

"Ah, yes, Gus. He's bad, but he made a choice to be bad. Heard talk in the village that he was a sweet child at one time."

The idea that people could be *good* was as foreign to her as the concept of *play*. "What about the people in the war? They're trying to kill each other." Even though everything she thought she knew was shifting, she knew the war had to be bad.

"You got me there." She pulled out a table chair and sat. "It's not the men who fight in the war, but those who start it. The leaders decide out of greed to invade other countries. The soldiers have no choice but to follow orders, rather like you with Mother Superior. You always did what she told you to do."

The words conjured up the stern-faced woman who might have staged everything as a test. The woman was fond of trying the sisters' faith. Once she left a sweet in the dining hall to see who might take it. Sister Andrew spent the night throwing up. Sister Gabriella whispered that bloodroot tainted the treat. The bitter herb caused vomiting. Her eyes searched the corners of the cottage for any sign of Mother Superior. If it were a test, surely she'd failed with her earlier gluttony.

"Meara, let's pin up your dress and transform you into my young cousin. Make the dress more your own than some obvious hand me down. You'll be my cousin from Cumbria. Travel is somewhat restricted with the gas rationing so I don't want you to have come from too far. The accent might be troublesome too. Try not to talk too much."

The sewing basket drew Eleanor's attention as Meara gave the mirror a final lingering glance. Her desire was to stay and watch the new creature she'd just met. Desires were not something she could give into since that led to Eve's downfall. Already she'd fallen to the same temptations as the first woman. No wonder there were no mirrors in the convent.

Her hands grabbed the full skirt of the dress and swished it as she walked. It fluttered against her legs, making a breeze. Quite a change from her heavy tunic that hung straight down due the weight of the fabric. "I like this dress. Why didn't the sisters have garments like these?"

Her hostess had her back to her as she searched for something, but her laughter carried. "Why don't the sisters have dresses like the one you have on? I imagine a few did before they entered the order. Then they exchanged it for a plain black habit."

"Why?" Even though she'd spent her life surrounded by women in black, she couldn't understand the deliberate choice of no color when there were so many to pick from. She'd assumed material only came in black, white, and deep brown. Black reminded them of their need for repentance, while the white undergarments emphasized purity. Her brown garb emphasized she wasn't a member. Even inside the walls, she didn't truly belong.

Eleanor brandished a brush with a wink. "Your hair will need a good brushing, but first the dress." She gestured to a small footstool. Even in the convent, she'd had her tunic hemmed. The difference being she had hemmed it after it was pinned. Oscar stretched and made a plaintive *meow* before strolling over to investigate their actions.

The cat head butted its owner, who ignored him. He kept up his actions until Eleanor stopped pinning long enough to rub his head as she spoke.

"As for the nun's garb, I always thought it was to inform people that they were different and to keep their distance, especially men. Ordinary people might rub up against them and soil them some-how."

Her mouth twisted as she tried to visualize one of the sisters casually bumping into a villager, and then recoiling in horror. "The sisters never left the convent as far as I know. Whatever we received came through Mother Superior who dealt with the villagers."

"Hmm, that's probably the way of it. I can't say I've seen any of the sisters in the market." Her fingers nimbly folded the material above the ankles and pinned it.

"Won't my dress be too short?" Her cast-off garment was always catching on trees, loose bricks, she had tripped on it more than once. Still, Mother Superior insisted no part of the leg should show. Only the tip of a sister's slippers could show as she walked. While this may have worked for someone moving in a slow and contemplative manner, it caused issues for her.

"Country girls tend to wear their dresses shorter to keep them out of the mud. All a man is going to see is a sturdy pair of work boots." Eleanor added with a nod.

"As your cousin, what name would I use?"

The woman stopped folding the dress to rock back on her haunches. "What did they call you in the convent?"

"Mary." While she was used to the name, she preferred to leave it behind.

"No surprise." Eleanor rolled back to her knees and continued to pin. "What name would you like to be called?"

"Meara," she spoke without hesitation. "My mother chose that name. Uncle Simon said it meant *sea*."

"It does. Meara, it is." The woman stood and pulled at the waist of the dress. "I could tighten it here, but it would cause interest of the unneeded kind."

So many things about this outside world that she wanted to know, but the dominant question centered on why Eleanor had been at the edge of the woods to meet her. "How did you know I'd be in the woods?"

"Oh, that. Your father woke me up and told me to hurry to save his only child."

In a world of Zeppelins, soldiers hiding in the woods and benevolent lights, this somehow made sense. "You just jumped up and went into the woods?"

Eleanor cocked her head and peered up from her kneeling position. "Now that I think about it, the urgency I felt was unusual. The closer I came, the smoke and noise validated that you could be in trouble. The voice that woke me hadn't been clear on what I was to do to save you. I was glad to see you standing there. Not sure if I would have had the gumption to run into a burning building.

"As I walked, information came to me, or maybe I thought of it on my own. Before I met you, I bumped into a few townspeople who told me what was going on. That's how I knew no one survived and what the one bitter sister said before she died."

The chaos of the place burning, along with the looting, made her wonder if any of the sisters had time to escape. "You told me some of the sisters escaped. Did you see them?"

A sadness took up residence in the woman's eyes. "While I didn't see any of them tiptoeing over the broken wall with a hobo bag in hand, I still felt them. Their spirits flew away like newly released doves. Later, when they count the bodies for burial we'll see how many remained."

"Will someone from the Church come and take the bodies?" The bigger question was would anyone count the bodies? If they did, would they know the number of sisters that resided at the Holy Rosary? They could assume some burned up in the fire.

"I suppose they will be notified but with a war going on, nothing will come of it. The sisters will be interred in the convent grounds. The officials won't come around until the war is over. I imagine by that time there will be little left of the place since scavengers will take whatever they can use, including the stones that make up the walls."

Meara hoped the fleeing sisters would find a better life, more suited to them. Who knows? She might see them again. If they met, should she act like she knew them? Would it ruin their new lives? Perhaps someone would grab them and bring them back to a nunnery, only one with higher walls and possibly a silent one.

Even though she knew almost nothing about this world, she was determined to learn more. "Tell me what I need to know to be your cousin."

THE LAST THREE days faded into one another as Eleanor schooled her in the ways of the outside world. People, mainly men, had endless choices of where they could travel or what job they could take. Women had fewer choices, with the number one decision being they could choose the man they married. The war opened up jobs abandoned by men going into the service, including factory workers and trolley operators. Women filled the positions of nurses, telephone operators, and clerks.

Uncle Simon should arrive in a few days, but she couldn't expect the man to look out for her forever. Eventually, she'd need employment. Her hands slid over the book Eleanor had found for her. The title *The True History of the Druids* excited her. Perhaps she might discover something about her father and his beliefs. On the book cover, a bearded man stood by a tree.

Eleanor approached with a filled wicker laundry basket on one hip. "Not sure if there's much truth between those covers. I heard the Druids weren't ones for writing things down. Those who chose to write about the Druids did it from their own viewpoint."

Meara pushed up from the table, realizing she should help with the laundry, considering that is exactly what a cousin would do. "What's a viewpoint? Why would a person write a book if it wasn't true?"

"Come, we'll do the laundry outside." She angled her head toward the back door.

Meara gave a last look to the bearded man book cover before following Eleanor out to the back porch where a wringer washer stood. Eleanor had already filled the tub with water.

"Back in the city, I had electricity. Here in the woods, I had to give up a few things for privacy. After I put the clothes in, grab hold of the agitator and move it like a butter churn. The wringer doesn't need any power except what we provide."

The gleaming white tub was a step up from the stone sinks in the convent. Working in the sunshine was another plus. "You never answered me about viewpoint."

"Give an old gal a chance." She pulled the sheets out of the basket and shoved them into the water. A measuring cup held the washing flakes, which she added to the water. "Go to it."

Her fingers slipped on the wet agitator until she interwove her fingers providing a good grip. She moved the agitator one way, then the other. Her biceps flexed as her thighs strained to keep her balance. No wonder Eleanor wanted help.

"Viewpoint." The woman cleared her throat. "It's how you see something. Doesn't make it right or wrong. It's how you believe it is. For example, you told me that Mother Superior wouldn't have taken care of you if she'd known your father was a Druid."

Meara managed a confirming nod as she twisted one way, then another. It was best not to think of the hurtful words, especially since she wanted to think charitable thoughts of the dead.

"Now, your Uncle Simon knew your father was a Druid, but had no issue with it."

The water splashed up on her as she tried to formulate a reply. "He said his da wasn't happy with her moving to a different country."

"That's to be expected." Eleanor bent to pour a bucket of water into a galvanized tub. "All the same, your uncle and Mother Superior had different viewpoints about Druids based on their beliefs and experiences."

It was hard to remember exactly what her uncle said. Something about his sister, her mother, was determined to marry her father. Fulmen, her father, appeared to be a respectable man. "I think I understand. What does this have to do with the book?"

A small grunt escaped Eleanor as she straightened up and her hand went to the small of her back. "I think viewpoints would be just fine if they stayed viewpoints, but so many are convinced they have to bring people over to their side. Can't stand it if someone is a different religion or prefers cornbread to yeast rolls."

Until recently, Meara only thought there was only one religion. "The book," she prompted, afraid her kindly hostess might go off on a tangent about yeast rolls.

"Oh yeah, that. Can't say I read it. I did hear once that the Romans had spread rumors about Druids being cannibals."

"Cannibals," she sounded out the strange word. She stopped twisting the agitator long enough to shoot a questioning look.

"That's when people eat one another."

Both eyebrows went up. Surely that would mean the Druids were devilish people.

Eleanor continued speaking, wrinkling her own nose. "I doubt it was true. The Celts resisted the Romans, led by the Druids. The Romans swept in and killed every Druid man, woman, and child. Hard to say if they started the stories before or after the massacre to justify the killing."

"The infidels truly are evil, going around killing everyone." She'd prefer to live in a world where life was celebrated as opposed to ended.

"Ha! You know your scripture. There was plenty of killing done in God's name. Much more went on after the scripture was written too. I put it down to wanting other people's stuff."

A tiny jolt of guilt zapped her. She'd longed for Eleanor's chipped teapot and mirror. She hadn't necessarily wanted them, but something that could belong to her. She'd cherish a photo of her parents.

"Anyhow," her hostess continued, leaning against the exterior wall of the cottage. "People's viewpoints come through no matter what they do. For example, the author of your book might believe Druids are bad and repeat old rumors. On the other hand, the writer could believe Druids to be the most perfect people on Earth and make up stuff about how wonderful they are."

"Why can't you just ask a Druid?" It seemed like the most obvious answer to her.

"It would make it easier. If any exist, they're keeping to themselves as you probably expect from their previous reception. As you may have noticed, your way can be difficult if you're different from the majority. It's one reason I chose to live in the woods."

"I thought you moved here because your family died." Meara cringed since she hadn't meant to bring up the painful subject.

"That too. If I do anything that seems off to the villagers, they attribute it to my grief. It gives me a great deal of leeway." Eleanor grinned.

Meara's lips turned up in an answering smile.

"It's about time I take you to town. Plenty already know you're here. We have to get the story straight before gossip takes over."

Her smile vanished. Town, villagers, pretending to be someone she wasn't would be a test. One she wasn't ready for.

Chapter Five

ELEANOR FILLED A basket with jams and jellies she'd made using the wild and domesticated plants near her home. She held out a jar to Meara.

"This is my rose hips jelly, which is very popular. It's full of vitamin C. Not as sweet as I'd like due to the sugar prices, but it's still a good seller since it helps with female complaints."

The slightly pink substance filled the jar, and the only notation of its contents was *Rose Hips* written across the lid in grease pencil.

"What female complaints?"

"Oh, the usual." Eleanor piled herbs in the other basket resting on the table. "Cramps, fatigue, having too many babies too close together, being married to an irritating jerk." Her lips tipped up at the last comment.

"Does it really help all of that?" The almost translucent substance didn't appear any different from the corncob jelly Sister Paul's family gave instead of a tithe. She remembered the excitement of having a sweet with their dry bread only to discover it wasn't that tasty. Sister Paul disappeared shortly after that. The jelly might have caused her transfer.

The woman smiled as she counted out coins and placed them in a small coin purse. "I'm not the one who boasted about the claims. When Leticia told everyone that it made her woman's time tolerable, I had an upswing in requests."

Meara tucked the jar in with the elderberry jellies and the blackberry jams. "There's magic in the jars."

Eleanor's laughter came so hard she grasped the table. After a few hearty gulps of air, she waved her hand in front of her face to cool down her flushed skin. "Ah, magic, I wish. If I had magical powers, I wouldn't need to go barter with the other folks for my necessities. All I put into the jars besides the jelly is the good intentions I stir in."

The expression, good intentions, wasn't foreign to her, but she'd never heard of anyone putting it in a jar. "How do you bottle it?"

"Well, it's there in everything I do." Eleanor pulled out a table chair and sat. "When I plant my seeds, I wish for a good harvest. Then I care for the seedlings and the wild plants by clearing undergrowth away so they can grow strong. The faeries appreciate this and reward my efforts with large fruit or sometimes they guide my feet to a berry bush I never knew existed, filled with ripe berries."

"Faeries again. They appear to be everywhere, but I'd never heard of them before. Where do they come from?"

"That's a good question." Eleanor's eyes flickered upwards as if recalling something. "The faeries existed before we people ever walked the land. They were friends with plants and animals, fishes and birds."

"What happened then? Why do we never see them anymore?"

Her hostess's shoulders went up in a shrug. "Don't know for sure, I think we may see them and not know it. Depends on who you talk to and all. Some describe faeries as being tall, slender, and beautiful. Others say they are tiny enough to fit inside a flower blossom. Legend says the faeries chose to hide. The humans' greedy and violent nature didn't fit in with the faeries generous and kind way of life. It didn't help that people were destroying the faeries' homes by putting in roads, building towns, and other such things."

"I can see how that would make them mad. Why would they help me?" While she hadn't constructed any roads or villages, she hadn't done anything useful, either.

"They love children due to their pure hearts and limitless imaginations. Often, only children can see the magical beings since they haven't hardened their hearts yet."

Her first response was to deny being a child. The conversation between Uncle Simon and Mother Superior was the first time she'd a definite clue about her age. While she knew she'd been small and had grown larger, she existed in an ageless limbo. The only reference to her age came in a scolding that she was old enough to know better.

Her mother had made it to the convent around seventeen years ago. Still, the idea of a child was something she didn't associate with herself. A child was the chubby baby ensconced in Mary's lap. The statue sat in a courtyard that visitors passed through when coming to call. The smiling mother had a serene expression on her face. Often, she wished that statue, instead of St. George battling a dragon, stood near the garden fountain. Did someone try to take off with the statues, too?

"I'm almost seventeen." She wasn't too sure when her birthday was since it was never celebrated.

"That's a fair age. Most girls would have married by now or at least selected a sweetheart. I think by living in the convent and away from the world, in some ways you're much younger. There's no malice in you. The faeries were bound to like that."

A pleased smile rested on Eleanor's lips. Was the woman teasing her as she had so many times previously? This constant smiling, snorting, winking and joking tended to confuse Meara after spending her life with women who labored to show no emotion. "Just like that, the faeries like me?"

"It may have been. Then again, it could have been your father. Didn't you tell me he was a Druid?" She cocked her head, looking at her with the alertness of a robin usually reserved for a worm before it was gobbled up for a meal.

"I did?" She wasn't sure what she'd said as Eleanor had guided her out of the woods. The shock of seeing her home in flames and the villagers looting it made it difficult to remember clearly.

"You did. Druids are friends of the faeries because of their respect for all living spirits. Faeries have very long memories. They do not forget a kindness. No surprise they chose to help you. They had to since it's part of who they are. They never repay a favor with discourtesy. Not helping you would be exactly that."

Her father was a friend of the faeries, which she assumed was good. An incomplete picture of her father took shape. She knew the man was persuasive if he had managed to convince her mother to come back to England with him. He loved her mother dearly. Apparently, he respected nature, and in turn became a companion of the faeries. It made her wonder why the faeries didn't save him. Obviously, his need was more than hers was. If they were his friends, it would make sense that they'd assist him.

"Why didn't the faeries save my father and mother?"

"Aye, that's a hard one." She shook her head sadly. "I wonder why everyone in my family died while I survived. There's no satisfactory answer. I've heard that faeries' natures are good. They can't withstand being in the presence of evil too long. Even as powerful, immortal creatures, hate, greed, and anger wears them down. Could be they tried to help. Didn't your mother escape to come here?"

The story of how she ended up at the convent had flowed out of her before she'd been in Eleanor's tidy cottage less than an hour. Meara was more confused than ashamed of her roots. What she wanted was someone to explain everything to her. Since no one even spoke her mother's name in the convent, she had little hope, but her new friend radiated a sense of ease and practicality.

"All I know is the letter my uncle received from someone who knew about the attack on my father. The writer went on to say he thought my father's death was accidental, but he wanted my uncle to be aware of what had happened. Not sure if he expected someone to show up for retribution, but at least he'd let Simon know the family property had ended up in the hands of non-family. Do you think it's my farm now?"

A warm sensation filled her body. Never had she dreamed of having her own property, but it had promise. The sisters had taught her how to garden and care for livestock. Somewhere, a farm existed, land her father died defending. It should be hers.

"Might as well wipe that smile off your face if you're thinking of marching into some place and claiming it as yours. Whoever is living there won't see it that way."

"Why not?" Perhaps she didn't know a great deal about the world, but she did know the property of the father went to the children.

Instead of answering immediately, Eleanor clucked with her tongue as she arranged things in her basket. "You have no legal proof that the land belongs to you. Even if you did, whoever lives there would claim it's fake."

"Fake?" She hadn't heard this word before. She shook her head not making sense of it. What's hers should be hers. Meara never thought of herself as a greedy person before, but that may have been a combination of the thought of eternal damnation for the sin of greed or not having anything to be greedy about. It was probably the latter.

"False. Surely, you've heard that word. Thou shalt not bear false witness."

"Lying. If I show up with legal proof, whoever is living on the farm would call me a liar?"

Eleanor hefted the herb basket onto her arm and angled her head toward the heavy jelly jar basket. She waited until Meara picked it up before answering. "Being called a liar would be the least of your troubles. More likely, he'd set the dogs on you or fire a warning shot over your head. Land's hard to get here and harder to keep due to the taxes being so high. No one is simply going to allow you to have the farm back."

This was so wrong. "Wouldn't the fact that my father died make them want to do the right thing?"

A slight pat on her shoulder and a sad smile served as a response. The door swung wide as Eleanor opened it and stepped outside. "Come on child, we have to get there before all the decent food stuffs are gone. We'll be left with the burnt bread and the day-old eggs."

The sky was rosy with the impending dawn as rays of light danced on the underside of leaves. "Why do we have to leave so early?"

Her hostess started at a vigorous pace, demonstrating the need for speed. "It's a fair piece. A bicycle would get me there quicker, but it wouldn't do well on the forest paths."

Meara had to hurry to catch up. "It would be simpler to live in the village." Even though she hadn't been too impressed with the villagers she saw looting the convent, she assumed people wanted to live with other people.

"You're right. I originally came to this village to stay with my friend, Lynne. She helped me through that dark time. My goal was to find a tidy cottage nearby when I discovered the house in the woods. No one claimed it, so I did. I supposed most wouldn't want to do without regular roads or electricity. In a way, I'm probably not much different than the man on your father's property."

A bluebird swooped down in front of the two of them and flapped away with furious movements. "Ah, the bluebird of happiness. One of us is in for a welcome surprise today."

Meara's denial that Eleanor was anything like her father's murderer died on her lips. "How could a bird, albeit a pretty one, predict happiness?"

"It's a common enough saying. Bluebirds aren't plentiful. Seeing one is lucky. The fact the little fellow tried to be seen meant he was imparting a message for one of us."

The idea intrigued her. "Do all animals bring messages?"

Eleanor's forehead furrowed as she hummed a little. They walked deeper into the shade where the early morning light didn't reach well. "Be careful, dear. A single root or stone could trip you."

The songbirds grew silent as they navigated the somber section of woods. Light shone ahead through the slender saplings highlighting the path. Wildflowers, purple and white, edged the trail ahead. Meara picked up her pace, as did Eleanor.

Back again, in the sunlight, they both heaved a sigh. Eleanor glanced at her and confided in a whisper. "Don't care for that stretch. People say it's haunted. Keeps troublemakers away from my home, though."

"Haunted?" Sister Thomas had mentioned rich foods, beautiful fabrics, and parties haunted her, but she thought that meant tempted. "The woods tempt you?"

"No." The woman broke into a wheezy laugh. "Goodness, we need to work on your vocabulary. Haunted means when something or someone undead comes back. They may haunt an area or person because they lived there or as retribution. Sometimes, if they died a violent, unexpected death, they can't move on."

It didn't sound like the same thing Sister Thomas mentioned. Meara always had the impression the woman missed the fine food, especially after partaking of the plain fare the convent had. "People fear these undead spirits? Can they harm anyone?"

If she'd known the woods were haunted, she might have run the distance instead of her fast walk.

Eleanor didn't answer right away, making Meara wonder if she'd heard her. "I said can these spirits ..."

"Heard you the first time." Eleanor snapped. "I may be old, but not deaf. I like to give things thought before just blurting out an answer. Something you'd do well to consider."

Chastened, she kept her lips tight as thoughts raced through her head. Had she chattered too much? Did she annoy her new friend with her questions?

The woman beside her sighed heavily. "Sorry I almost bit your head off. Truth is I've been haunted by the loss of my loved ones. There're times when I'm sure I hear them calling my name when there's no one there. The ghosts the people fear that haunt the woods are most likely those who came to a bad end. They're upset about their sudden demise and do their best to frighten travelers. As for them hurting folks, I don't know."

If Eleanor had meant to reassure her, she failed miserably. Meara glanced back at the gloomy section they'd left behind. "Will we go back through it on the way home?"

"Could. It's the quickest way, but we can go a longer route if you prefer."

"I do." Not even out in the real world a week and she was already proving to be a coward. Perhaps once she became familiar with her new surroundings, she'd be more at ease and braver. The idea of mingling with other people in the local market unnerved her. Her goal would be not to let it show.

What encounters should she avoid? A few might ask where she was from. It would be better if Eleanor answered those questions. It would serve her better if her hostess made her a deaf mute, but then she'd ruin it by talking. Could be most people would overlook her altogether.

The sounds of the town reached them before they exited the woods. The strange rumble of a horseless carriage like her Uncle Simon drove filled the air. The nicker of horses and the shouts of people accompanied the mechanical groan, providing a rough sort of background music. Her steps sped up as opposed to slowing due to the excitement of seeing the forbidden town.

The way some of the sisters had described the town she expected to see all sorts of depravity, from people running nude through the streets to murders. Her first glimpse of a mill with a large waterwheel and men loading grain sacks into a wagon proved disappointing. Eleanor huffed up behind her.

"Why did you take off without me?"

Meara smiled at the red-faced woman. "I wanted to see what the sisters were determined to leave. I've heard how bad it was."

"Couldn't wait, huh? It might not look bad on the surface. Most of the time it isn't, but some folks here have dark hearts and even darker intentions. I'll be your guide in that matter."

Eleanor bobbed her head before Meara even agreed.

Two middle-aged women in cotton house dresses and sweaters walked in their direction. The one with a scarf tied around her head waved at them.

"Good luck meeting you since I need some of your rose hips jelly." The woman reached into her own basket and flourished an empty jar.

Meara pulled out a matching container filled with jelly and handed it to Eleanor, who moved toward the woman. "Appreciate you bringing the jar back, Naomi. I'll give you a discount on your new batch."

The woman laughed. "That's why I always bring it back. My husband complains I don't need to be wasting money on your jelly, but with the discount, it's not so much."

A disgusted snort came from the remaining woman. "Men. What do they know of women's troubles?" Her alert eyes fixed on Meara. "Who do you have with you?"

Eleanor pocketed the money and stored the empty jar in the basket before answering. "My cousin, Meara, from Cumbria. She came to help me."

The woman's gaze unnerved Meara as she studied her from head to foot, cataloging her features. "Pure green eyes, porcelain skin, nice figure, and flaming red hair. Adelaide will not be pleased to make your acquaintance. She can't stand having anyone prettier than her around."

Before she could ask what she meant, Eleanor jostled her elbow. "Got to get going and set up my stall."

The women made their goodbyes as they strolled away. Eleanor tucked her arm into Meara's drawing her close. "You were about to ask who Adelaide was?"

Even though she had been, she shook her head.

"Of course you were. I know you well enough. Simply put, the girl thinks herself some type of princess since her father is the mayor. Doreen summed it up by saying Adelaide dislikes anyone prettier than herself. If inward beauty counted…" Eleanor hesitated, and then pointed to an aged draft horse straining to pull a wagon, stacked high with barrels. "Brutus has a bigger heart and more inward beauty than Adelaide."

The thought made Meara giggle. Her free hand covered her mouth, not knowing if giggling was permissible in town. Maybe she wasn't ready to be here. The sound of shouts and laughter distracted her. Three young men jostled one another as they carried baskets of produce to a nearby stall.

Her eyes remained on the three. Their sable hair and similar coloring marked them as possible siblings. Their varying heights suggested different ages and their open faces and good humor caused something in her to respond to them. The shortest looked back at her and nudged the male closest to him. The three of them stopped and stared at her. The tallest smiled, which caused a fluttering in her belly. Her face heated when she realized she'd been caught staring as well. Her lips lifted on their own before she could even decide if smiling back was the proper response.

Perhaps realizing Meara wasn't keeping pace with her, Eleanor stopped and gave her a curious look, then swung her head toward the unknown males. "Ah, the Douglas brothers. I'm sure that trio caused more than one female heartbeat to speed up."

Her hand slipped up to rest over her heart, feeling its rapid beat. How strange.

A sharp elbow to her ribcage knocked her hand down.

"Stop that. Quit staring. The Douglas brothers, especially

Braeden, aren't for you."

Braeden. The name was unfamiliar to her, not one of the saints' names.

"Make haste before he comes over here."

Her footsteps hurried to keep up with her new friend who had reached an empty stall of large cinder blocks and a broad board. Eleanor pulled a cloth out of her basket and spread it across the board before placing her herbs on it.

Meara placed the jelly jars next to the herbs. Eleanor quickly plucked all the jars off the board except for four. Noticing Meara's astonishment, her friend explained.

"It's better if a customer believes they are getting the very last jar or next to the last. Something there isn't that much of is more desirable."

A woman who had been fingering a patchwork quilt at another stall immediately dropped the material and headed in their direction. Her tired countenance brightened as she managed a hopeful smile. "Do you have any chamomile?"

"I do." Eleanor's fingers wrapped around a delicate looking herb. "Normally, I'd tell you to use it sparingly, things being the way they are, but it looks like you haven't had a good night's rest since your son left for the army."

"You're so right. I wish it were all over. Thank goodness the Germans haven't made it to England."

Meara's eyes cut to her friend who nodded as Eleanor spoke, "I know. I want you to make yourself a strong tea. You're not doing yourself any favors by not sleeping."

"Aye, I know, but..." the woman fished in her pocket and brought out two small coins, "...this is all I have, not nearly enough."

"Don't fuss. Keep your coins. I'll consider this my contribution to the war effort."

The heartsick mother took the proffered chamomile and hurried off with whispered thanks and a tear sliding down one weathered cheek. Meara's potential comment about money not being made dried up on her tongue.

Braeden Douglas weaved his way through the shifting crowds to their stall. He stopped in front. Taller up close, his eyes sparkled as he grinned in Eleanor's direction.

"Good morning, Miss Eleanor."

The woman narrowed her eyes but had the manners to return the greeting. "Good morning to you, Mr. Douglas. I do not think you have any need of my jellies or herbs."

The normally friendly woman didn't return his smile and at best seemed only civil. She practically told Braeden she had nothing to sell him. Why couldn't she see this vibrant man meant her no harm?

"I was wondering," he flicked a look in Meara's direction, "if you could introduce me to your charming helper?"

Instead of answering, she snorted. Braeden stood stock-still, waiting. When it looked like Eleanor would say nothing, she rushed to introduce herself.

"I'm Meara. Her cousin from Cumbria. I came down to help." The few words exhausted her backstory and earned her a dark look from her companion.

"Hello, Meara from Cumbria. I'm Braeden from here." He chuckled as if he'd made a big joke.

She found herself laughing along with him.

"Tell me, Meara. Did you leave a sweetheart or a husband behind to fend for himself?"

Before she could answer truthfully, Eleanor pointed in the distance. "Isn't that your fiancée, Adelaide, looking for you?"

The man's eyebrows went together as he shot Eleanor a disbelieving look. A feminine voice carried over the market murmur.

"There's my sweetheart, Braeden." A blonde-haired woman dressed in a blue ruffled dress sashayed toward the dumbstruck man.

Until now, Meara thought her dress was the nicest thing she'd ever seen. Even an inexpert eye such as hers could easily tell Adelaide's dress was newer and more expensive. The townspeople gave her room as if they were the Red Sea and she Moses.

Adelaide tucked her arm into Braeden's and seared Meara with a venomous look before towing the man away. "I've been looking for you. There's no need for you to waste time chatting up pathetic war widows."

The two moved away slowly, allowing everyone to admire what a handsome couple they made. Braeden gave Meara a pleading glance that reminded her of the vixen she'd freed from a trap.

Eleanor clucked beside her. "Exactly what I was afraid would happen."

"What do you mean?" Her gaze remained on the swath of blue she knew was Adelaide. What must it be like to be a couple?

"I suspected you might jumpstart a few male hearts, but I was hoping it wouldn't be Braeden's."

"Why?" She rocked up on her toes, hoping for a last glimpse of the eldest Douglas brother. None of the bearded statues with their flowing robes even suggested a man could be beautiful. All she wanted was another look.

"Might as well stop gawking before you start talk."

Her heels hit the dirt as she exhaled slowly.

Eleanor brandished her index finger. "I keep to myself, but that doesn't mean I don't know what goes on in the village. Miss Adelaide is a spoiled child who gets whatever she wants, no matter what the cost."

It was hard to imagine a big, strong man trapped by a slender female. "You can't buy people."

Eleanor lifted one eyebrow. "Well, you'd be wrong. Adelaide's father can cause a great deal of trouble for the Douglas family. You'd do well to forget Braeden before Adelaide causes mischief for you."

Chapter Six

ELEANOR'S PRODUCTS SOLD out fast, giving the two of them no reason to linger in the village. After purchasing some flour, eggs, and salt, they headed back toward the woods, Meara carrying the heavier basket. The sound of the dying market crowd resulted in one last reluctant peek at the bustling scene. At first, it had been overwhelming, all the sounds, smells, and colors. After an hour, she could pick out the booming voice of the brewer extolling his beer. Lillian, the flower seller's light, airy voice, floated above the crowd rather like her blossoms' scents that rested on top of the cinnamon bun aroma and the hot, pungent smell of so many people in close quarters. When Simon arrived, and whisked her back to Ireland, she could visit the market there any time she wanted.

"How will we know when Simon comes back?"

The dappled shadows of the woodland path brought with it a stillness that insulated them against the outside world. They strolled deeper, surprising a hare into leaving its hiding place. "Look, a rabbit! Better hop to it."

"What?" That didn't answer her question at all. "What should I hop to?"

Eleanor wrinkled her nose. "I'm not sure. My granny used to say that whenever she saw a rabbit. It meant to keep doing what you're doing or stuff would start happening rapidly."

"What stuff? What does that have to do with Simon looking for me?" A particularly long shadow enveloped Meara, chilling her. True, she may not know much about the outside world, but she could tell when something was being withheld from her.

"My granny never told me what. It was an inner knowing. Perhaps something that had been heavy on my mind. The animals served as messengers to indicate all was well or to discontinue a venture. As for your Uncle Simon, I'm not sure. Do you remember his last name?"

"Cleary. He's a Cleary from Galway County."

"Mmm." The woman walked a few steps, and her lips pursed as she thought.

The absence of any sensible response unnerved Meara. Had she missed her only opportunity to connect with her family? For a moment, the life she'd known had changed with her uncle's arrival. Family, connections, a place where she belonged, it had all arrived when Uncle Simon claimed her as niece. It reminded her of being in a particularly dark patch of woods and sunlight beaming through the branches illuminating everything. An ill-placed bomb detonated that particular option. It could be her uncle and his friend suffered a mishap. Her footsteps slowed as she considered the loss of her recently found relative.

Eleanor's clear voice reminded Meara she wasn't alone on the dark path.

"We could write a letter to your family in Ireland. I'm not sure how many Clearys live in Galway, but surely one Cleary must know the other. If the letter even gets to a cousin, we should get a reply."

Although she'd never written a letter before, she did understand the process. The very fact that some unknown boy had written a letter that had started Simon combing the countryside cheered her a little.

"How long would it take to hear back, especially considering Simon isn't in Galway and was planning an expedition?"

"That's a problem." Eleanor planted her walking stick ahead of her and pulled herself forward demonstrating her weariness.

"What choice do we have?" Could this be what the rabbit was

warning her about?

"Outside of hanging out near the convent waiting for your uncle to appear, I can't think of anything else."

She had thought about going to the convent, possibly going into what remained of Mother Superior's office. The tea set would be long gone, but possibly something Simon left would still be there. Paper wouldn't be of interest to scavengers. If she returned, all she might find is the singed earth and the impression of where the bricks once sat.

"I could go to the convent and wait." It seemed like the most plausible solution. She knew enough not to add anything about ferreting through the remains. Sister Matthew, who had nursed her mother before she died, mentioned a hiding spot in the office while in her delirium. She spoke of a fine necklace her mother wore on entering the convent, a locket of some sort. The only thing she managed to get out of her rambling account was her mother had been stripped of the necklace before Meara's birth. On one level, she knew enough not to share the information. Now would be the time to look.

Eleanor whirled around showing surprising energy. "Don't even consider it!" Her eyes flashed a duplicate warning as she stabbed the ground with her walking stick.

"It would help." No need to explain her desire to search for Simon's address or her mother's locket.

"Help who? Those who fear every stranger, every odd sound, anything that isn't the way it has always been. Those would see your appearance at the convent as an omen, a sign. Some would call it a clear admission of guilt returning to the place you set on fire."

The words battered and mystified her at the same time. Her hand flattened against her chest. "Eleanor, you found me, told me my father sent you. How could you believe such a thing?"

"I don't. People like things tied up in nice packages. There're many who want the mystery of the fire laid at someone's door.

Preferably, someone they can grab and put away. You, a stranger, hanging around the convent would be enough."

People would accuse her, just to solve the fire's cause. It resembled the paranoia most of the sisters embraced about the outside world. Could there be truth to their fears? Her brief excursion outside the walls included an encounter with foreign strangers and a faery rescue. Perhaps she should heed Eleanor.

"I understand. Say no more." Even though she mouthed the words, her mind returned to the idea of searching the convent. If she could find her uncle's address, it would make it more of a certainty she could contact her family. Hadn't the bunny told her to hop to it?

They strolled the rest of the way in silence. Meara mentally debated why she shouldn't visit the convent. When bored with the practical side, she assumed the other view. After all, it was her heritage. Everyone else knew his or her people and even their ancestors. For as long as she lived, except for this short week, she had accepted her mother appeared one day without any real explanation.

The small cottage came into view signaling the end of the trip. A strident meow let them know how Oscar felt about their time away. Eleanor picked up her pace, hurrying to the spoiled pet. "We're home. I suppose you feared you might have to fend for yourself. No worries."

Meara followed slower, taking a leisurely review of the tidy house and garden. They were a step above the convent life, but she knew this wasn't her place. Eleanor's granny spoke about an inner knowledge. As much as she'd like to stay here, it wasn't her future. That much she knew.

"Hurry up, you slowpoke. I set the beans simmering before we left. They are almost ready. I'll add a handful of flour to the corn mix I already have, and we can have some cornbread, too."

Her stomach grumbled, reminding Meara she needed to eat as she planned her future, a rather frightening prospect when she got right down to it. The basket dropped the slight distance to the table as she released it. The empty jars clanked together.

"Have a care," her friend warned from her location by the stove, stirring the beans. "I don't have the coin to be buying new baskets or jars."

"Sorry." Another reason she needed to leave. She ate Eleanor's food and used up her supplies. What did she do in gratitude? Stir up trouble in the village. "Do you think Adelaide will cause trouble because of Braeden speaking to me?"

The woman blew across a spoonful of beans and then tasted them. "Needs salt."

Meara passed her the salt shaker.

After a heavy shake and another taste, Eleanor answered. "I wouldn't fret on that matter. Men notice pretty girls. It's a natural reaction. In the end, Adelaide brought Braeden to heel and paraded him through the market for everyone to see. In our small town, Braeden is the best as far as young men go. His family is prosperous and well respected, and I'm sure you noticed he's not difficult to look at."

For a second, she thought to deny his attractiveness but realized her dumbfounded expression on seeing the man had said it all. Meara nodded, choosing not to speak, not wanting to interrupt her friend.

"Aye, women like Braeden. He has a good heart and is kind, too. Adelaide had been to Lancaster where her father hoped to match her up with a wealthy merchant. Turns out there are plenty of beauties in the city with much sweeter temperaments. The mayor only has sway over local families, so a local boy will suit for a bridegroom, and she picked Braeden."

The idea that the indulged female could pick a groom from the town's populace the way she picked berries irritated Meara. "What if Braeden doesn't care for being picked?"

The metallic banging of pans made Eleanor's response somewhat garbled. "Pretty girl. Young enough to have children. Money to her name. What's not to like?"

"What if he doesn't love her?" The words popped out of her mouth before she had fully formed the thought.

Eleanor laid the cornbread pan on the stovetop. "Love?" She balled both hands on her hips and cocked her head. "I know the sisters never gave you any such ideas. People make advantageous marriages. Men want children, a warm body to snuggle up to, and a hot meal on the table when they come home. A fat dowry sweetens the deal."

"What do women want? Don't they have any choice in the matter?"

"Most want the same thing apart from a dowry and a hot meal. Most want to leave their father's house and have a responsible husband that provides for them. It's even better if he's not a drunkard, skirt chaser, or beats her."

Her lips twisted as Meara considered the dark picture. *Good* was when you didn't marry a drunkard who beat you when he wasn't out chasing other women. *Bad* didn't bear thinking about.

"Oh, you don't want a husband who gambles, either. Then you'll always be worrying about feeding your family."

Another worry to add to her list. "It's no wonder so many women choose to become sisters."

A snort came from the stove where Eleanor held a bowl against her belly as she measured out the flour with one hand. "Most of those women didn't take the veil as their first choice."

"What do you mean?" Being a bride of Christ was a higher calling that few heeded.

"Just goes to show how little you know. Catholic girls who become pregnant without being married end up in the convent. The baby is given to a Catholic family to raise while the mother is shuttled off to the nunnery."

This was something she had never heard before. "Did they become pregnant by the Holy Spirit? Is their child blessed?"

"Goodness, girl." She placed the bowl on the stove and laughed. "We need to talk. Better that I help you reason things out than one of those randy village boys."

"Talk about how the Holy Spirit visited the future sisters." Her mind raced as she considered which sister might have a child on the outside. Sister Gabriella came to mind. No wonder the woman needed to escape to visit her child.

"Not exactly. The father could have been a Tom, Dick, or Harry, but in the end, they didn't stand up and do the right thing." She motioned to the pan.

Meara took down the pan and smeared some lard over the bottom to prevent sticking. "What's the right thing?"

"Marriage, of course, especially since he got her in the family way. The man had his fun, but many refuse to pay the piper."

Piper? Fun? She watched as Eleanor cracked an egg against the bowl. "Is it fun for the woman?"

"That's a hard one. It depends on the man and the woman. In the end, if the woman turns up pregnant, she's called a loose woman and her child a bastard. The Catholics give the woman a ticket to the convent. Protestants don't have such an efficient system. Sometimes the girl disappears to visit some far away relative and returns nine months later. Then there is the girl who has no place to go and has to bear the scorn of the locals."

"That's not fair. What about the man?" She had thought the cloistered world hadn't been fair to women, not even bothering to have any female saints besides Mary. It looked like the outside world had the same double standards.

"Most women won't name the father, deluded into believing the man loves her, or he could be married, or even a relative who took her against her will. In the end, people mumble something about men being men."

"No wonder the sisters had no use for men."

"I imagine some saw the cloistered life as a sanctuary, but I don't want to give you a one-sided experience. I married and considered myself happy. My husband, Donald, while not wealthy, was comfortable, which meant I had a comfortable life. Some marry for status and freedom."

Freedom? "How does marrying make you free?" It made no sense. She bent to fill the oven tinder with slender logs and twigs before lighting it.

"As a young girl, like yourself, your movements are very restrained. Everywhere you go you have someone watching you. The real reason is females are worthless if they aren't virgins. Once you marry, you are someone's wife. The ring on your finger serves as a magical cloak that keeps other men away. If they make the mistake of talking to you, once they see the ring, they wander away. As a married woman, I could shop on my own, even ride the trolley in the city. These were things I couldn't do as a young girl."

The whole discussion confused her. "You can do these things now."

"Yes, I can, but I'm a widow now. I hear with the war on there's a lot less men to look out for the young women. Here they must look out for themselves, often traveling in groups when using the underground or traveling to their wartime jobs."

Heat rose from the oven. Eleanor wet her finger, held it above the heat. "Not quite." The wood had to burn down enough to bake the bread as opposed to frying it in spots.

"Underground? Wartime jobs? Virgins? Am I a virgin?"

"Of course you are." Eleanor held open the over door and licked her finger again. "Almost there."

"If I'm a virgin, does that make me holy like Mary?" She'd never considered herself particularly sacred since none of her sisters treated her as such.

"Ha, that's a good one. You'd think something like that with men going on and on about only marrying a virgin. If they only knew. No, you're a regular female who hasn't met up with a smooth-talking man who managed to get into your drawers."

"Why would some man want to wear my drawers? Wouldn't he have undergarments of his own?"

Eleanor slid the pan into the oven and regarded her with an amused look. "Didn't you have any livestock around your place? I know you had a rooster since I saw it leave. Haven't you ever witnessed the rooster mounting a hen?"

"No way could I miss all the crowing and clucking. People do that?" It was hard to think of some of the solid citizens she met today resorting to such antics.

"Similar, perhaps without all the clucking. Although the men still like to crow." Eleanor rested her open hand on the table as she collapsed into a chair. "If a man wants to walk with you, sometimes he simply wants to walk. Other times, he's like the randy rooster, hoping to mount you."

Relationships between men and women made her wonder how humanity managed to exist. "Well, I guess I should avoid all walks with males."

"I'd highly suggest that, but if you stay with me, there will be men who want to court you."

Sister Thomas had mentioned this before in the context that her male relatives would prevent the wrong type of man from courting her. "Who will warn me of the good and oily sorts?"

"I will. Even though I live in the woods, I know the character of local boys. Braeden caught your eye, but his younger brother, Grayson, is a fine fellow. He's closer to your age, too."

Everything seemed so surreal. Days ago, she knew she had a family, and her only luxury was slipping into the woods to commune with nature. Now, her companion speculated on her marital prospects. It seemed that no matter where she was, she exchanged one position of imposed servitude for another. What would it be like to be free to do as she pleased?

After a hearty meal of beans and cornbread, Eleanor yawned.

"It's a nap for me. I bet there's some watercress near the river. Afterward, maybe we could pick some if the light holds."

"Where would you look for it?" It would be nice to do something for the woman who had done so much for her.

"Ah, it's beyond where I found you. More north. All you really should do is listen for the water. Surely, you've had it at the convent." Her words slurred as she made her way to her comfortable chair and ottoman. The woman was almost asleep on her feet.

Instead of explaining they had watercress a few times when someone brought it as a tithe, Meara cleaned up the dishes. The sunlight filtering through the windows promised several hours of light. Her hand gripped a foraging bag, which she slung over her head. She'd be back before her benefactor even woke.

Since she'd only trod the convent path while in shock, Meara tended to second-guess every move. A few steps on a path to her left felt wrong, and she ended up doubling back to the original path. After what seemed forever, the trees she remembered lined the path. Even the bird songs resonated. This place, she knew. A small break in the trees revealed the broken stone fence and smoke darkened convent walls.

She glanced at what had been her home. Her memories felt as if they belonged to a stranger. Off to the left, she could see the cemetery outside the convent walls. There were fresh mounds of dirt indicating new graves. Curiosity propelled her forward. Had they conducted a service for the women? There were no wooden crosses with their names carved into them. No one in the village would know their names. Some caring person must have buried them. It was something to be thankful for, but it bothered her that the women passed on without anyone speaking their names, feeling a sense of loss at their passing. It was as if they never existed.

There had to be something she could do. Meara glanced around, puzzled about the lack of birdsong. Death hung over the place as if a shroud. The chill on her back could be the icy finger of death stroking her. The urge to flee battled with her need to honor the women. The shell of the convent reared up behind her. The living areas had taken the most damage. The entry courtyard and Mother Superior's office were untouched by the fire, which meant possibly that her uncle's address existed still. Truthfully, she never told Eleanor she wouldn't look.

She made each step as silent as possible in her heavy work boots. No need to say anything to Eleanor if her search didn't yield results. Did that make her a liar? The line between truth and lie tended to blur more than she'd realized previously.

Broken crockery splintered under her boots. Abandoned loot that someone may have dropped. Most of what the sisters used was very plain and worn. It made her wonder about the penury that would make such items valuable. Even though the sisters had taken the vow of poverty, there could possibly be those worse off, though, on occasion she had wondered why Brides of Christ were not treated better.

The broken chicken coop reminded her of gathering eggs. The berry bush that hid her escape hole remained untouched by the flames. Plump blackberries glistened on the bush. On the way out, she'd harvest the berries, which should mitigate Eleanor's anger.

The long, windowless halls received a spill of light from open doors making visibility limited. Although she'd walked the halls enough in the dark to know her way, the prospect of walking blind through them wasn't one she wanted to repeat. The stink of smoke hung heavy in the narrow corridor, choking her. Her hacking cough echoed through the empty place. A few more steps and she'd be there. Gus, the local opportunist, had probably emptied the office.

Her mind reconstructed the room. There were four padded chairs, a small tea table, and an oversized desk from behind which Mother Superior held court. An ornate crucifix adorned the wall. There had been a tea set on the table and a carpet on the floor. Besides that, she couldn't remember much more.

A spill of color at the end of the hall prompted another memory of the stained-glass window in the office. It was an ornate rose design that was a smaller version of the one at Notre Dame. Sister Matthew called it a *vanity* once. Since Meara had never seen it before then she hadn't known what a vanity was. After seeing it, she deduced a vanity was something that existed just to be beautiful.

Inside the office, the sunlight streamed through the rose window, leaving spots of color on the bare floor. The carpet was an obvious casualty along with the furniture. Nothing remained except the window, which was too high to reach, and the crucifix. Perhaps scavengers had qualms about touching religious items. More likely, they had no need for a six-foot cross with a tortured man on it. Thank goodness for that. Sister Matthew's ramblings included the location of a secret compartment behind the cross. Had she meant to tell her? Did it even exist?

The stillness of the place unnerved her. Though the sisters normally kept conversation at a minimum, there was sound from the bells announcing the hours, a swish of fabric denoting a passing sister, or even the clang from pans in the kitchen signaling meal preparation.

Meara's hand pushed on the base of the oversized cross not expecting it to move. It trembled, startling her, resulting in her jumping back as it fell to the floor. Dust flew up and hung in the air, making a cloud for the color stained sun rays to penetrate. Her hand covered her mouth, muting her involuntary scream. The plaster body smashed into dust except for the head that rolled to the corner of the room where it stared back at her. The dust settled enough to see the broken wire on the cross. It was probably seconds from breaking. Her movement had sent it hurtling. Some of the sisters would have called it a sign.

Since she remained unhurt, it had to be a positive omen. A swatch of purple light highlighted the wall where an indentation indicated a small door. Sister Matthew had been telling the truth, but something being in there might be a different matter.

She slid toward the wall, ready to jump out of the way if something else should fall. The only thing left was the window. Her hand felt the outline of the door, but it had no handle or knob. How did a person get it open? Her short nails couldn't pry it open. After trying for several minutes without success, she slapped the panel with the heels of her hand. Every corner received a hard hit doing little more than bruising her hand until her final rap. The door flew open fast, banging her chin.

Another sign, possibly. Her fingers rubbed her chin. At least she wasn't bleeding. A bruise would show by tomorrow. Didn't matter since she so seldom saw anyone. Inside was a metal box with a lock. Obviously, she wouldn't try to open it right away. The box was the size of the ornate Chapel Bible. It weighed down her forage bag and left no room for berries or watercress. Her innate sense of preservation urged her to leave now.

The familiar winding hallways spooked her with their silence. It wasn't as if they'd been filled with chatter and noise before, but at least she knew living sisters existed behind the closed doors. Now, she hurried past them. An occasional open door threw out a stream of light along with the vision of a ripped mattress and a rough wooden trunk with its lid open. If anyone hoped to find something of value in the nuns' cells, they'd been disappointed.

An urge to visit her own room tempted her. Her worldly treasures consisted of a needle, a stone, and a candle stub. She didn't even have an extra tunic to her name since her growth spurt two years ago. Her boot steps echoed off the walls, making it sound as if someone trailed her.

"There's no one here. Just me."

Her brave words did nothing to reassure her or to slow down her racing heart. A large swath of sunlight indicated the outside door, which meant she was very close to her room. Maybe she would grab the stone she'd found on one of her forest trips. The smooth stone had a hole in it that went all the way through. She had considered getting a piece of string and wearing it under her tunic. Often, in the dark, she'd run her fingers around the stone. Even though it didn't make any sense, simply touching the rock comforted her.

Decision made, she pressed her room door wide only to hear something behind her. Her muscles tightened as she held her breath. *Nothing.* The closed shutters left her room in darkness. Her urge to retrieve the beloved stone dissipated. The room, which had been hers for years, emanated an air of malevolence. Her hand rested on the door as she peered into the shadows. Her forgotten slippers stood by her mattress as if waiting for her to don them. She darted into the room, grabbed her slippers, and rag bundle from under her mattress. A loud clatter caused her to run into the courtyard without bothering to look for the source.

Meara stopped behind the courtyard statue of St. George. No one had taken off with the ugly statue, although his lance showed hammer nicks as if someone had tried to separate the lance from the gloating knight. The dragon had always intrigued her more than the sadistic saint determined to kill anything in his path. Her breath slowed as her hand caressed the carved dragon scales.

In the strong sunlight, her fears retreated. A bunch of blue wildflowers caught her eye as she exited the convent. The sight of the bare graves had her reaching for the flowers. It wasn't much, but it was better than nothing.

At the graves, she placed a single flower on each grave, murmuring a name of a sister who may have perished in the fire. There were fewer graves than she expected, which supported Eleanor's belief that some sisters used the fire as an opportunity to escape.

As she placed the last flower on the grave, she heard voices.

"Look, it's her."

A quick head swivel revealed Adelaide standing with a finger pointing in her direction. A brown-haired girl stood beside her. They both spoke about her as if she couldn't hear, or she didn't matter.

"What's she doing with the graves? She must be gathering grave dirt to put a hex on someone. Maybe she bewitched Braeden."

"Braeden's mine." Adelaide growled the words.

It was enough of a warning for Meara to flee into the woods with the forage bag hitting her leg with every step.

"Let's get her."

The sound of running steps spurred her into greater speed until a large tree root tripped her. They'd be on her in no time. Life in the convent hadn't prepared her to deal with jealous females. Her hands, braced against the ground, felt the vibration of their running footsteps. Must hide somewhere. Too late to climb a tree.

Meara crouched behind a prickly bush. The two girls thundered by shouting instructions to one another.

"I'll hold her down. Then you'll mess up her face. No one would find her pretty then."

"What if she tells?"

Meara couldn't determine which one expressed doubts at the cold-blooded plan.

"No one will believe her since she's a stranger."

Who knew strangers had fewer rights than women? Strange women had no protection whatsoever. Her leg muscles burned due to her crouched position. How long would she have to stay like this?

Chapter Seven

A LOW BUZZ followed by running footsteps and screams helped her locate her would-be attackers as they sped past her, followed by an angry swarm of bees. She waited for the girls to pass before slipping back onto the path. No bees followed her, which made her wonder if they were really bees.

The lack of bird song made Meara glance over her shoulder, expecting the mean-spirited girls to be on her trail or the villainous-looking St. George statue to come to life. Sister Thaddeus explained that George was a great martyr who not only saved the king's daughter from a gruesome death, but also rooted out evil wherever it existed.

The forage bag hung heavy on her shoulder, reminding her of her actions. She had stolen from a convent. Did that mean she robbed God? Her eyes flickered upward, expecting gathering storm clouds, complete with lightning. The sun still shone. A break in the leafy canopy revealed a few fluffy clouds traveling across the blue expanse. A bird trilled near her, breaking the ominous silence. Another responded farther away.

Overreacting, that's all. She'd let her emotions get the best of her. It wasn't theft if it belonged to her. Convinced she had done no wrong, her pace slowed. Eleanor might not see it the same way, though. It'd be best if she opened the box before she returned to the cottage. Besides, the woman was sleeping. How she'd pry it open was the question.

Lost in contemplation on how to best open the box, the sudden appearance of a breathless Eleanor startled her.

"Mercy, child. Your father practically screamed in my ear. Something about you in danger."

Danger? Well, she had been in something. "I'm fine. Some village girls planned to mess me up so no one would find me attractive. They're gone now." She'd shrugged her shoulders, knowing she left a great deal out in the telling.

"Ah, that's all. Where did this happen? I haven't had any issues with people strolling close to my cottage." Eleanor fisted her hands on her hips and narrowed her eyes.

Meara swallowed, aware she'd been found out. "You said my father woke you?"

"He did. I could hear him as clear as I can hear you. It surprises me that he can yell orders at me when my own family never stopped by for a final goodbye."

Eleanor's hands slipped from her hips as her shoulders drooped. Sadness. Meara easily recognized that emotion. For all the talk against emotional displays, sadness existed within the convent walls. Usually, it was despondency due to the wretchedness of humankind. Still, she didn't want her friend to suffer. "Your family is happy where they are. They had no need for you to do anything for them. They're in Heaven, floating around, plucking their harps."

A snort, then a hoarse laugh served as a response to her ethereal explanation. Eleanor's lips tipped up in a smile before she cuffed Meara's shoulder, making the forage bag shift a little.

"I see what you did there. Changed the subject. I can't imagine my Thomas playing a harp." She gave another chuckle, but her eyes dropped to the forage bag.

"The girls. You never asked me what happened to them."

Eleanor's gaze stayed on the bag as she asked. "Go ahead, tell me. In fact, why not tell me where you saw them. I wasn't asleep long enough for you to journey to the village and back."

A trip to the village hadn't even tempted her. She knew so little about how to act around village people. If the girls were any indication, they could be both unpredictable and dangerous. "One of them was Adelaide. I recognized her from our trip this morning."

"Not good." The middle-aged woman shook her head, and then muttered, before clearing her throat and addressing Meara. "You'll want to stay out of her way. That one, despite having everything given to her, has a mean streak a mile wide. I knew no good would come from Braeden speaking to you."

Even though Meara knew Adelaide's dislike came from her short conversation with Braeden, she defended him. "He didn't do anything wrong. Braeden was being friendly."

"Aye. The way males always are to pretty girls. You didn't notice any men chatting me up."

The idea made her wonder. Before she could voice her question, Eleanor held her finger up.

"Yes, you're pretty. Braeden thinks so. All the same, Adelaide has chosen him. He might as well get used to the idea. The sooner your Uncle Simon gets here the better off you'll be. Once you get to Ireland, you'll find another young man like Braeden or one even better. The Irish have a charm the English lack."

Meara exhaled, aware there was no one like Braeden, but she knew enough not to mention it. Village people deserved to be together, not that the mean-spirited girl was good enough for the handsome man. Meara wasn't good enough. Still, Braeden thought she was pretty. It was a small thing that no one could take away from her. She'd hold it close and bring it out whenever she needed a reason to smile.

"Should I ask why you're grinning like a cat that lapped up the cream, as if I didn't know?"

Her smile faltered. "I guess I was thinking about the girls running from the bees."

Eleanor reached for Meara's arm and pushed up the sweater sleeve. "Not a sting on your face, arms, or hands. How did you avoid the bees?"

Her shoulders went up in another shrug. "I don't know. The bees came out of the woods directly at the girls as if on a mission. They hadn't disturbed their tree or anything. As they ran away, I went in the opposite direction."

"This happened where?"

Eleanor, in her single-minded determination to ferret out the truth, could even put the Mother Superior to shame.

"Near the convent."

A wagging finger punctuated Eleanor's words. It went up and down as she spoke. "I warned you not to go there. See. I didn't caution you just to hear myself talk. Plenty of villagers get some type of precarious thrill visiting a place where someone else has died. What was your excuse? I imagine it has something to do with whatever is weighing down your bag."

"You were worrying about how to contact my uncle."

"Hah, I see you're going to try to put this at my door. Not even out of the convent a week and you're already as wily as the rest of us."

Unsure of what wily meant, Meara debated finishing her explanation. She suspected it wasn't a compliment. "I needed an address to find Simon." It felt good saying his name, knowing she belonged somewhere.

"I'll give you that. Did you find it?" She angled her head in the direction of the bag.

The strap bit into her shoulder. Her fingers wedged under the strip of cloth and lifted it over her head. "I don't know. I ran when I thought someone was in the convent."

The bag landed on the dirt with a small thud. The cloth bag dipped a little, exposing a corner of the metal box. Eleanor knelt beside the box and lifted it free. Her fingers tugged at the lock with no luck. A dull thunk and metallic rattle came from within. "It's heavy, which means there's something inside. I'm shocked Gus didn't find the box. How did you locate it?"

"Gus didn't nurse Sister Matthew as she died. The woman had been a special friend of Mother Superior. While she was feverish, she spoke of a hidden place in the office. I found it behind the crucifix."

"Good reason Gus didn't find it. He'd have no need of a crucifix. Could be he drew the line there, but somehow, I doubt it. Did you have no fears about moving it?"

Truth was the fear came later. "When I pushed the cross aside, it fell from the wall almost hitting me, then the body on the cross shattered. The head remained with the dark eyes staring right at me."

Eleanor shook the box again. "Interesting." She cocked her head, like a bird listening for something. "The fact you escaped being crushed and set upon by jealous biddies shows you're magically guarded."

Magically guarded? The idea bemused her. "I don't know what you mean."

The woman tucked the box under her arm and sauntered down the path toward her house. "The way I see it, things happen to ensure your safety. Everything, from your mother having you at the convent, to the bees chasing the meddling girls, equals an extraordinary force working on your behalf. I think you have an important mission ahead of you."

"I don't think so. How could I when I know nothing about the world." Even though she often wondered in the wee hours before dawn what her life would be, she never expected a daunting purpose.

"You'll learn. Maybe I outlived my family to help you on your way. Makes sense, especially when I consider the ease with which your father orders me around."

Even though it should be ludicrous that a dead man was constantly giving orders, it wasn't. "Why do you listen to him? Couldn't you just ignore him?"

Eleanor's laughter trailed behind her. "If only it was that easy.

Urgency compels me to do as he asks. It's like a psychic boot in the pants. Trust me. I didn't want to get up in the wee hours and look for someone who might be a figment of my dreams."

"I'm glad you did." Her lips tipped up, imagining the resistance the woman had put up while wandering the mist-shrouded woods at her father's original request. "All the same, I'm doing my best to relieve you of the burden of my presence."

"Pshaw, you hardly eat more than a sparrow."

The comment caused her eyebrow to lift in disbelief.

Eleanor crinkled her nose. "Make that a couple of sparrows." She winked before tacking on, "Maybe a good half dozen."

Birds ate twice their body weight. Was her hostess hinting she ate enough to tip a wheelbarrow or only the weight of a dozen sparrows? "I didn't think I gobbled that much."

"Probably enough to keep a growing girl going."

Not the insult she imagined. Her eyes dropped to the metal box she'd swiped. A certainty that something inside the box belonged to her stayed with her, even as she'd fled from the mean-spirited females. She'd do well to avoid them in the future. "I think maybe I shouldn't make any future trips into the village." Not waiting for an answer, she reached for the box. Even though she'd never seen the tarnished box before today, she felt an odd proprietorship toward it.

Eleanor sighed and allowed Meara to take the heavy box back. "It's my fault. I should have suspected the havoc a new pretty face would cause in a closed community."

The box safely back in the bag, she swung it over her head. A feeling of rightness settled over her that she couldn't explain. The two of them strolled side by side when the path permitted. The sun filtered through the trees, bathing them in warm light. A hare hopped across the path, giving the two of them an unconcerned glance before hopping away. It was hard to believe only minutes before she'd ran for her life. If she hoped to make her way in this world, she needed information to survive.

"What's a closed community?"

"Hmm," Eleanor hesitated, before pointing to a small puddle off the path. "That puddle is a closed community, as is the village, and your convent was one. There are certain known living creatures in the community. They aren't all necessarily good, but people know who to watch out for."

"Like Gus."

"Yeah, like Gus. The man would take anything not nailed down. Still, it would take more than suspicion to put him away. Others shame those who've had something stolen about not taking better care of their treasures. Truthfully, no one sees Gus take anything, and the man is too smart to keep the stolen goods around his house."

"We saw him." The memory of the sly man with his bulging bags still stung.

"True. Perhaps he wasn't as careful knowing the original owners were dead. Besides, he had to compete with the other villagers. War times have made scavengers of us all. I heard a farmer carrying a load in Durbin had a mishap, throwing his load of potatoes and onions into the road. Dozens of people showed up to help them, which pleased him. After the truck was loaded with his bushels of produce, he found a marked decrease in what he had."

"Some could have rolled into the undergrowth along the road," Meara suggested, as she veered out of the reach of a prickly bush.

Eleanor laughed. "That's what I like about you, your willingness to believe the best of others. Talk was that it was also the only road to the marketplace. His planned *accident* relieved him of his foodstuffs. Anyhow, I digress. As for the closed community, whenever someone new shows up, there's a reaction."

Sister Thomas was the last new person to enter the convent in a long time. Even though the Mother Superior was glad to welcome her and her money, most of the sisters were indifferent. "I think I understand. Right before the fire, a new sister came into the convent.

I liked her. She was the only person who talked to me about the outside, although I didn't understand half of what she said. A few of the sisters reported her for infractions as opposed to warning her."

"Sounds about right. They felt threatened. One of the reasons I stay in the woods is to appear harmless. I don't want to usurp anyone's status in the village pecking order. Nor am I interested in any man who might have a sweetheart or even someone with an unspoken interest in him. People generally assume I'm a relative of the Collins family since we bear a strong resemblance. I usually save back some of my jams and jellies for them, being kin and all."

Meara almost corrected Eleanor since she'd previously told her she had no family left. The woman's broad wink confused her. "Are you related to the Collins?"

"Ah, we're all related in some manner, since Adam and Eve were the original parents."

Her answer, while an accepted one, confused her more. All she did know so far was people tended to be reactive when a new person entered a closed community. "If people thought you were related to someone in the village, they'd be friendlier?"

"You could say that, although, I'd go with less suspicious and hostile. I had to prove to people that I serve a purpose. The rose hips jelly was my foot in the door. I guess we need to find one for you. Being pretty will endear you to the men, but not any of the women. Is there something special you're good at?"

Her eyes rolled up on her own as she considered her simple existence with the nunnery walls. "I know several prayers in Latin. I can even sing *Our Father* in Latin."

"Laudable, but I can't see anyone having any use for that."

Her world had been so limited up to now. "I can read and write, even do some calculations."

"Then you're better off than most of the village girls. The fact you can obviously read and speak Latin could go against you. I wouldn't mention it to anyone."

"I guess I should say nothing about the smattering of Hebrew I picked up, either."

"No." Eleanor's head swung slowly side-to-side. "Too many people in the village are illiterate. Either they were pulled out of school at an early age to work or they never went. Many of the women stayed home helping their own mums. Any talk about Latin or Hebrew would just get their backs up. Say nothing. Your reading and writing ability will help you, but no reason to brag about it."

Bragging was a sin in the convent. It marched in step with pride. Meara never considered herself guilty of either. "I won't." The shape of the cottage pushed the uncomfortable discussion of closed communities to the back of her mind. Soon, they'd pry the box open and find whatever called to her.

Oscar delicately picked his way toward them, meowing his welcome or possibly a plea for food. Even though she'd only been with Eleanor for a brief time, the sight of the thatched bungalow caused her to heave a sigh.

"Old Oscar serves as a sentinel of sorts." Eleanor reached down to scratch the cat's head.

"Does he guard the place?"

The woman's hearty laughter danced in the air. "I suppose his constant weaving between an unwelcome visitor's legs could result in a fall. Mainly, he'd annoy them with his constant demands. He's more of a watchman than a guard dog. I'd know if someone was coming."

The two of them walked into the shadowy cottage. Meara opened the shuttered windows after depositing the forage bag on the table. Eleanor placed the kettle underneath the kitchen pump and worked the handle until water sloshed across the rim. The two of them worked together as a team without any words. If the convent taught her nothing else, it taught her to anticipate what someone might want. As the youngest, she usually fetched and carried for several elderly nuns. Food, water, retrieving a dropped prayer book, even opening shutters, or handing another a needed utensil she could do with almost no conscious thought.

Unfortunately, there were situations to which she didn't know the right simple response, such as Adelaide and her vicious machinations.

Meara stoked the fire in the stove before taking a seat at the table. The box mocked her with its lock. Sure, there had to be a key, but for all she knew, it went into the ground with Mother Superior. As desperate as she was, she drew the line at digging up graves.

"Tea will be ready in a couple of minutes," Eleanor spoke, as she placed a large hammer and chisel on the table.

Meara grabbed the chisel and rammed it into the half circle the padlock hung from. If she tried to batter the box from a sideways position, she wouldn't be able to deliver much strength in her swing. Her hands arranged the box so it balanced on its end, which would allow her to strike downward. Her left hand held it in place as she battered it with the hammer. After a half dozen attempts, the metal ring splintered off the box, leaving a matching pair of jagged holes.

"Careful." Eleanor leaned closer. "A metal cut can result in tetanus or even lockjaw."

Both sounded like something she'd rather avoid. Her fingers skirted the jagged holes and pried at the seam to no effect. "I can't get it open."

"Here, let me." Eleanor pushed her aside as she grabbed the heavy hammer. "Probably age and the damp climate rusted it shut. All it needs is a good blow."

The woman choked both hands up on the hammer handle before raising it as high as her head to hit the box with a deafening crash. The metal top bent in with the impact, then surprisingly popped open, spilling out some bags, papers, and jewelry across the table.

The smell of age and disuse filled the room. It reminded her of how the corridors smelled after a wet spring when water slipped in through cracks in the walls and holes in the roof. Holy Rosary only repaired the chapel and common rooms when needed. Since the population had greatly diminished over the years, a nun had only to move to another room if her cell leaked. Most did this under the cover of night to prevent the accusation of pride.

Eleanor picked up the various bags and shook them, causing them to clink. "I think it's money. Gus would be so upset if he knew." The idea caused the woman to giggle.

"It's tithes. Each nun had family who would pay a tithe towards the upkeep of the nunnery. Often, we'd get food, occasionally, feed for the livestock. Someone like me, who has no one, was a drain on the convent."

The clatter of coins hitting the table drew her attention. Eleanor was busy organizing coins into certain piles. "What are you doing?"

"Counting. Looks like most of the sisters' families were not generous givers. There are some pounds, but mostly pence coins."

"We need to send this back to the families."

Eleanor quit counting long enough to throw a sympathetic look. "Do you know any of the sisters' actual names or where they lived?"

"We were forbidden to speak of our past."

"Makes it hard then. Instead, consider all you've done for the nunnery. You've gardened, cared for the livestock, and nursed elderly nuns, even helped in the apothecary. You did all of this without a single pence as far as compensation."

It wasn't too hard to figure out where Eleanor was going with her rationale. "I was doing no less than the other sisters. Sure, I was younger and better suited to the activities."

"No doubt they were glad for your strong arms and sharp eyes. Still, the other women made a choice to go into the nunnery. They knew what it entailed."

Sister Thomas may have thought she knew, but the conversation they shared indicated regrets for her hasty actions. Apparently, Sister Gabriella regretted her decision also. "Not all."

"No matter. They made their choices. You were born in servitude. You were little more than an unpaid slave. If the Zeppelin hadn't mistaken the convent for their target, you'd still be there working, possibly until your death."

Her instinct was to argue that she wasn't a slave, but she wasn't so sure. She'd never been around a slave so it would be hard to compare. Would she have stayed there all her life? It was hard to say, but Mother Superior hinted that her behavior was not fitting as a bride of Christ. She assumed it was to curb her wayward behavior. It could be her time at the convent was limited. Would she vanish rather like the sister whose family donated corncob jelly as their tithe? "I'm not so sure."

Eleanor had gone back to counting her money and arranging the coins in neat piles. A pocket watch sat next to the empty money pouches. Her uncle had a similar watch, only not as ornate. She picked up the watch and flipped it open. Inside the lid was an inscription, "To Griffin, my soul mate. You hold my heart forever. Marjorie." The words resonated within her. There was no way she'd know a Griffin or Marjorie.

She showed the engraving to Eleanor. "What's a soul mate?"

"Ah, mostly, it's wishful thinking on a women's part. Every now and then two people meet, and somehow it all works together. They don't just marry. Their souls unite, and it's painful to be apart from their husband. I like to think my husband and I were soulmates, but maybe not."

"Why not? You loved him."

The woman's face folded in a resigned expression. "I did. I've heard soul mates can't live without their mate. They usually die when separated from the other. The fact I'm still here tells the story."

Meara folded her arms feeling a juxtaposition in their relationship. "It just means you're stronger than those other women. More capable. Lack of vision, not lack of love, killed them. They were unable to see beyond the walls."

"When did you get so wise all of the sudden?" Eleanor cocked her head, arching a brow.

"Not sure, but I do know I'm right. My parents loved each other. Some people might say my mother died because of my father's death, but I don't think so. Gabriella told me it took extreme determination for a very pregnant woman to flee in absolute terror through miles of forest over a series of days. Her only goal, I believe, was to find a safe place for me. Once she had, she allowed herself to die because of all she'd experienced."

"Aye, on that I'd count you're right. Your poor mother. No one should go through such travail, especially when carrying."

The watch's claim to eternal love forgotten. Meara's thumb rubbed over the etched words. *I'll find Marjorie someday and return the watch. I only wish I knew I knew how it ended up in the box.*

A tangle of chains and the glitter of jewels caught her eyes. A small, delicate silver crucifix, appropriate for any sister to wear tangled with a long string of pearls. There were more pocket watches with long chains, even some men's signet rings. Not the thing someone would give as a tithe. Eleanor donned a large topaz ring and held out her hand to admire it.

"I can't imagine a wealthy family sending their daughter to the nunnery. Surely, she could have married well."

Something didn't seem right about the jewelry. Sparkling jewels of an assortment of colors spilled across the table as she dumped out the treasure to find one object that had exerted such a pull on her emotions. It had to be in there somewhere.

A few loose gems rolled across the table. A dull clang and a slip of ribbon with a cross attached had Eleanor reaching for it while Meara's fingers stilled on a tarnished silver locket. A flash of energy sizzled through her fingers and up her arm.

"This is a Royal Red Cross medal. Queen Victoria gave them out to some of the nurses who served during the war. Florence Nightingale was the first to receive one. I can't believe any nurse would give away a medal the queen gave her. There's something fishy about this entire box of goodies. Even if families did give the convent their worldly goods, it wasn't exactly like Mother Superior could exchange a string of pearls for a year's worth of flour."

Her brief tour into town gave her a basic understanding of the village economy. "Some of your customers paid you with honey, eggs, and flour. How would pearls be any different?"

"Hmm, true. Times are tough with the war on. In some ways, a jar of honey is more valuable to me than money. Jewelry, watch fobs, and medals are worth more than a simple villager could pay." Eleanor held up a necklace with several gold medallions hanging from it. Inside each medallion was a red stone. "I think these are rubies. My husband, Walter, scrimped and saved to buy me a locket with a birthstone in it for my birthday. I can't imagine anyone here would be able to afford any of this stuff."

Her words made Meara wonder why the roof was never fixed with so many valuables hidden behind the crucifix, while her fingers pawed through the tangle of chains and an occasional coin or loose gem. An inner urge resulted in goose bumps and a compulsion to find *it*. Of course, she didn't know what *it* was, only an assurance she'd know when she found it.

A smooth silver case with initials on it intrigued her. She stared at the elegant E, H, and C twined together. As beautiful as it was, she knew it wasn't the item. Envelopes with faded lettering she passed by, knowing it without picking them up. An oval shimmered, pulling her gaze. The chain attached to the oval fell free of the other chains when she touched the necklace.

Meara brought the oval closer to her gaze. The play of light that originally attracted her dulled on closer inspection. Tarnish coated the item, making it hard to distinguish too much about the design.

Eleanor crowded closer. "Must be old to be so badly tarnished. Looks like a simple locket, which could have been traded easily enough. Makes me wonder why Mother Superior held onto it so long. I have just the thing to clean it up."

The dull oval had a name etched into it. She pressed the oval close to her heart and closed her eyes. A sense of comfort enveloped her.

The sound of rustling meant her hostess was up to something. Meara opened her eyes to discover the woman had assembled vinegar, baking soda, salt, and hot water. From a small wooden box, Eleanor withdrew some silver paper. Perhaps feeling the weight of Meara's gaze, she explained as she pressed the silver paper into a small pan. "I saved the foil wrappers from Tober chocolate bars knowing I could use them to clean silver. I line the pan, place the jewelry on the bottom, and then add the hot water, salt, baking soda, and vinegar. The hot water loosens the tarnish. The vinegar, baking soda, and silver foil cause a chemical reaction while the salt serves as grit to scrub away the tarnish. I'll need the locket."

Instead of handing it over, Meara ignored the outstretched hand, reluctant to let it go. Her ragged thumbnail caught on a latch. The struggle to free her nail resulted in the locket slowly opening, exposing two pictures. The bearded man with the kind eyes she recognized immediately as her father. He appeared the same in her dreams. The gorgeous woman with an easy smile and a sparkle in her eyes had to be her mother.

"Mother."

She whispered the word, but loud enough to cause Eleanor to strain her neck to peer at the portraits. "You have the look of her. The man, your father, was handsome, although he tends to be a bit demanding in the afterlife." She chuckled at her own remark before adding, "You'll want to pop the photos out before cleaning. You're lucky to have them."

No one had to tell her twice as she used the side of her nail to loosen the photos. How fortunate they hadn't fallen prey to damp that permeated the convent. The closed locket must have kept them dry, Once the photos were out and on the table, she handed over the locket for cleaning.

The sound of splashing along with a slight hiss and bubble drew her eyes to the pan where the mixture frothed and heaved. It reminded her of how she pictured the red sea when it closed over the Egyptian soldiers, with the exception that it had been red as opposed to the white. "Are you sure it won't hurt the locket?"

"Goodness no, child. Silver is a treasure of the Earth. Your locket will outlast both of us, although it's a wonder why it stayed in the box as opposed to providing for a need within the convent." Eleanor dipped a small brush into the liquid, then picked up the locket and scrubbed it. Already, it was lighter.

The woman held the brighter locket up to the light as it spun in a slow circle. "The answer why it was never sold is due to the engraving."

On the front side was her mother's name. Elegant script spelled out *Sorcha*, confirming the identity of the owner. Meara didn't need the name to know the locket, the photos inside were part of who she was. On the back was a stylized dragon.

"It might be a bit awkward for the Holy Mother to show up somewhere trying to sell a necklace with a woman's name on it."

"She could say it was hers. No one knows the sisters' real names."

"Ah, she could that, except the dragon on the back, which was probably a Druid symbol, has an entirely different meaning in the Christian faith."

Meara couldn't help but think about the statue where an angry St. George had speared a small dragon. The armored man was upon a battle charger and the small animal didn't even reach past the horse's forelegs. "What's so special about the dragon?"

Eleanor shot her a look of disbelief. It made Meara wonder if this matter had already been explained to her while she was caught up in memories of Braeden's gorgeous smile.

"It stands for all the Pagan religions, especially Druids. That's why you see so many saints battling dragons."

Now it made sense. Her finger went up. "The dragon St George battles in our courtyard is the size of a dog. It hardly seems fair."

Eleanor shook her head slowly. "That's what you call propaganda. It was important for the Church to show the old ways as small, annoying nuisances, nothing to merit true fear."

Would she bother to kill something that might annoy her but would not hurt her in any significant way? Normally, she brushed away the flies as opposed to killing them after Sister Gabriella had explained they only lived for weeks. "Why did the saints feel the need to wipe out the old ways?"

"There's no reason in it. Some humans will not suffer competition in any form. Consider Adelaide. The girl has so much going for her besides her father's position in the community, her inheritance, and beauty. Still, it doesn't stop her from destroying anyone who deflects attention from her."

The idea both confused and terrified her.

Chapter Eight

WITH THE CONFUSING day behind her and the benefit of a good night's sleep, Meara decided Eleanor had to be mistaken. Why would Adelaide view her as competition? She had nothing to offer. No family, no history, no status, and most of all she didn't have a pound to her name. Living inside cloistered walls even prevented her from learning the simple skills that every female knew such as marketing and cooking.

Sister Augustine, while never an exemplary cook, refused help in the kitchen. Simple tasks such as carrying firewood and water were all she tolerated. Even then, she stood guard over whatever was cooking as if someone might peek in and divine their dinner contents. At the time, she considered it pride until she recently tasted Eleanor's meals. Sister Augustine had nothing to pride herself on. Then again, something else could have been going on. More happened in the convent than she ever realized, especially considering Mother Superior's suspicious collection of expensive jewels and one of the sisters slipping out at night to meet an old lover.

The rosy glow of the rising sun washed both the cat and sleeping owner in a flattering pink light. Meara gazed at both wondering where she'd be without the wise woman's help. Alone, without a friend, she'd have to throw herself on the villagers' mercy. While some might have taken her in, the others would be quick to give her a fate like her father's.

Her unexpected discovery along with her timely escape had erased all thought of watercress. If she left now, she could return with a delicious surprise for her hostess. A chilled finger of apprehension touched her neck and continued down her spine. A wiggle of her shoulders shook it out. Spoiled, rich girls would not be out at sunrise. No, they'd sleep in until a maid brought them hot tea in bed. An unimaginable luxury Eleanor insisted was true.

No one would be out, she reassured herself, as she closed the door slowly, trying not to make a sound. Outside, the birds were warming up for their part in the nature symphony. The soft filtered light kissed everything with a gentle touch. It must be how a mother woke a beloved child.

The slim transition period between night and morning was also the liminal period when faeries were often afoot. Sometimes, a sensation of watchful eyes occurred. Instead of creeping her out, she felt protected while in the woods. Still, she hoped for more of an encounter than tiny lights that were reminiscent of glowworms. Her gaze passed over the dew-covered wildflowers, up the shaggy bark trees, up into the leafy canopy overhead in search of the magical creatures. No mischievous faces staring back at her. No rustling in the brush indicating movement.

A clear, haunting whistle carried through the forest. The melody, slow and charming, halted her steps. Didn't faeries love music? It wouldn't surprise her if one chose to serenade the dawn. It called to her. Obviously, the faeries understood her wishes to know them better and sent her a sign. Perhaps they could converse, and she'd ask them about her father. They could tell her where her father died and where his bones lay strewn. Even though she went from unknown orphan to having a family in less than a week, she still wanted to honor them.

The sound lured her off the path into the moist underbrush. Not everyone classified faeries as helpful and benevolent beings. There were stories of enchanting music luring people away from their homes never to be seen again. Could be one of the darker sorts had decided to trick her. Just about the time she decided to go back the way she came, a crouching form straightened in front of her.

A thrill of awareness raced down her back, awakening her senses. A handsome male towered over her by a few inches, looking nothing like a faery, but very much like Braeden Douglas. Her hand touched her hair that she hadn't even bothered to brush in her desire to get outdoors. With her unruly curls, brushing seldom helped anyway. Besides, the man wasn't in the woods to meet her.

"What brings you in the woods so early?"

"The prince brings me to the woods." The man grinned as he delivered his cryptic statement.

"I didn't expect the Prince of Wales to be walking through our bit of woods."

Instead of laughing as she expected, Braeden tilted his head and graced her with an inquiring glance. He had an off-white foraging bag that he reached into, pulling out a mushroom with a flattened top and loamy soil still clinging to the roots. "This is a *prince* mushroom. It fetches a fair price in the city at some of the fine restaurants."

It was hard to imagine some place beyond the village, but it would be the most likely place to sell the goods contained in the metal box. Perhaps she should know more about it. Her uncle went to the city. She thought he had said London, but wasn't sure. "Are you going to the city?"

Braeden pushed a leaf out of the way with the toe of his boot, exposing three white capped mushrooms. His long fingers plucked the three and held them at chin level for inspection. "Field mushrooms, normally you'd find them in a—"

"Field." She finished his sentence. Perhaps she shouldn't have done that. Mother Superior was always warning her about her habit of talking when she should be quiet. Her shoulders hunched, expecting an angry reply or a scolding, but Braeden laughed, easing the tension.

"I see you're a smart one. I can't impress you with my simple mushroom skills." His nose crinkled the slightest bit.

Her initial action would be to deny any sort of intelligence. After all, she knew nothing about how average folks acted. Instead, she looked down at her folded hands.

Braeden shuffled closer. His unexpected actions brought her head up. Her heart chose that moment to lurch into a rapid beat more suitable for running. His hazel eyes hypnotized her with their gentleness and good humor. How could someone with such eyes hurt anyone? Sister Thomas warned her about men but took relief that her uncle would handle things. What would Simon do if he were here? "Could I help you pick mushrooms?"

"I'd appreciate that." He reached into his pocket and withdrew a battered pocket watch. "I probably have fifteen minutes before the truck leaves." He closed the watch and returned it to his pocket.

That answered her question about the city. A tiny squeeze caused her heart to skip a beat. Her heartbeat tripped as if something gave her heart and a fierce squeeze. "How long will you be gone?"

He winked as he slid the mushrooms into the bag. "Will you miss me?"

The creature, which had taken to squeezing her heart, gave it another hard crush. "We don't see one another on a regular basis. How could I miss you?"

He placed his right hand on his chest and staggered backward a few steps. "I'm mortally wounded with your logical response."

What had she done? Meara rushed to place her hand over his, resting on his chest. "Are you ill?" Perhaps he had some medical condition she knew nothing about. Somehow, she had triggered an attack. Sister Nicodemus had fits that required rolling her to her side to prevent her from swallowing her tongue, although she never understood how you could swallow something that was attached.

Braeden's hand was warm under hers. His body stood straight and strong, no sign of tumbling to the ground or seizures. His hand turned under hers, grasping her fingers and gently carrying them up to his lips. He brushed a soft kiss against them. Even though she never experienced a kiss before, she recognized what it was, as did her heart, which managed a somersault in her chest. Never had the organ caused her as much distress as it did today.

His eyes held hers as he spoke. "I'll be delighted if you promise to walk with me on the morrow."

Relief that he was coming back to see her had her half-sighing her answer. "Yes."

"That's what I need to hear. It will get me through the long day. I'll be waving goodbye to my best friend, Grant. He's joining the Army. I have half a mind to enlist too, but now I have something to keep me at home."

Adelaide's enraged face took form in her head as he mentioned having someone at home. Of course, he had a girlfriend, even a fiancée. How had she forgotten? "Adelaide," she murmured the same way a housewife might acknowledge rain after hanging out her laundry.

Braeden dropped her hand and took a step back. "Not you too. Everyone has me all but married to the female. I try to be respectful since it's the right thing to do. Still, I have no desire to marry her, ever, and have said as much to her."

The words cheered her, but they were just words. He probably meant them, even believed them. Still, Eleanor's prediction that Adelaide always got what she wanted felt more real. If she got between Adelaide and her chosen bridegroom, she'd only delay the inevitable and suffer the consequences. She knew she'd have to break her half-made promise to meet. Her fingers interlaced with one another trying to still her nervous hands. "As for tomorrow—"

"Don't say it. A promise is a promise. I'm not sure why everyone is so scared of her. If it makes you feel any better, then we'll meet in the woods."

She nodded while wondering if maybe Braeden fretted more than he was willing to admit. Why else meet in the woods? Their relationship would go nowhere, but she was willing to delay the inevitable ending by a day. Braeden probably never heard the hatred and something darker in Adelaide's voice.

"Be here by sunrise tomorrow. I'll bring you something nice from my travels."

"I will." Her fingers touched his lifted hand. For a second, it felt like all their inner thoughts were flowing between them where their hands touched. Before she could say anything else, he turned to leave. His tall form weaved between the trees until she could no longer see him.

A nearby birdcall startled her. Meara blinked at the sound, before returning the way she came. Maybe she hadn't met faeries today, but something magical had happened. There was still time to gather watercress and talk herself out of meeting Braeden.

The watercress she found by the stream easily enough. As she bent down to pick it, she spotted a frog on the bank. "Hello, frog."

When she first started her adventure outside the walls, she got in the habit of talking to the animals. It made sense since she was stepping into their world. A few may have dipped their heads or fluttered within eyesight a few wingbeats longer. None ever spoke to her, until now.

The frog's liquid gaze captures hers. "Why is Braeden not for you?"

Not only could the creature talk, it obviously read thoughts, too. "Um, well you know. Adelaide has picked him to be her husband. What Adelaide wants, she gets."

"Croak," served as the frog's only response.

Perhaps, she had imagined it talking at all. Could faeries talk through animals? She wasn't sure. Eleanor might know.

On the walk back, she argued her case for not seeing Braeden. Unfortunately, part of her very much wanted to see the man and forget about the consequences. Why not? Have some fun. What will it hurt if they met and spent some time together?

No one would be the wiser. It wasn't as if Braeden would fall madly in love with her and be determined to have her. No, that would never happen. After all, she was a stranger with a vague background. People feared outsiders just as suspicion greeted the few sisters who joined the convent in last few decades. It took years to be accepted. Some never were, such as Sister Gabriella. No wonder she chose a cell away from the others. It also made outside trips possible.

People were never what she thought they were. Her growing attraction for Braeden made it easy to understand why the sister slipped out to meet her lover. The part she couldn't understand was why the woman was in the convent in the first place. Did she have a story like Sister Thomas of a conniving brother-in-law out to wrestle her fortune away from her? The little she talked to the sister, it sounded as if she'd already regretted her hasty decision based on fear and possibly spite.

An owl swooped down close to her head, making her look up in alarm. A slight breeze from its passing rustled her wayward tendrils. Her fingers tucked a curl behind her ear. "Why out in the day, friend?"

Meara waited, not expecting the animal to talk, but so many unexpected things had happened already. The bird continued its graceful flight without a hoot or a backward look. Owls were often associated with darkness and death. The hoot of an owl signaled someone's imminent demise, usually a mouse's. Still, she couldn't accept that the sighting of such a majestic creature could be unwelcome news. Perhaps, it signified wisdom. Finally, she was learning something about the mysterious outside world.

Smoke drifted from the cottage chimney signaling Eleanor had started the stove and put on the kettle. The idea of a hot cup of tea and possibly a tasty breakfast lightened her step. Odd how in such a brief time she had accepted luxuries such as tea as her own. Things could be different in Ireland. Maybe there she'd make do with a cup of well water to break her fast. Whatever it was, she'd deal with it since she'd have family and a place to belong. She folded her arms, hugging the prospect of her new life close to her. Of course, when she left, she'd leave Braeden behind.

Her step faltered as she blinked, keeping back incipient tears that arrived without thought. "Doesn't matter. Nothing will come of it."

The door swung open unexpectedly. Eleanor peered around her. Her furrowed brow announced her confusion along with her query. "Who are you talking to? Nothing will come of what?"

The door opening along with the abrupt question startled her. "Nothing will come of me and Braeden."

"Of course not." The woman shook her head as if she couldn't believe Meara fancied she had a chance with the gentle charmer.

While she'd admit the same to herself, hearing it from someone else's lips made it sound harsher, especially when Eleanor had been so much kinder to her than anyone else had.

"I agree, but what makes you so sure? Besides Adelaide?" It was hard to tell if she wanted confirmation to forget about the brief interlude in the woods or the tiniest spark of hope. If Eleanor's reasoning didn't make sense, she'd permit herself an early morning walk in the woods tomorrow. Her shoulders went up and forward as preparing herself for a blow.

"Ah. Already, you dislike Braeden's name linked with another. Adelaide is always an issue, but surprisingly she's not the only one. Braeden is not only going into the city to sell produce but is also taking his friend Grant along."

Meara opened her mouth to tell her she knew this, but never had a chance. The woman kept talking. A sense of lightness filled her. If Adelaide wasn't the issue, whatever obstacle should be easily overcome.

"The two of them have been thick as thieves forever. Grant is enlisting in the army. I wouldn't be surprised if Braeden enlists, too."

Eleanor went to the stove and pulled off the steaming kettle to make tea. She hummed as she measured out the tea leaves, unaware of the shock she had just delivered. An owl did dip down in front of her on the path earlier. Still, that could have nothing to do with Braeden. Besides, the hoot signaled impending death, not just sighting the bird.

"Braeden told me he had a reason to stay here." Her emphatic tone raised Eleanor's eyebrows as she laid out the cups and plates for breakfast.

"Ooh, I didn't know the two of you talked so much." She placed a spoon and knife by each plate, not looking up from her task.

"Well, I…" She made sure her tone was softer. "We met in the woods by accident. He was mushrooming." She shrugged, not knowing how to explain the serendipitous occurrence. "We talked."

"Hmm," Eleanor straightened and brought her thoughtful gaze to Meara's face. "I suspect it was no accident."

"No, it was. I went out to look for watercress and before I was very far from the cottage coming back, I saw Braeden."

"That only shows he's a very resourceful man. While I consider my home hidden in the woods, plenty know of the general location. Most would not make the time or effort to go through the dark section of the woods. I consider that strip of the forest as my fence. Only a male pursuing a female would show up in the wee hours."

It didn't make sense to her. "How would he know I'd be out looking for watercress?"

The woman's eyes brightened as she laughed. "I keep forgetting how ignorant you are about the ways of the world. First, a male will do almost anything to get to a desired female. I've seen the animals brave flood-swollen streams, jump huge spaces, battle other rivals, even get up in the middle night to be in the forest just in case a certain young lady decides to wander outside."

"No, you have to be wrong about that." She shook her head. "Besides, he had mushrooms, he showed me."

"Doesn't mean he couldn't do two things at once. He probably told whoever was waiting for him that he'd pick a few mushrooms before the trip. No doubt Grant, or whoever else was there, offered to go with him, but oddly, he tells them he'll do it on his own. His mission wasn't to just pick mushrooms."

When Eleanor spoke with a knowing gleam in her eye, she made it sound like meeting Braeden out in the woods really was no accident. The idea thrilled her, but along with it came the knowledge that the woman could be right about other things, too.

"Tell me how you knew about Grant enlisting?" She wanted to add something about Braeden possibly joining the army, too, but she didn't. No doubt, a faery whispered the information in her ear or it arrived via a dream.

"I heard it several times from the women I do business with. It's pertinent news since most of them have daughters, and Grant would make a good son-in-law. Of course, he wasn't pledged to anyone. Good thing, since no one knows how long the war will last or even if he'll come back at all."

Meara's hand fluttered and landed on her chest. "Do you think he might be killed?" Maybe that was the reason behind the owl, but still, it shouldn't have come to her. It could be a bird returning home after an evening hunt.

"It happens in war. The generals send all the young boys up front, protecting the decorated officers. They call the new enlistees cannon fodder." Eleanor retrieved a loaf of bread from the keeper and sawed off thick slices.

"That's horrible. Why would someone want to enlist?" Fighting, especially when it involved fighting someone else's battles, not even your own, made no sense. All the stories in the Bible about the Jews going into towns and killing everyone, even the babies and animals, horrified her. She'd never told anyone. Whenever there was a scripture reading about it, a few of the nuns wore matching faces of smug complacency, convinced they were on the righteous side.

"The recruiters show up and talk about God, King, and country.

They also promised the boys a chance to see the world. They never mention they'll be crawling on their stomachs through the mud with bullets flying overhead. Still, some need a job. The military is a legitimate job with fair pay, and most of the time, England isn't at war."

When put that way, she could understand why Grant, whom she hadn't met, might join. "Why do you think Braeden will enlist?"

The crock of butter ended up on the table alongside a jar of rose hips jelly. Eleanor acted as if she hadn't even heard as she moved items around the table.

"You never answered me." Normally, Meara would never be so rude to point out someone was avoiding a question. Her stomach clenched and rolled, afraid of Eleanor's answer and at the same time, fearful of no answer. Her imagination could always supply frightening possibilities. It had already with the owl. She wiped her sweaty hands on her dress preparing herself for whatever Eleanor would say.

"Come sit down. The tea is ready, and I think you'd fare better with some food in your belly.

Not what she wanted, but the thought of tea and buttered bread tempted her into sliding into a chair. The two of them had already assumed roles in their impromptu living arrangements. Eleanor poured as the cottage owner.

"Meara, why don't you pour the tea today? It would do you well to get some practice. I have no clue where you'll end up in life. You might work in some fancy household. Most wouldn't think pouring tea is a skill, but it is, and you'd be judged harshly if you couldn't pour it properly."

Her hands gripped the chipped porcelain pot. "How do you do it right?"

"Start the nose of the pot near the cup. Some showy fools start high. It makes a cascade of tea that splatters and cools the tea in the process. If we had sugar, it would go in the cup first along with the milk. Never fill the cup to the brim. It makes it hard to lift without spilling. If you go into domestic service, you'll find out each person likes their tea a bit different. Right now, I'm giving you general knowledge."

Did Eleanor expect her to become a domestic? She gently tipped the pot, imagining Eleanor to be a grand lady as she carefully poured the tea. She had no experience with grand women of any type. Most of those she read about in the scriptures were mainly queens who often beheaded or killed the saints. Mother Superior was strict, often critical, but she never had beheaded anyone, although she had never helped, either.

With the tea poured, she took her seat and waited. Eleanor spread the butter across her bread, then the jelly, prolonging the silence. Had she forgotten she was going to tell her why the army appealed to Braeden?

"Boys Braeden's age are on the cusp of their future. They're full of emotions and impulses. Often, they do things without thinking, which is the reason mothers warn their daughters to be on guard."

The aromatic tea teased her taste buds, leaving behind a sense of wellness as she sipped. Even though the concept of daughters being on guard puzzled her, she wouldn't mention it, afraid it would cause Eleanor to sidetrack into a different topic.

"In my opinion, the young men don't know exactly who they are and fall prey to every strong emotion. A recruiter appeals to their sense of patriotism and bravery. Young men are ready to rush into battle because they operate on urges as opposed to methodical thinking. The fact that Grant, his best friend, is enlisting may tempt Braeden to enlist. Shouldn't friends have each other's backs?"

"A friend could also convince the other not to enlist." It was the most logical solution.

Eleanor shook her head slowly. "Men have to make their way in the world. Although Grant is a responsible young man and works hard on his family's small farm, he's the third son."

The emphasis fell on 'the third son', making her think that made the difference. She remembered the story of Esau and Jacob. Jacob tricked his blind father into giving him the firstborn's inheritance. Apparently, everything automatically went to the first male in the family. Nothing had changed too much. Those not lucky enough to be born first had to make their own way. "So, Grant is joining to have a career?"

"Possibly. There's also the lure of leaving the village for the city."

As a person who just discovered the village, she wasn't very interested in anything bigger yet. "Do you think that will tempt Braeden?"

Eleanor bit into her bread and chewed. She shook her head, which wasn't much of an answer. Oscar the cat butted against Meara's leg, reminding her of his location.

"Do you mean Braeden doesn't want to move to the city? Or that he won't enlist?"

A hasty swallow had the woman following it with tea before answering. "Can't say. He's the eldest, which means his family's holdings rest on him. If the war keeps up, he may have no choice but to fight. I wouldn't have even considered him enlisting, except he shows a marked preference for your company."

It didn't say much for her if she drove men to enlist. The army could use her as a recruiting tool. "Why would that make any difference? You told me Adelaide plans on marrying him."

"True. True. Everyone has accepted it as fact, except for Braeden, who has been dragging his heels about a wedding, even to the point of refusing to call Adelaide his fiancée. I guess he has a point if he'd never asked her to marry him, but it is almost to the point of shaming Adelaide with his foot-dragging. It's no wonder the gal harbors hard feelings toward you."

An attempt to mess her face up rated more than hard feelings. She shuddered thinking about it. "How does this affect Braeden enlisting or wanting to do so?"

"Don't you see? He'd enlist to get away from Adelaide. A girl should marry by a certain age or she's a spinster. Men don't marry spinsters. They carry dual labels of *difficult* and *unwanted*. They certainly suit Adelaide." The woman snorted at her assertion. "Still, the army takes you for years, and that's too long to wait to get married. All the other girls in the village would be married by then. No, Adelaide would have to scramble for a new prospect."

"They could marry before he left." Her nausea returned with her very practical suggestion.

"No doubt Adelaide would say the same. With that in mind, don't be surprised if Braeden doesn't come back."

An emptiness swept over her, but it didn't dampen her determination to wake early on the morrow just in case Braeden waited for her. She had no clue life could be so complicated. Unexpectedly, she had found someone who liked and valued her. Then fate stomped the possibility before it had even taken fire. Her people were not meant for happy endings.

Chapter Nine

MEARA STARED UP in the darkness, listening to the soft combined snores of Oscar and Eleanor. She hadn't even known cats could snore, but then she hadn't been in that close company of one. Oscar might be a special case. Outside, she could hear the hoot of an owl. That she could do without, especially if it were a precursor to death.

Eleanor had mumbled something to herself when she mentioned her fears about the owl. The woman explained that all the old wives' tales often involved death since people died all the time. Obviously, when an owl hooted someone could die, but he didn't die because of a bird's call. Instead, they died when it was their time. Thinking of it that way made the nocturnal sentinel's call less ominous, although it did sound lonely.

Meara blinked. Her eyes were dry from holding them open way past bedtime. It occurred to her that she might not awaken in time to meet Braeden, if he came. From Eleanor's take, the man would enlist just to stay out of the web Adelaide had spun.

She'd get up before dawn and slip out of the house. That was her last thought before her eyes fluttered shut. A piercing whistle nearby woke her. The sun's rays outlined the shutters and peeked through the cracks. How did that happen?

Eleanor was already up and preparing Oscar's bowl, which caused the cat to meow his instructions. The woman glanced at her and angled her head to the door. "You best go see what he wants. It's the third time he's whistled, and it's beginning to rile up the birds.

She rushed through dressing but remembered to pull a brush through her curls before tying them back. Eleanor held out a mint leaf to her.

"Chew on this. I imagine he came for his goodbyes. They might as well be sweet-smelling."

How would Eleanor know why the man came? She didn't waste time asking. Besides, the woman had been right so far.

She opened the door slowly and slipped out without closing it properly. Braeden waited near the edge of the clearing.

"Meara, I thought you'd forgotten or maybe didn't want to see me, but I couldn't go without seeing you."

"Oh no, I wanted to see you. I fell asleep." A noise of a pan dropping reminded her of her unseen audience. Braeden touched her elbow with his hand.

"Let's walk." They took a few steps on the path that led to the convent. "A weird thing happened on my way back home yesterday."

The woods hosted everything from talking frogs to protective faeries. Which one had Braeden encountered? "What was it?"

"I met a stranger near the convent. He asked me what happened to all the sisters. I told him they all burned up due to some evil cooked up by a newcomer."

The possibility that the man could have been Simon excited her. Even hours ago, she'd been pining to belong to a family, but now the thought of leaving Braeden chafed. "What newcomer?"

"I don't know exactly. My mother told me the sisters had taken in some evil female who repaid their kindness with death. Had to be possessed by the devil. It doesn't matter anyhow since she burned up in the fire, too."

Now didn't seem like the best time to confess his mother could have been referring to herself. "What did the man do?"

"He thanked me, turned away, cursed, and walked to his automobile."

It didn't sound like Simon had even stayed to search for her. A bitterness welled up in the back of her throat. Her hands fisted as Braeden continued to talk, unaware of her inner turmoil. If she knew a family member could have died, at least she'd have searched for them, for something, even if it was only a grave. After all, he did ask to see Sorcha's grave. Maybe Braeden got it wrong.

"Are you sure he left? Which way did he go?" Even now, Simon could be looking for her, knocking on doors in the village. Surely, if the man searched for her and his sister for seventeen years he wouldn't allow one ill-informed person to end it all. Her jaw felt tight as she regarded the handsome farmer with irritation. Unfortunately, she had found something the man wasn't good at, relaying accurate information. Too bad it was at her expense.

"He had to go back down the convent road to get to the main road." He gestured to the long tree-lined road that made an abrupt dogleg turn. "I couldn't see where he went from there. Still, if he'd hung around, I think I would have heard about it. My mother knows everything that happens five minutes after it does." He chuckled as if amused by the idea.

Meara wanted to add that his mother probably reshaped actual information to put her own malicious spin on it. "You think the man left for good?"

Her comment caused his eyes to narrow. "Why do you care about the movements of some unknown man?"

"I don't." Of course, now that she denied interest it would be much harder getting any more details. Her shoulders went in a shrug, denying any lingering curiosity about who she assumed was Simon. Maybe it was someone else, such as Angus.

"Anyhow," he continued, shoving his hands into his pants pockets." I didn't come to talk about him, but about us."

Her earlier irritation melted away at the mention of *us*. Meara slowly eased one foot closer. The rest of her body followed. After all, if there was an *us*, which technically there shouldn't be, they should be standing closer together. "Go on," she urged with a shy smile, lifting the edges of her lips.

He moved closer so they were almost touching but not quite. The warmth from his body wafted off him in the cool morning air and wrapped around her before dissipating.

"Grant, my best friend, joined the Royal Army. I was sad to see him go, but it got me thinking." He paused, waiting for her response.

Eerie how his words reflected what Eleanor had told her. She cleared her throat as she searched for the right comment. "I'm sure you'll miss him."

"I will. We've been together forever. Grant is only a month older than I am. Our mums used to put us on the same blanket to play when we were babies. I've known him longer than I've known my own brothers. I didn't want him to go. Even begged him not to, but he told me it was time to take charge of his own destiny." His head shook slowly.

"What did he mean about his own destiny?" It might be useful to know since she was somewhat in a comparable situation.

Braeden winked at her. "How did you know I asked that very question?"

Her shoulders went up in a shrug. There was no appropriate answer.

"He told me living in the village everything would be the same as it had been for the last two hundred years. People would slave away to make their patch of land produce, while often nature didn't cooperate. There'd be births, marriages, and deaths. He wanted to change the outcome, and the only way he could do that was to leave. Of course, to leave the village, he needed somewhere to go and money. The army provides both. He's also fighting for his country, which is the noble and right thing to do."

Eleanor's description of cannon fodder came to mind, but she dared not repeat it. "This will change his destiny?"

"I believe it will. The life in Hogstead moves on as it would anywhere. Any girl who might have hoped to marry Grant will marry someone else in his absence, even if he decides to come back after his enlistment is over. Things would be different. He certainly wouldn't be the same man, having survived the atrocities of war. Good chance he might find another occupation or another place that might suit him better. In the city, there're all sorts of factory jobs. With a little training, a man can be a clerk or a scrivener. With Grant's skill with horses, he could even be a teamster or any other profession that works with horses. Pay must be better or at least regular.

"As the third son, Grant would do little more than work for his brother who would inherit the land. Farmers spend most of their year in famine only to have a few short months of feast when a good crop comes in. A poor year keeps the farmer hungry. That's why I should do extra, such as mushrooming to have some personal funds."

She could see how this mattered to Grant, but not to the newly formed *us*. "I'm not sure how this involves *us*?" A tingle slipped down her spine from even saying the word.

"I was getting to that part." He removed his left hand from his pocket and held it out to her.

She entangled her fingers with his warm ones. A feeling of right-ness descended upon her, similar to a fine mist only noticeable to the person touched by it. Was this how her mother had felt when meeting her father?

"Grant's decision started me thinking. Am I in control of my fate? Any villager would tell you Adelaide calls the tune. Better yet, her father does, as he hints for a marriage between our two families."

Meara attempted to tug back her hand clasped by Braeden's callused one. She didn't want to hold hands and discuss Adelaide. Even thinking about the woman soured her stomach. Instead of releasing her fingers, his hand only tightened around hers more.

"Stop it. Listen to me. I don't want to marry Adelaide."

She stopped using her other hand to pry Braeden's fingers from hers. Saying he didn't want to marry Adelaide wasn't the same as not marrying her. People often ended up doing things they didn't want to do due to circumstances. Hadn't she spent almost the entirety of life in the convent with no choice of her own?

"Do you have a choice?" Eleanor had made it clear he didn't.

His face scrunched up, then smoothed out again as he sighed. "Not here, I don't. My family would suffer if I didn't marry her. However," he gave her hand a squeeze before continuing, "if I wasn't here, but fighting for King and Country, then she'd marry someone else. She's twenty now, which puts her on the shelf. Plenty are already mothers by twenty, some twice over."

She almost didn't hear the rest of his words, so struck by the idea of Braeden leaving and being neck deep in battle. It wasn't what she wanted, but she could see how it would get him out of an untenable situation. "Reminds me of a fox chewing off its legs to get free of a trap. Are you sure this sacrifice in necessary?"

He swung up their clasped hands, turning hers so it was on top and kissed it. The tender brush of his lips radiated out to her fingers. She inhaled deeply, savoring the moment. The soft rush of air had her looking up as an owl flew by.

Not again. The nocturnal creature showing up in the day struck her as ominous, especially after Braeden's declaration to join up. "Do you have to do this?"

Even though Eleanor thought most of the young men would eventually end up on a battlefield, it didn't make it any easier.

He held her clasped hand against his cheek, rubbing his cheek against it. After a long silence, which allowed Meara enough time to create horrible mental pictures of war, he answered. "Aye, I do, if I ever want any kind of future with you."

He wanted a future with her when she hadn't even dared hope for such an outcome. She would have been happy with a stroll, handholding, and even a stolen kiss. Her breath sounded labored to her own ears. Would she be happy with just that? It would have been more than she ever had, but it would be a great deal, like Eleanor's biscuits. Once she had one, she had to have another.

Would a tiny bit of Braeden be enough for her? Other girls her age had the opportunity to fall in love, marry, and have families. Why wouldn't she want to do the same? Inside the convent, she had no real choice, but now she was outside. Why did the life she wanted come with so many extenuating circumstances? "Tell me about our future."

He grinned and squeezed her hand. "Glad to see you're coming around to seeing things my way. Well, I've talked to Grayson, my brother. He's next in line to the farm. Once I leave, I can't ever come back. I know my brother has been sweet on Adelaide for some time, but she'd never consider a second son. We talked on the way back from the city about him taking my place on the farm. When the farm does well, he could pay me a little until eventually he bought my share. After the war, I'll settle somewhere else on a piece of land to call my own."

They could farm her father's land. Excitement bubbled up in her, imagining the extensive farm and grounds and what a fine dowry it would be. She rocked up on toes wanting to share her news. Only a few things held her back. She had no clue where the farm existed. There was also the issue with someone already living on the property. It would involve her explaining about her father being a Druid as well.

Her eyes roamed his face, memorizing his strong chin, clear eyes, and his nose with a slight bump on it that did nothing to distract from his handsomeness. It was hard to say how he might react, knowing he was holding hands with the ungrateful wench blamed for the fire. A chill touched her, pebbling her skin at the thought. Never mind that she knew different. It was what people believed that mattered.

"You couldn't do that here?" It wasn't what she wanted to ask, but she needed to say something.

"Oh no, I couldn't do that to my brother. Adelaide doesn't hold any great love for me. She looked over the village bachelors and decided I'd do. It would be no hardship for her to marry Grayson, who would treat her better than I would. He'd put up with her tantrums and consider himself lucky to have her. If I returned, especially to marry you, and you agreed, it would be hard for her to swallow. I'd be a reminder that I rejected her. With me gone, she'll tell everyone she gave me the boot. With me in town, she'd take out all her unhappiness on Grayson or you. I don't want that for either of you. With me gone, it would be easy for everyone to forget. Besides, the villagers usually accept whatever story is out there."

Marry. Perhaps she'd heard wrong. It didn't sound like much else unless he was talking about the Holy Mother. It didn't seem likely since he mentioned Adelaide in the same sentence. Her heart did a double beat at his casual statement. Braeden's eyes searched her face for a response. It probably wasn't the time to explain she'd spent her entire life in a convent and never considered marriage as an option, while the village girls probably had their potential husband picked out by an early age.

Braeden angled his head as if expecting an answer.

"True." Meara agreed readily. After all, they'd accepted the story of the convent burning down as somehow associated with the Druid whelp. A bird trilled nearby catching her attention. Another bird answered its call, making her smile. Nature went on with no real change. It took no notice of a war raging near England's coastline that was subtly making inroads into the countryside, if the bombing of the convent was any indication. Braeden moved ahead where the path grew narrow.

"Do you think the people of Hogstead have anything to fear about the war?"

Braeden's head swiveled sharply, directing his attention from the path to her. The way his brows shot up announced his incredulity at her inquiry. "Of course not. That's one reason I'm joining is to protect the village and to keep us from speaking German."

"What if the Germans are already here? In these very woods?" With everything that had happened, she'd reassured herself whomever she'd met in the woods had vanished. Good chance they hadn't or even worse, there were many more.

"Goodness. Where do these ideas come from? Next thing you'll be telling me that the convent was bombed as opposed to simply catching fire." He chuckled as if the idea amused him.

Shouldn't Braeden be the one most likely to believe her? Yet, he dismissed the truth with a laugh. Eleanor didn't even know about the two who had attacked her. While her terror felt very real at the time, the more distance from the incident made it less real. She'd almost convinced herself it was a dream.

Weird, when she accepted faeries and her dead father talking to her as real. With a small effort, she managed a laugh. "Why would Germans bomb a convent?"

"They wouldn't. Weapons storage, military bases, utilities, even the Parliament would be more likely targets. Still, I guess accidents could happen. I heard some of the bomber pilots carry bombs in their laps and drop them by hand as they fly over a target."

"Pilots?" The word was unfamiliar to her.

Braeden gave her an indulgent smile as he reached for her hand and pulled her close. "I would think even in Cumbria they'd heard of planes. A lightweight vehicle with wings allows men to soar through the skies. From up high, they can see the enemy's movements and report. It could be a game changer for England. Before, they had to rely on tethered balloons for information on troop placement."

"Wouldn't that be noticeable?" Perhaps that's why the Zeppelin flew at night.

"It was definitely a problem, but usually the enemy didn't have weapons capable of shooting that far, but with a machine gun the balloon would be an easy target."

A shiver shot down her back. "You're not going to fly, are you?" The idea of soaring through the skies somehow represented a world she knew so little about. While she'd been behind the walls, people used horseless carriages to get around, some had planes, and there was some deadly weapon called a machine gun.

His shoulders went up in a shrug. "No. Planes aren't that common in war. Besides, they need someone who knows how to fly. I'll be infantry, a humble foot soldier."

Instead of reassuring her, the thought of Braeden sneaking through the woods in enemy territory scared her more than being in the sky. At least he could hide in the clouds. "That's dangerous, too. Why did you join?"

He must have told her, but fear crowded out any logical thinking.

He stopped walking and pulled her to a halt. The two of them stood without speaking. The only sound was the cheerful gurgle of the stream, which sounded out of place in such a somber moment. Braeden's dark eyes searched hers as he reached for her other hand.

With him holding both her hands, staring into her eyes, and the body heat wafting off him, carrying the scent of the woods, earth, and Braeden, everything suddenly felt right, and yet she knew it wasn't. Throwing himself into a war could never be right.

"I need to take charge of my own life. This is the only way I can with honor. Haven't you ever felt the need to determine your own destiny?" He rested his head against hers.

The touching of foreheads calmed some of her anxiety. It made no sense that a simple touch could have that effect, but it did. At least it did with Braeden. Inside the convent walls, there had been very little touching. Could he read her thoughts? Did they flow from her head to his? If so, he'd know how she both questioned her world and her place in it almost every single day of her life.

He drew back and wrinkled his nose. "Silly question, I know. Girls don't have to go out and make a living."

His easy assumption made something rebel in her. Did men think women had it so easy? Eleanor told her men believed women needed to be looked after, rather like newly hatched chicks. Sister Thomas entered the convent because she couldn't expect a second favorable marriage, and somehow her brother-in-law could wrestle her fortune away from her with the help of the law. She didn't truly understand it all, but it appeared as if the law favored men.

"Some do. Eleanor does. Even those who are married are quick to tell you that being a mother and wife is work."

His expression cleared as his eyebrows shot up at her rebuttal. "It's work they welcome."

Maybe. It would be hard to say. Eleanor enjoyed being married and having children, so it might not be too bad, but Meara had just left the iron rule of Mother Superior. The thought of another boss, even if he had gentle eyes and an inviting manner, invited caution. "Perhaps. I can't say they all welcome it. I saw plenty of housewives at the market that talked negatively about their husband and children."

Instead of answering her, Braeden dropped her left hand while retaining her right and started walking as if he expected her to follow along. Meara dug in her heels, determined not to casually follow the man. Even though she liked him, more than a little bit, it didn't seem right to hand over her life, especially since she finally had some say in it.

Two steps were all it took before he threw a questioning look over his shoulder. "What's wrong?"

Unaware of how to make herself understood, the question caused a gusty sigh. As much as she wanted the security Braeden represented, she still needed to stand on her own two feet. "You never asked me what I wanted. You just assumed whatever you said would be perfectly okay with me."

Confusion chased across his face, followed by a furrowing of his brow as his lips pulled into a straight line. "Is it me? Do you prefer someone else? Who?"

The last inquiry he bit out with more emotion than the other two. Meara shook her head slowly. Seriously, she didn't know anyone. How could she prefer someone else when she really hadn't met anyone?

"No, it's not that." How could she explain that she couldn't commit to anything when she knew so little of the world and her own history? Her free hand found its way to her mouth as she bit a nail, a habit the liberal use of pepper hadn't cured. How could she explain it without exposing her origins? With time, she suspected Braeden would come to accept her, especially when he was away from the household that included his gossipy mother. She dropped her hand to speak. "I want to be wooed."

"Wooed?" Braeden repeated the word.

Maybe she hadn't said it right. According to Sister Thomas, it was a grand thing to be wooed.

He stepped back, ducked his chin, and stared into her eyes. His hand found her free one before she could bite her thumbnail again.

"Ah, Meara, I will woo you. I'll even do it properly. I needed your promise to wait for me before I left for battle. It will keep me strong when the going gets tough. It will also bring me back to you. Then I'll dance with you, giving you whatever you want from flowers to poems, and especially kisses."

Her head tilted up at his last word. His well-formed lips were inches from hers. An image of the venomous Adelaide kissing Braeden made an unwelcome appearance in her thoughts. "Did you ever kiss Adelaide?"

Braeden jerked slightly as he regarded her with a quizzical expression. "Good heavens, no. I've spent years trying to discourage the girl. A kiss would have sealed my fate. Why would you—"

Before he could finish his question, she rocked up on her toes, barely able to reach his lips, but managed a brief touch before dropping back to her heels. Her actions silenced the man, who wrapped his arms around her, drawing her close to him. He rested his head on top of hers. They stood wrapped in each other's arms, saying nothing, absorbing the moment until a chaffinch's chattering call sounded nearby. Braeden shifted, lifting his head, and loosened his arms.

"If I could, I'd stay in your embrace forever." He sighed. "I'm fortunate the recruiter allowed me to come back to say my goodbyes. Most don't, but I explained I had to talk to you. Will you wait for me? Allow me a chance to woo you?"

The space between them enlarged in her mind as she envisioned Braeden far away in another country, diving for safety as the enemy pelted him with bullets. There was no fairness in the world if a man had to endanger his life to escape marriage with an indulged female. Even in her uncertainty about what the future held, she knew she could not send the man away with a vague promise to think about it. "I'll wait for you."

His eyes sparkled as he leaned down to kiss her. His lips touched hers, stirring up something inside her she didn't recognize. Her left hand gripped his shoulder, feeling the rough texture of his wool shirt under her fingertips. The pressure increased as she pushed up toward him, returning his kiss with equal vigor. Warmness filled her as she pushed closer, their bodies touching from lips to hips with almost no space between. His arms tightened around her as her knees went soft, unable to hold her up. No one had ever warned her about the power of kisses.

His lips left hers, making them feel abandoned. Meara stared into his eyes, willing him to kiss her again. His head ducked as if he would do just that when a shout carried through the woods.

"Braeden, it's time to go."

Grayson stood a stone's throw away from them. He had probably witnessed the kiss. Meara inhaled deeply, returning her eyes to

Braeden. It didn't matter if Grayson saw her or not. This might be the last time she saw Braeden. Her hand on his shoulder tightened, gripping his shirt. "Don't go!"

"I have to. It's a matter of honor. I'll go with an easy heart, knowing you're waiting for me. When I get an address, I'll send it home. Grayson will bring it to you. We'll be able to write one another. It won't be the same as now, but it will give me strength to persevere. Do you know how to write?"

She laughed, knowing she could at least thank the sisters for that skill. "I can write, and I will."

"Of course, it was foolish of me to ask. You strike me as a female who could do just about anything. Give me a kiss and seal your promise."

Meara tiptoed to reach his lips for a kiss that was much too short due to their impatient audience who shuffled and snorted, reminding them of his presence.

Braeden smiled as his embrace loosened, and he stepped away. "I should be back in weeks, possibly months. No way the Germans can beat stout-hearted Brits."

The two men meandered through the woods, talking softly as they left her behind. A few weeks wouldn't be that long. Good chance she'd still be here. It would be hard to know if Simon would come back in that time. The only thing she did know was she'd have to find some way to reach her uncle while staying in contact with Braeden.

Chapter Ten

HER FEET STIRRED up the dust as she shuffled back toward the cottage. If she picked up her feet, there'd be less dirt to wipe off her boots. It didn't matter. Nothing mattered when unknown soldiers would be using Braeden for target practice for no other reason that he was British. Why was there even a war?

Eleanor came around the curve in the path still wearing her apron. "What's with you? If your face were any lower, I'd have to tie it up with a scarf to keep it from dragging on the ground. Braeden must need some help in the wooing department if he leaves you with such a woebegone attitude."

A spark of anger brought her head up. "His wooing is fine. I'm sad that he joined the army and is off to fight the Germans."

Eleanor whistled as she drew abreast. She placed her arm around Meara and snuggled her close to her side. "I can see how that would upset you. I expected some of the village boys to be drafted. Did Grant's leaving cause Braeden to volunteer?"

She sighed, feeling exhausted. A lethargy settled over her, pushing her down, except for a tiny spark that flamed up at Eleanor's innocent inquiry. "Adelaide, that spoiled brat, has Braeden's family in a stranglehold. He's put off marriage as long as he can, but she's getting impatient, which explains why she tells everyone they're engaged, hoping to shame him into the union. The only way he saw of not marrying without any retribution on his family was joining the Royal Army. Who could argue against fighting for King and Country?"

"Hmmm," her companion responded. They took several steps more before Eleanor shared her thoughts. "Adelaide won't like this one little bit. She'll throw the mother of all fits. I pity anyone close to her when she finds out."

"I'll keep myself hidden." She had no desire to encounter the vindictive woman.

Eleanor snorted beside her before adding, "Well, you should. I'd be the first to tell you the girl is past spoiled, but she isn't stupid. She'll recognize Braeden's entry into the army as the ultimate insult despite the locals applauding his patriotism. No, she'll see that he'd rather face possible death than marry her."

Meara winced at the word, although she had thought it herself.

"Sorry. Still, many men return from wars. If they hadn't, there would be hardly anyone left to populate England. There are plenty of people in the countryside and even more in the city."

"You're right." She wanted just one person to return, not most of the English army. She regretted her thought as soon it occurred. There had to be other women, mothers, wives, sweethearts left behind yearning for the return of their special someone. "Why is there a war?"

The cottage came into view with Oscar waiting patiently by the back door. Eleanor gave her a little squeeze. "War has always puzzled me too. There have been wars throughout time. It's always the same. Someone, somewhere, wants more power and land. They fancy it up by calling it a holy war. Sometimes they mumble about taking back something that should be theirs. In the end, it's all greed. Young men so full of life and potential die for a few people's avarice."

The continual reference to war equating to death did nothing to reassure her. The cottage became wavy as tears clouded her vision and slid down her cheeks.

Eleanor clucked beside her, the sound loud in her ears. "Ah, child, I'm sorry. I guess I wasn't thinking. Braeden will be fine. I'm sure he made his promise to return to you."

The memory of him asking her to wait for him revived her uncertainty. "Well, he asked me to wait for him. I didn't promise to marry him, but told him I'd be willing to be wooed."

Eleanor's laugh cheered her some.

"Good girl, make the man work. Don't let him assume anything."

Her lips twisted to one side as she considered her actions. "I'm not sure I wanted to make him work. It was just that I got away from the convent where I had no choice about any action, and I didn't know if I wanted more of the same with a kinder master, but a master all the same. I heard the women complain who came to you, hoping for relief with the rose hips jelly."

"I can see why you might think that." Eleanor pushed the door open. "Let's have a cup of tea and some bread. We can talk it over on a full stomach."

Meara helped her set the table as they both waited for the water to boil. "You were happy in your marriage, weren't you?"

In the process of measuring out the tea leaves, Eleanor stopped, her eyes taking on a faraway look. "If you'd asked me while I was married, I wouldn't have said I was happy. Depending on the day, I might gripe about my husband's snoring keeping me awake or that he'd left his dirty clothes on the floor instead of putting them in the basket. Now, I see what incredibly small offenses they were. Sometimes, I want to shake the woman who complains about their husband slurping his soup or falling asleep after dinner. At least they have a husband. To answer your question, yes, we were happy. I didn't realize how happy I was until I no longer had a husband."

Eleanor went back to measuring tea leaves, signaling the moment of self-revelation was gone. Too bad. Meara wanted to know more. Her companion's heartfelt revelations helped her to make sense of life. "What made you realize it after his death?"

The steaming kettle took precedence as Eleanor lifted it from the stove and poured the water into the waiting china teapot. She capped the pot to allow it to steep and pulled a tea cozy over it. "Ah, my Donald." She collapsed into a kitchen chair with a wheezy exhale. "He wasn't a flashy man who drew attention to himself, which meant I didn't know half the things he did for the family until later. He often worked long hours to give me luxuries such as French milled soap or taking a seashore holiday. Instead of taking up expensive hobbies, he spent time with the children. He even helped me with the simple chores. He made sure I had a village girl to help me around the house. When I had all that, I didn't think about it. It just was."

"He sounds like a kind man." Her simple question had turned her normally jovial hostess reflective and somber.

"He was. I married young. I never ever realized it was a man's world until I didn't have one." Eleanor poured tea into the two mugs.

Sister Thomas had said something similar. "How's it a man's world?"

"Being in the company of women your entire life made you ignorant of male hierarchy." She dipped the knife into the butter crock, loading it with the creamy substance, then spread it and on her thick bread slice. "Even though the convent was run by women, the church is headed up by a man, the Pope. All his Archbishops, bishops, even priests are all men. Women aren't trusted to have any type of authority in the church. It's the same in the government and business."

"Mother Superior had charge over the convent and reported to no man."

"Ha. That's what she wanted people to think. There was some man over her, demanding a tithe from the convent. Although, that treasure box you found makes me wonder if something else was going on with her."

"If women are so inferior in men's eyes, why didn't a man run the convent?" All this talk perplexed her. Mother Superior was not one to back down easily. The stern taskmaster practically snatched her back when Simon he took her hand.

"I bet there would be many a man who would volunteer for such an assignment." She blew on her tea as she raised it to her lips. After taking a sip, she spoke. "The Pope wouldn't allow any of the brothers or priests to take such a position. They've taken a vow of celibacy, and women would tempt them to break that vow. Besides, most regard women on the same level as animals. I blame an old fellow by the name of Socrates for starting that rumor. There would be no honor in riding herd on women."

"Why did people even listen to this," she sounded out the unfamiliar name, "So Crat Teas."

Eleanor rolled her eyes, before giving her a weary smile. "He was a man. I suspect half the time men fear women getting together and turning things upside down. Which is why they came up with the nonsense that women are inferior to men."

Braeden expected her to wait as if she hadn't anything better to do with her time. How many men kissed their wives and sweethearts goodbye expecting the women to shut themselves away like a broom in a closet? A tiny sting of irritation curled her upper lip. Why were women always blamed for tempting men?

Meara had sat through the 'Receiving the Habit' ceremony when Sister Thomas entered the community. "I know the sister takes a vow of chastity. How could they tempt a brother?"

"Ah, there's the rub. They do it by simply being female. It all goes back to Eve and the apple. Somehow, Adam never owned up to his own disobedience. It's always Eve's fault for suggesting eating the fruit."

"I always wondered about that. If Adam wanted to obey God, then why didn't he? It would be the same with the brothers if they broke their vow of celibacy, then pointed their finger at women for causing their stumble." She slipped the tip of her finger into the tea to see if it was cool enough to drink. It was. She took a long sip thinking how she'd never grow tired of the taste of tea.

"I think you're starting to get a notion of how the world works. Of course, I didn't get my education until after my children and husband died. Men came, saying my husband owed them money. At the time, my grief was so strong I gave them what they wanted just to have them leave. It never occurred to me they would victimize a grieving widow. My Donald had served as a barrier between me and the ugly side of humanity. Fortunately, I shook off my bereavement before I gave away everything. I soon realized I couldn't live as I did with what money I had left. I sold the house and most of its effects. I probably didn't get a fair price in my anxiety to leave the area. Everywhere I went, inquiring about a place to live, they wanted to talk to my husband. Even as a widow, they expected a man to step in and manage things for me."

"How did you end up in this cottage?"

A glint of the jovial Eleanor showed as she winked. "Do you want the story I tell the villagers or the truth?"

"Both. The truth first." It would benefit her to know both, especially if someone ever asked her in the village.

"Ah, well, you remember I mentioned staying with my friend Lynne?"

She bobbed her head as she chewed her jam loaded bread slice.

"It was a good thing I did. It gave me a connection to the village. The two of us used to go into the forest searching for rue, feather-few, gilly, and marjoram. We passed the abandoned cottage a few times. The man who lived there had wandered off, never to return. I took a liking to the place. Lynne inquired without any luck. The woods are common property, making it likely the original tenant never bought the land."

"Then why did it matter if you contacted the original owner?" Perhaps she could find a friendly cottage in the woods to call her own.

"It's about appearance. As an outsider, I couldn't afford for the villagers to take a dislike to me. Lynne found a relative of the former resident who gave me permission to use the cottage. I moved Oscar and myself into the place and started making repairs. That's how I ended up here."

If she could fall into something similar, it would suit her fine. "You never worry about the man coming back to find you in his home?" An impression of an angry man pushing an upset Eleanor out the door disturbed her, although her friend kept drinking her tea, obviously not feeling the same alarm.

"It's been years now. I've worked hard to make my concoctions a needed item in the local community. The old man who used to live here did little more than threaten those who came near his cottage. I'm betting the villagers would take my side. I would not give up without a fight. Truthfully, I have nothing to lose. He'd get more teeth and nails from me than a cornered badger."

"Well, for the man's continued good health, let's hope he doesn't come back. Could be he came here to think something over. Once he did, he returned to wherever he came from. So, you think the village would support your claim over his?"

"Yes. He was an outsider who had no relatives to stand by him. People assumed Lynne and I were cousins. She didn't dissuade that belief. For whatever reason, people tend to trust people they think have family ties to someone already in the village. The man could be a wastrel, but people would give him a pass because he had people."

It made her think of her father who came to claim his birthright only to end up dying for it. The voice she attributed to her father sounded in her head. *I didn't die for the land, but to keep you and Sorcha safe.*

It didn't erase the hatred she felt toward her father's killers, even if his death was unintentional. Years spent trying to marshal her emotions dissolved when she found out about her mother's panicked flight and her father's murder. Her days since were awash with fear, surprise, delight, anger, even love.

"My father was killed even though the farm was his inheritance. Someone wrote my uncle a letter detailing how my father died. Apparently, some of the villagers were worked up due to the fact he was an outsider. You'd think as a real relative, they would have accepted him."

Meara only trusted Simon, Eleanor, and Braeden. Unfortunately, Braeden and Simon both left her.

"Hard to say what happened without being there. People often make up the facts after the incident occurred. I suspect your father could have been aware of any hatred directed toward Druids and wouldn't have made mention of it. Whoever had their eye on the land became upset that it had been snatched out of his grasp, when your father, an outsider, turns up with an Irish wife claiming the land. It would be easy to concoct a story sure to frighten the ignorant."

Did it happen that way? It may have. Still, she needed to know more. "Why would it matter if my mother was Irish?"

"It doesn't matter to me." Eleanor topped off her teacup and did the same for Meara. "I'm not sure how much recent history you know. England has a way of taking over countries, including Scotland, Wales, and Ireland. Most accept it, but there are always rebels fighting against English rule, thumbing their nose at parliament and the king. It tends to make the ordinary Brit think of the Irish, Scots, or Welsh as untamed, dangerous folks."

"I'm sure my mother wasn't like that. My uncle told me she was a woman of strong opinions who chose to marry Fulmen and relocate in England." How could anyone have anything against Sorcha?

"A woman who did as she pleased. That would be enough to scare some of the local men. Still, I think a scandalous tale was concocted that had the men forcing their way onto the farm. It is neither here nor there since you'll never visit the place where your father fell."

The thought had occurred to her before. She should see where her father died. "It should be my farm now."

Eleanor put down her cup to cover her hand with hers. "Forget about it. Haven't you heard anything I said? You don't even know where this place is. I'm sure a slip of a girl like yourself would be laughed off the property, even if you did know where it was. Be happy with what you have. Consider that Braeden is the pick of the village men, and he wants you to wait for him."

She didn't need to point out he might not come back, or he could come back and no longer feel the same way about her. Should she even make such decisions without contacting what was left of her family or seeing where her father fell as he lay dying?

"You're right. I'm a very lucky girl." Too bad she didn't believe her words. She had to discover who she was before she could commit to Braeden. Her hips shifted in the hard chair as she wrestled with her restlessness. The urge to dash out of the house after Braeden consumed her. The man would be long gone by now. Even if she did catch him, what would she say? How could she explain her feelings when she wasn't even certain what they were?

Her inner struggle must not have shown since her companion continued to talk. "I know it's hard for you. The waiting. What you need to do is to stay busy. The best way to do that is helping me to make more rose hips jelly for another market day. Plenty of women will trade eggs and butter for a miraculous cure."

Eleanor grinned and waggled her eyebrows. Was she doubting her rose hip jelly or ridiculing the women who put so much faith in it? Perhaps Meara should try it. Would it help her be any more certain about what path to take?

"How did you know you were in love?"

The woman cocked her head and bestowed Meara with a knowing look. "Now you think you're in love. Not too surprised. Most young people think they're in love whenever they see a pretty face or a handsome pair of shoulders. Love isn't a one-time thing. It's a live, growing entity."

Somehow, she made it sound like a plant springing up between two people. A rose or stalks of lavender depending on the depth of their bond. "Why isn't it a one-time thing? Are you saying people will fall in love again and again?"

The woman placed her hands flat on the table and pushed up into a standing position. Her fingers wrapped around the teapot as she cleared the table. "When you're young, like you and Braeden, love is a feeling."

"Are you saying it isn't a feeling?" Sometimes it felt like Eleanor spoke another language for all the sense it made.

The clatter of dishes competed with her words. "Love is an action." She hesitated, glanced toward the mantle where all the family photographs sat. "Back when Donald was courting me, he told me he loved me. I believed him. After we were married, he showed me every day."

The possibility that an action could demonstrate love caused her heart to skip a beat. All she had to do was watch for that act to know. The idea made her eyes glow. Who knew it was so easy? "What did he do?"

Sister Gabriella told her about what the courtiers did for Queen Elizabeth, saying, "In the evenings, he could take her hand and recite a poem on bended knee." At the time, she thought it was supposed to demonstrate their dedication to the crown. Another sister scolded her for the story, pointing out our loyalty was to the divine king.

"Ah, it was several things. He got up early and started the fire so the house would be warm when I awakened. He went to work every day to support the family. No matter how burnt or inedible dinner had been he always thanked me for fixing it." A wistful smile found its way to Eleanor's face.

It was not what Meara expected, but she thought how her cell at the convent was often cold. It would have been nice to wake up in a warm room. She'd not given much thought to men's jobs. If she had, she'd assume they did it for themselves. Eleanor showed her working every day was for the family. "I understand, I think. By doing these things it made you feel loved."

"That and more." Her hand fluttered up and rested above her heart. "Sometimes, it was what he didn't do that demonstrated his devotion."

Meara's nose crinkled as she considered a simple question for which she expected a yes or no answer taking a convoluted route. "What?"

"Some of those women who buy my jelly have husbands who spend their free time in the tavern, shooting the breeze with like-minded men, drinking up the extra money, and flirting with the barmaids. My Donald wasn't like that. He occasionally liked a pint with his meal, but he didn't need to head to the local watering hole to do so. At the time, I thought my husband was a good, decent man, but I never realized how much he loved me until he was gone."

"I'm not sure I understand."

"Not surprised." She placed a work rough hand on Meara's shoulder. "Going to the tavern wasn't bad, but those men only cared about themselves and their ease. They never thought about their children being tucked into bed without a father's loving kiss. Their thoughts never strayed to a wife who darned his socks while he was out carousing. Love happens over time. The wait could be a proving time for the two of you."

Those weren't her exact thoughts, but she thought something similar. It was more along the lines of searching for Simon while writing to Braeden. "You could be right."

Her companion's eyes twinkled, announcing she knew she was right. "Ah, yes, perhaps. Let's get this table cleared and get the jelly started. You go out to the shed and get me ten jars with lids."

THE DAY PASSED quickly with the rose hip jelly steam scenting the air. Eleanor issued instructions as certain as any general. Meara rushed around the room, sanitizing jars, pushing Oscar off the table, and stirring jelly. Before long, they had ten cooling jars. Sweat dotted her brow and tendrils escaped from the rawhide strip she used to tie her hair back. In a couple of hours, a grease pencil would serve to mark the lids.

She emptied out the canning water onto the back flagstones. Eleanor stood close by clucking to herself.

"Did I do it wrong?" While the cook in the convent kitchen had never let her help, there couldn't be that many ways to dump water.

"Hmm, no, I was just thinking about blackberries. If we found some we could make jam. Then we could have used the same water."

Jams and jelly-making was a hot, messy job. Meara sighed, realizing there would be a berry walk in her near future. The woman was determined to keep her busy, leaving no time to think about Braeden. As soon as she thought his name, his face crowded into her mind with gentle eyes and smiling countenance. Where was he now? Had they reached town yet?

"Grab your basket. Day's a-wasting." Eleanor pushed past her with a large basket hanging from her arm.

Meara found a basket on the hook inside the house. The small cottage had a hook or shelf to keep everything in order. Eleanor's voice, lifted in song, made her smile. **"My story to you I will relate concerning of a pretty maid, concerning of sweet, lovely Joan as she sat milking all alone."**

The woman wasn't singing about Joan of Arc. The sisters didn't mention her much, even after she gained sainthood after her denouncement as a witch and a heretic. It could be because she was a female who blazed her own way as opposed to following rules.

On the way out, she herded Oscar in front of her. The cat would be better named Joan, since he did exactly as he wanted. If left alone, he'd probably knock over the jelly jars. "I'm ready," she announced as she used her foot to move the cat out the door.

"Good. We need to hurry. We won't be the only ones foraging.

I've seen some berries close to the creek."

"There's a big bush inside the convent walls if you don't mind going there." Since her last experience involved running for her life from Adelaide, she hoped her suggestion would be vetoed.

"Most of the villagers wouldn't know about the bush. I think we should visit."

The woman picked up her pace as if racing possible pickers who would beat her to the bounty. Not the reaction Meara had expected. Why did she even mention it? Her steps slowed as a weight of contradictory emotions settled around her with the fear of encountering mean-spirited girls overriding any others. There was probably little chance of anyone lurking around the convent. Surely, a close encounter of the bee kind would keep them far away. Nor might they not be as bold with Eleanor as a witness.

A DARKNESS, NOT like the night, but more like dark silty mud, clung to her whenever she entered the burnt convent walls. Instead of feeling familiar and comforting, it seemed like the very walls mocked her for not knowing her identity. Another part of her pushed her forward, whispering about the possibility of Simon or Angus returning to look for her.

The address she needed could still be hidden in the office. Last time, a giant crucifix almost crushed her. What type of divine retribution could she expect next?

Eleanor stood unmoving in the shadows close to the break in the convent walls. She held one hand up. Young voices shouting and the occasional squeal, indicating play. Oddly, it was something she'd never done. The village youngsters chasing each other through the busy marketplace was the first display of playing she'd ever seen.

Her companion nodded at her, then cupped her hands around her mouth emitting a ghostly moan. "Whoooo goes there? Disturbing my bones. A curse on you. Flee now before I have your own bones for supper."

Two children she recognized as the offspring of the chicken snatcher, scrambled across the wall, screaming.

"Did you have to do that? Scare them?"

"Yes, did you forget how you were almost crushed by the crucifix? Now, they'll avoid the place for a time. When they get their courage back up, blackberry season will be over. Sometimes you've got to do the tricky thing for the right thing to fall into place."

They pulled up their dresses to scramble over the walls. The berries glistened in the sunlight. The top berries had been bird pecked, as expected. The rest were full and glossy. Her fingers plucked the berries while avoiding most of the thorns. Sometimes you had to do the hard thing to do the right thing.

Eleanor popped a berry into her mouth and sucked on it noisily. "Good berries. Now that Braeden isn't on the scene, I think you should go to the local dance they're having this week."

It wasn't the right thing, "Why?"

First, the ditty, then scaring the children, now an outrageous suggestion. Did she even know this woman?

"You have to show Adelaide you aren't afraid of her." A few more berries went directly into her mouth, bypassing the basket. She hummed her opinion of the fruit.

The only problem was she was afraid of Adelaide. "What purpose would that serve?"

"It would keep her from harassing you every chance she got. It will give you a chance to make friends. The more friends you have, the safer you will be. This is the perfect time since she'll be too busy with Braeden's desertion to concentrate on you."

A cloud passed over the sun as she tried to comprehend Eleanor's rationale. The cloud continued on, allowing the sun to shine down unfiltered. "Going to the dance would be the challenging thing."

"Exactly."

"How do I know what the right thing is?" Would her foray into village life result in Simon's return?

"You never know what the right thing is until it happens."

Chapter Eleven

THE FLASH OF light and a frightening boom woke Meara. The gray silhouette of the table and stove reminded her of her location. Her hand pressed against her chest as she tried to catch her breath. The cannon roar must have been the thunder. That's all it was. Nothing more. A tear slid down her cheek, followed by another.

The German soldiers, Zeppelins flying overhead, and the blinding blast of artillery shells appeared whenever her eyelids closed. Along with the noise of gunfire, she could hear talking. "Douglas, I need you to scout out the ridge ahead."

She wanted to shout, "No, don't do it! It's a trap!" even while caught in a waking dream. Could she be seeing the future? If so, she should warn Braeden, before he made a fatal mistake. A half roll took her and the blanket to the cold slate floor.

The chill of the stone chased the last dregs of the dream. She crouched as she pushed up, doing her best not to make any noise.

"I'm awake," Eleanor called from her bed in the corner. "Been awake for a while. I wasn't sure if I should disturb you. The way you threshed around I knew you were having nightmares. My first inclination was to interrupt them, but thought maybe it was something you needed to experience."

Needed to experience? "It was horrible! Smoke from all the shooting and cannons darkened the sky. Braeden was there, I knew it. Even though a man called him Douglas, I knew who it was. The man told Braeden to scout ahead, and I knew it wasn't safe."

"Could be a vision. I'd be surprised if you didn't have the sight

141

from your parents." Her hostess sat up in bed and turned down a corner of the blanket as if undecided if she'd remain in bed or get up. "Want to talk about it?"

Her bare feet maneuvered around the table and chairs as she paced the shadowy room. "No, I don't want to talk about it. I don't want to remember anything." The thunder rumbled, sounding close, when a bright explosion caught her in mid-stride, startling her and sending her to the floor. Her hands covered her head as she whimpered. Bare feet slapped against the floor, but the soft-pawed Oscar reached her first, rubbing against her arms, his plaintive mews questioning her behavior.

"I'm fine."

"You're not." Eleanor held onto the frame of a chair and knelt beside her. "If lightning sends you to the floor, you're not fine. Talk to me. If it's a vision, there may be a message for you."

It wasn't message she wanted or needed. Meara dropped her arms from her head and shifted into a sitting position. "I'm not sure how it could be a vision. Sister Thaddeus saw a vision of the Holy Mother in a pail of milk. This wasn't like that. People rushed past me. The smoke made it hard to breathe. It was dark until an explosion lit up the night."

Goosebumps formed on her arms as she described the night terror. Eleanor placed an arm around her and guided her to her bed. Meara climbed into the still warm bed and allowed herself to be tucked in. The blanket, tight around her, offered some comfort. Was this what it would have been like to have a parent?

"Better?" Eleanor perched on the edge of the bed and patted Meara's arm outlined by the covers.

"Some. I wish I hadn't even had the dream. That would have been better."

Instead of answering, Eleanor held up two fingers to her mouth, as her eyes grew vague. Oscar jumped on the bed. His loud purr filled the silence as he kneaded a place on the bed to rest. The movements of the animal relaxed her. A sigh brought her attention back to her reticent friend.

"I think it was a vision," Eleanor offered.

"No, it couldn't be." Meara scooted into a sitting position, irritating the cat who voiced his discontent at her movements.

"Listen." She held one finger up, shushing any denials. "I'm aware that many people claim to see the Holy Mother at various times. Sometimes it is on the side of the church, other times on a bit of toasted bread, or in a pail of milk. What they see are a few lines they interpret to be Mary. They see what they want to see. Sometimes, it brings them recognition and attention."

"I'm sure Sister Thaddeus would never do anything to draw attention, especially if it wasn't true." Meara regarded all the nuns with equal amounts of awe and fear.

The woman chuckled and shook her head. "When it comes to innocence and believing the best of everyone, you outshine all the sisters. People, even sisters, like to feel important sometimes. A vision of Mary would do it. It's rather like *The Emperor's New Clothes*."

"What?" She knew they had a king, not an emperor.

Eleanor waved her hand as if erasing her words. "Forget about it. It's a faery tale. I'll tell you about it over breakfast. Now, I want to talk to you about your vision."

Meara shook her head, unaware of why the woman insisted on calling it something it wasn't.

"All right." She held up both hands as if surrendering. "We'll call it a premonition. Some of the things you said made me wonder. There's no way you'd know them unless you'd been in battle yourself."

The vivid tableau she'd thought seared into her memory was fading around the edges as if burning away. "What did I say that made you think that?"

"My husband had a brother, Eldon. He served in the Boxer

Rebellion and lived to talk about it. Too bad cholera did him in. I remember him telling me that while in service, he felt like no one knew his first name because it was never used."

How did a conversation from a deceased man figure into her dream? "Oh, Douglas. Someone called Braeden by his last name."

"Yes." Eleanor nodded before continuing. "How you describe the smoke being thick and choking. Eldon was in the thick of the fight. He manned one of the cannons and described how half the time he couldn't even see what he was aiming at even though it was day. The darkness made him think he'd gone blind."

"Yes, that's it! I thought it was night." She couldn't remember being on the battlefield but instead, she hovered above it as if a cloud or an angel. "I peered down at the scene as opposed to being on the ground."

"Interesting." Eleanor's fingers wove together, allowing her to steeple her index fingers. Her eyes stayed on her own fingers as if transfixed as she spoke. "People are always in their own dreams. It makes no matter if it is a good dream or a bad one. The person who's having it must be in it, but you felt like you were watching it from far away like a guardian angel."

"Ha! Mother Superior would have never used my name and angel together, but it was something like that. Can you explain it to me?"

Her lips twisted one way, then the other. "No, I can't. It sounds like you saw a brief second of battle. Something that hasn't happened yet."

"How's that helpful? Am I supposed to find Braeden and tell him not to scout over the next hill?" She sat up and leaned forward, wrapping her arms around her bent knees and rocked back and forth, waiting for any type of wisdom to flow from Eleanor.

"Did you see anything bad happen to Braeden?"

Her question surprised her. Braeden had jumped up at his name, snapped a salute, nod an acknowledgment, and then headed toward the dark ridge. "I figured ammunition flying everywhere was bad enough, but no one was shot. I felt apprehensive about him following orders."

"Aye. I can understand that. Eldon told Donald that his sergeant warned him womenfolk didn't need to know what went on in battle. He mistakenly thought a female would be too frail to understand. Could be he knew those at home would worry, knowing there was nothing they could do. I will say this perplexes me. It's too soon for Braeden to be at the front. The best you can do is think good thoughts and try to go back to sleep."

That wasn't going to happen.

Eleanor slid off her bed and ambled toward the fireplace to poke with a long metal poker at the smoldering embers until a spark flickered. A handful of sweet grass created a blaze that she fed with twigs, then sticks, and finally a log. Once the fire caught, the flames illuminated the weary creases in the woman's face. More than an unexpected startle in the night had caused the creases to be etched there.

"You must have slept through the night before I came along." Meara slipped out of the warm bed, smoothing the blanket with her hand. The fire meant they were both up for a while at least. The wind whistled and chewed on the thatched roof. Her eyes rolled up to the shadowed ceiling expecting a gap, exposing the night dark sky or possibly a stream of water.

"You'd be wrong, especially on nights like these." Her hand gestured upward. "There are leaks. You'll see them soon enough. Help me gather the pots and buckets."

Even though she had an inkling where everything was, more light would help find it. Her fingers gripped the cold glass globe as she lit the lantern. The clatter of metal indicated not only had the buckets been located, but also one had been dropped. Meara held the light aloft to locate the dropped item. "I got it." She scooped up the bucket with one hand. "Where should I put it?"

"Center that one on the table. I usually get a decent size drip there." Eleanor spoke from her crouched position near the wall where she lined up another pot. "If you weren't here, I'd still be awake, trying to hold off drowning inside my own home."

"Wouldn't be an issue if your roof was patched." Water dropped on her head and eased down her neck leaving a chill behind. Meara peered up to see where the troublesome rain was coming from and got a big fat drop in her eye. "Oh! I think you may have been wrong about the leak."

Eleanor looked upward as she walked to the table. "I always put it the middle." A solid plunk indicated the table pot received water too. "Where?"

A raindrop bounced off Meara's pointing hand. "There."

"Stay there. I'll get a bowl since we're out of pots."

The water splattered her slowly, getting her wetter and wetter as the search for a large bowl continued. They spent the rest of the night emptying bowls and pots as the storm raged on. Soggy and exhausted, Meara opened the back door to empty another full bucket. The horizon lightened with the approaching dawn and a bird sang nearby. "It's finally stopped." She closed the door and leaned against it. "Eleanor, when I take possession of my father's farm, you'll be welcome there. I'll make sure the roof doesn't leak."

"Ha! I'd like that," she called from her slumped position in the kitchen chair, still clutching a bucket. "Could you make sure it has electricity, too? I hear that's grand."

"Of course." She decided not to ask what that was since it was probably something else everybody knew about, except her. Life outside the convent walls would take some getting used to. What she really needed to do was locate her uncle and find her way to Galway County. Her eyes shut as she considered the voyage. It would help if she knew which way to go.

"How would I get to Ireland?"

The woman murmured to herself as she picked up buckets and

pans and carried them to the door. "By boat." She added as she neared Meara, "I suspect after the storm last night, you could build an ark and sail away."

"You have the right of it. Which direction should I go?" She swung the door open and helped Eleanor empty the receptacles on the flagstones. The crisp, green smell of the woods greeted her, reminding her that after every storm was a morning like this. A large spider dangled from the roof mere inches from her face. The multi-legged creature turned as it worked its way up a single gossamer thread. The diligence of the arachnid impressed her as it climbed to a still intact web glistening with water droplets.

"A spider," Eleanor remarked, noticing where her attention was. "It's a symbol of change, feminine energy, protection, fate, and death."

Meara could have done without the last one. "How did you learn so much about the inhabitants of the forest?" Her hostess did have a habit of quoting odd axioms usually related to nature.

"I came out here a broken city woman. My friend was forever wandering in the woods collecting herbs. She taught me some. I read a book or two, but mainly," she gestured to the outside world, "nature taught me. It's hard not to learn when you live alone in the woods. Every flower, every bird song, even a mushroom popping up after a storm has wisdom to offer."

It made sense in some ways, but in others, her cryptic sayings clearly contradicted each other. "How can protection and death be contained in the same symbol?"

"You've a lively mind, for sure. Used to confuse me as well, but often death is just change, rather like the seasons. It doesn't mean we're pleased about the change and often mourn it, like a physical death."

It reminded her too much of her dream. "Like Braeden leaving?"

"That's one." Eleanor agreed, tapped her shoulder, and motioned her toward the fire. "It's starting to die. Get it going and I'll start breakfast. There's many more. Missing your uncle could be a change or death. It doesn't mean you won't see him, but the uncomplicated way of having him gather you up as he passed through won't happen either."

Her shoulders straightened as Meara stepped away from the open door. The cheerful birdsong lifted her spirits. The feathered creatures who endured every type of weather and could still sing represented hope. "Why does everything have to be so hard?"

"Ah, if I knew the answer to that, I'd be a rich woman. I'd sit on my mountain and allow people to offer me gifts in search of that answer. Take heart in the fact that as long as you have trials you won't turn into a nasty piece of work like Adelaide."

Another cryptic remark that left her confused. A sharp twinge of annoyance spread through her body. Why couldn't people say what they meant? Then again, maybe Eleanor was doing exactly that. Meara's issue was she had so little information as a base. It made it difficult to decipher various sayings that most took for granted. "Why is that?

The woman puttered around the dry sink filling up the teapot from a pitcher of fresh water as opposed to roof water. "Well, I wasn't here when Adelaide was born, but I heard her mother died in childbirth. Daughters have a habit of winding their fathers around their finger while mothers teach them practical skills. If her mama had lived, I doubt if she'd tolerate her tantrums whenever she didn't get what she wanted. Her father has worked long hours at the mill and hired women in the village to care for her. I think everything was fine until one of them tried to correct the lass. Supposedly, her wails of discontent could be heard through the village and had her father fearing she'd die on him, too."

"What happened then?" She moved closer as to not miss a word.

Eleanor shook her head slowly. "The woman lost her position. Extra money is hard to come by in the village. The miller paid in coin, too. The next woman never did anything to upset the girl. A few times the woman suffered harm as she threw herself on top of a fire Adelaide had started or pulled her out of the way of a runaway horse. I even heard one villager refer to Adelaide as the devil incarnate."

"If she's that bad, why do people bother with her? I plan on avoiding her."

The mug clumped on the table as Eleanor sat them down and gave her a long look. "Have you learned nothing? Braeden left since he was unable to escape the tendrils of obligation that Adelaide wound around him, tighter than any spider's web. There are those who have power and those who don't. We are the ones without power."

Just when she thought she'd worked matters out, another obstacle presented itself. "Doesn't her father see how bad his daughter treats everyone?"

"Easy for you to see because you have empathy for fellow creatures. Adelaide has none. I'm fairly sure her father is devoid of that particular emotion as well." Eleanor shrugged as she sniffed. "Could be the man now sees what a monster he created, and his only goal is to unload her on another man. Her father, Herman, is still young enough to marry again, but no woman will enter his house as long as Adelaide resides there."

"How do you develop empathy, and why is she missing it?" None of the sisters mentioned the virtue of empathy.

"Another good question that I've given some thought." She held out a thick slice of bread to Meara. "Do you want to toast it over the fire?"

She took the bread and speared it with one of the sharpened green sassafras sticks near the hearth for such a purpose. The heat from the fire washed over her, warming her and drying her clothes, making them stiff as her bread browned. "What did you learn from your musings?"

"When something bad happens, you have two choices. Could be

something as small as not getting a desired item."

The idea puzzled her since she'd never expected anything. Even at Christmas, the sisters could not accept gifts from their families since they had taken the vow of poverty. "What else?"

"A friend could betray you. An illness like polio could sideline you from a life you expected to have. It could be a death of a loved one. People feel sorry for themselves, feeling as if life tricked them. They go about with a sour expression and equally ugly attitude."

It reminded her of a couple sisters. She'd figured the unhappy expression was part of the habit they donned every day. The convent hadn't been their life's aspiration, or maybe they thought it would be different. "Tell me the second one." Her bread toasted, she stood and returned to the table, where she slid into a chair.

Eleanor cracked an egg against the skillet sizzling on the wood stove. "For a while there, I was the first. I felt like a victim, constantly asking God why he was punishing me. I finally realized people get sick and die. Thousands died, not just my family. As far as I can tell no one deserved to die, especially the children." She threw a fierce look at Meara in case she'd challenge her assumption.

"No, children should never die."

"Aye, you're right on that, but they do every day. When I came to realize there was nothing I could do, I accepted it and moved on. Didn't forget. It still hurt, but after a while, everyone loses patience with the grieving woman. If I had to cry, I did it in private. Eventually, I could go through a day without crying. Whenever I met a woman who had lost a husband or child, I felt her hurt. My ability to share her loss somehow made it a little less."

It made sense in some ways. If she ever met another orphan girl raised in a convent, then she'd understand some of her feelings. The likelihood of finding such a person was improbable at best. "Which one is Adelaide?"

"Ah, that's the strangest one yet. A person who has everything she ever wanted and every obstacle removed from her path by an indulgent father."

The memory of Braeden's departure filled her throat as if a swallow of unchewed food rested there. Eleanor poured the steaming water into her mug for tea. Without thought, Meara lifted the mug to her lips and took a sip of the scalding liquid. It singed her tongue and burned her throat, causing her to gasp.

"Good heavens. What are you doing? Trying to burn yourself?" Eleanor put down the kettle, poured a jelly jar of water, and rushed it to the table. "Drink this."

The cool water soothed her burnt tongue and throat. What was she trying to do? She'd not confess the pain of Braeden's leaving caused her to forget basic things such as checking the temperature of her tea before drinking. It would make her sound like a victim. All the same, she needed to say something. "With Braeden leaving the way he did, that's something that didn't go Adelaide's way."

"Yes. I don't want to be the person who tells her. She'll turn on the messenger and savage them as if a cornered bobcat. She might even do more harm than a frightened feline. It's not telling what she'll do. The girl will not blame herself. It will be someone else's fault."

Meara tested her tea with her pinky and found it now warm, as opposed to hot. A sulfuric stink had Eleanor bolting from the table. "Oh no, the eggs. They're ruined."

"I'm sure they're fine. Trust me. Whenever we had eggs at the convent, we had two choices, runny or burnt. I'm sure yours is in between."

The woman gave her weak smile from her spot at the stove. "They're not runny. I'll give you that." She gave a chuckle as she dished them up. "In the end, it's a bit of protein, which we can both use after being up all night."

Oscar meowed his comment, which could have been a suggestion to offer the food to the cat. The plate with the firm yellow center and the egg white curling up along the edges looked good to her. "Not sure what you mean. This egg looks perfect."

"Everyone should have your attitude." Eleanor moved the skillet to the dry sink before carrying her own plate to the table. The two of them forked down their breakfast as the fire crackled in the background. A suspicion developed as she chewed. Growing larger, she hurried to swallow, seeking reassurance that it was another thing she had blown out of proportion.

"Who will Adelaide blame for Braeden leaving?"

Eleanor hoisted an eyebrow with her egg-laden fork almost to her mouth. "You, of course."

Chapter Twelve

MARKET DAY ARRIVED a few short days later. Eleanor insisted Meara didn't have to accompany her. Numerous filled jelly jars crowded the kitchen table along with the bundled herbs. An unexpected find of berries and rose hips resulted in a bounty of merchandise. To use every available jar, Eleanor dumped out spices onto the table for their containers.

On the high shelf where Eleanor usually stored her bottles of spices, a row of tightly woven dried grass containers stood. Some were round while others resembled boxes complete with tight fitting lids. Meara reached for a basket container. A scrap of cloth lined the basket before she held it against the table lip and used her curved hand to brush the spice into the container. It was a stopgap measure that wouldn't keep out the dampness. Still, pride had Meara straightening her shoulders. As far as accomplishments, there wasn't much she could lay claim to, but she could weave a tight basket courtesy of Sister Gabriella's instruction.

Where was Gabriella? Was she happy? Why couldn't she be more like Gabriella, forging her destiny instead of hiding out in the woods just to avoid a possible confrontation with Adelaide?

A sharp crack and grunt came from the doorway where Eleanor was pulling in a thick tree branch. Rivulets of sweat traced their way down the woman's face as she pulled the branch closer to the table. Smaller branches stuck out from it with a few dead leaves still attached.

"What's that for?" Firewood chopping happened outside.

Eleanor wiped her brow with her sleeve before answering. "I had an idea. The milkmaids used to carry milk with a yoke across their shoulders. Somehow, it balanced out the weight and allowed them to carry more than they would have by using their hands. I thought I'd give it a go."

Not too long ago, Meara had tried such a system only to have the yoke break under the weight of the water buckets. "It doesn't work as well as you might think." Using the hatchet, Meara trimmed off the extra branches and both ends, creating a limb that was about a foot taller than she was. A slight bend marred its symmetry.

"I'm surprised at you. I wouldn't have taken you for a doubting Thomas." Eleanor wrapped her hand around the cleaned branch and brandished it. "It will work."

The remark about a doubting Thomas stung. Out of all the disciples, he was only second to Judas when it came to how-not-to-act. Still, she eyed the branch thinking of the narrow path that twisted around the trees and undergrowth. Most of the time, they had to walk single file. No way could Eleanor manage with her dubious yoke. "I'll go with you."

It wasn't what she wanted, but how could she allow the woman who rescued her to tote all the jellies to market on her own? The extra expense of feeding another person forced her into making more merchandise and visiting the market more often. It would be churlish of her not to assist.

The branch popped and broke as Eleanor bent it once, then she bent it again until she had several foot size pieces she placed in the kindling box. "I wasn't too sure how far I'd have to go with my ruse. I dragged in the deadest branch I could find."

"I don't understand." Meara rubbed her neck muscles that tightened with tension whenever she encountered a perplexing situation. There were plenty of opportunities outside the convent walls to stress her mind and body. "Why didn't you tell me you wanted me to go with you?"

Eleanor clucked as she scooped up a large, sturdy basket and filled it with jars. "It had to be your decision, not mine." She tucked in the bundled herbs between the jars.

"I would have gone if you had asked." Her fingers continued to rub the back of her neck, but the muscles got tighter as opposed to relaxed.

"I have no doubt. What you needed to do was come to a decision on your own. I love having you here, but I started thinking I'm no better than your Mother Superior telling you to do this or that." Her thin shoulders went up in a shrug. "It's not what you need."

Meara's fingers released their grip on her neck. No amount of prodding or pinching would relieve the tension until she found her place in the world. "What do you think I need?" She was curious if Eleanor's answer would line up with the one she'd sketched out in the wee hours of the night.

"Well," she pushed away the basket she'd been fussing with, "you need to make your own decisions. Stand on your own feet. I treat you like a child, but you're a woman grown. One who should be examining her own mind on what's right or wrong."

A few short weeks ago, what to do and what not to do involved very few, if any, thought processes. She'd memorized entire chapters of scriptures, repeated the prayers by rote, and fought daily with such sins as sloth when she lingered in the woods too long. Everything she'd believed came to a crashing halt when Eleanor calmly insisted the woman stealing the convent's chickens wasn't committing a horrible sin. Was she any worse than the sisters who used the fire as an excuse to escape an unlikable life choice? No. They made their choice to join the order while she'd been born into it. Still, the high walls, the bells, the somber habits, the unending services were all a part of who she was. Now she had none of it. It didn't matter if she liked it or not. It was what she knew. The trembling started at her knees and spread upward. Meara stumbled toward a chair and collapsed into it.

"What is it, child? I'd thought you'd be excited about overseeing your own life. It's a privilege few women ever have." Eleanor moved closer and stroked Meara's hair.

A deep breath, then another, slowed the trembling in her legs, but her mind raced and refused to calm. "Back when I used to sneak into the woods, I longed to be in charge of my own destiny if only to steal a few more seconds in the woods. A moment or two, nothing more than that and possibly a mirror. Now," she held out her hands palms up, "everything is up to me. Somehow, I have more power than the average woman does over my fate. How can that be?" Her outstretched hands dropped to her legs.

"Ah, poor, sweet dear." Eleanor brushed a kiss on Meara's crown before pulling out her own chair and sitting. "As a mother, I let my children make small choices. Sometimes, it was as simple as what food they'd like to eat or what chore they wanted to do. Most of the choices weren't huge, but they allowed each child to experience some control. As far as I can tell, you didn't get to make any decisions. I can understand why this would be overwhelming."

She reached for Meara's hand lying on her leg. "Still, you're going to have to stand up and make your own choices. Fight your own dragons. Most women go from their father's house to their husband's abode without making a single major decision. They think they have power, but they don't. Often they think they picked their own bridegroom when in truth the father did the picking."

"Do they not resent their limitations?" It had been hard reconciling herself to a world without absolutes. Were the females who left their childhood home for their new role more discerning than she was?

"I remember myself at that age thinking I knew it all when I knew nothing. Most are unaware they have limitations. The life they have is the one they expected to have. Consider this as we walk to the village. You have more control over your life than most of the women you'll meet today."

"This should be a comfort to me when Adelaide attacks me for stealing her beau?"

Eleanor stretched out her legs in front of her and folded her arms. "I blame myself for your apprehension, me and my big mouth. I doubt the girl will show unless she's already developed her cover story."

If she didn't have to worry about Adelaide, then she acted the coward for no reason. Meara rolled her shoulders, then neck, which felt significantly looser than before. "Let's go."

It didn't take them long to pack up, and they were on their way. The cloud cover made the woods gloomier than usual. A sense of foreboding settled into the leafy canopy overhead. "Do you think it's going to rain?"

"It's England. What do you think?" Eleanor joked and then laughed at her own perceived wit.

The brief glimpses of the sky bothered Meara. The grayness didn't resemble storm clouds, but more of a low hanging fog or smoke. Could something be on fire? If so, why couldn't they smell it? The possibility worried her since a lone cottage in the woods would be vulnerable.

Dozens of people crowded the main road leading into the village. Instead of heading to the weekly market, they stood in groups, whispering as if afraid they might be overheard. A few stared up at the sky and pointed.

One red-faced farmer drove three fat hogs through the street grumbling something about no kraut would take what was his.

A familiar woman from the last market approached, waving her kerchief. "Eleanor." She jogged the last few steps to reach them. "Did you hear about the bombing?"

Before either of them could answer, the woman went on to explain. "My husband Marvin claims they were probably trying to hit a port city but fell short. They hit the granary in the next county. It caught fire. With all the stored grain and hay for fuel, it's been burning the entire night."

Eleanor sent Meara an indecipherable glance. Was she warning her against mentioning that the convent suffered a similar fate? Another bombing so close indicated their corner of the world was far from safe. Ireland, besides representing family, appeared more and more like a sanctuary to her.

The women gathered around Eleanor and chatted. One woman took two jars of jelly, afraid that she might run out at an inopportune time. The woman put up her hand to shield her mouth and her words. "It's a terrible thing the Germans did, but my Marvin thinks it may result in higher prices for our hay since the supply will be limited."

Meara knew that less of little was often none. Those with some knowledge of the woods such as Eleanor could eek out an existence, but soon others would be collecting the same berries, nuts, and watercress.

Shoppers worked their way through the market in bursts of speed, acting more like startled woodland creatures than people. They darted from one stall to another. Those unable to break into a run settled for a fast walk while their heads pivoted side to side, trying to ascertain where the danger lay.

Not everyone chose to hoard luxuries such as the rose hips jelly. A few regular customers came to apologize to Eleanor for not buying any. They mumbled something about saving for necessities, which Meara translated to mean food.

A few girls close to her age scurried by. One dark haired girl glanced back and smiled at her. Meara held up a hand in response. Outside of Braeden, she was the first person near her age who'd been friendly. The girl hung back and then watched her friends move past the stall.

One spoke in a carrying voice. "There's nothing there for us. That's just for old ladies."

Eleanor, instead of taking offense, chuckled. "They're making the mistake the young often do, thinking their youth is eternal."

The dark-haired female stood in the street, glancing at Meara, then at her fast-moving group of friends. Decision made, she darted toward Meara with her hand out. "My name's Rosemary Callahan. Pleased to meet you."

A sharp elbow in the ribs from Eleanor had her shaking the girl's hand. "Hi, Rosemary. I'm Meara." What would she do for a last name? Her father had one, but she didn't know it. "Ah, Cleary. Meara Cleary." A sense of rightness settled on her. Hadn't Angus commented how like the Cleary family she was?

"I imagine my cousin is so pleased to meet you," Eleanor prompted.

Ah, yes, a hint. She should say something. "I'm happy to meet you." The words sounded forced, but Rosemary grinned at her, possibly not noticing her stilted speech.

She glanced up the street where her friends had faded into the crowd. "I need to go. Maybe we could talk again. There's a pitch-in dinner and dance happening Friday night at the exhibition barn. You should come. I'm hoping that the recent fire and Grant and Braeden leaving won't put a pall on things."

Her first impulse was to ask about Braeden, but she could feel Eleanor stiffen up beside her. "Oh, I'd like that."

Before she could say anything else, Rosemary held up her hand and darted down the street. Eleanor sighed heavily. "Goodness, I thought you were going to show your hand there."

"Why? Because I didn't know to shake hers?"

"Not that." Eleanor's gaze lifted to the milling people in front of her. "Women shaking hands is relatively new. Just the young people do it. My grandfather told me men shook hands to demonstrate they didn't have a knife to stab the other man. No, I meant you saying something about Braeden."

"I didn't. Why would it have been wrong if I had? Obviously, it's the news of the village." She shrugged, wondering why it would have even mattered, especially when Rosemary was being friendly.

"Ah, there's where you're wrong. If you were my cousin from Cumbria, then you wouldn't know Braeden. At best, you saw him in the market last time. No reason for you to be concerned if he stayed or left, especially considering he's Adelaide beau."

"He's not!" Even though she knew most considered Braeden and Adelaide were a done deal, the idea sickened her.

"Hush."

Eleanor bumped into her as if reaching for a jar, but Meara knew better. It was her way of reminding her where she was. "I get it."

"See that you do. It might be good for you to go to the shindig."

Had she heard her, right? She shot her companion a look of patent disbelief. Her original plan was to hide out in the forest until Simon showed. Had Eleanor forgotten?

"I've pondered the matter. You're new. Folks your age will want to meet you. An average girl would want to be around people her age."

"I could say or do something wrong."

"When in doubt, smile. I'll run sample conversations with you. In the end, you should be able to talk to people to get on in this life. When you go to Ireland, you'll have to talk to your cousins. Think of this as practice. As long as you don't mention Adelaide or Braeden Douglas you're good."

The blonde beauty broke through the crowd on the arm of Grayson Douglas. "Did I hear my name?"

Despite Grayson's attempt to move the agitated female in another direction, the woman stood at their booth, narrowing her eyes at the two of them. What other name sounded like Adelaide? Gabriella admitted to having a younger sister named Annalise. She even told Meara that she reminded her of her little sister. "We were talking about my sister, Annalise. She's considering being a nun." She clamped her teeth together aware that her mouth tended to run off on its own. Not sure why she added the nun part, but it was all she knew.

Eleanor bobbed her head in agreement. "There's an order in Braintree she might go to."

Adelaide yawned widely, not even having the manners to cover her mouth. She drifted away without comment. Grayson's gaze caught hers. An unspoken message passed between the two of them. He knew why Braeden left and was more than ready to be the stand-in fiancé for Adelaide. He could know where his brother was, hopefully nowhere close to enemy fire.

Once Adelaide faded into the crowd, Meara's fear of the woman dissipated. She knew better than to think Grayson would turn the mean-spirited female sweet overnight, but maybe he could have a gentling effect on her. She'd seen her at her worst as her tenuous grip on Braeden slipped. Since Braeden was beyond her reach, she had to regroup to make everything look like her choice when it was anything but.

Did Adelaide fool anyone? Would mothers use her as the main character in cautionary tales about what happens when you're too demanding regarding a bridegroom?

"Stop your woolgathering and help me pack. I'm taking more back than I would like. The bombing, whether intentional or accidental, isn't good for business. Too many are squirreling away what they have in case they need to leave in a hurry."

"Where would they go?" Meara grabbed the heaviest basket, still half-full of jars and herbs.

"Most would head farther north. City people come to the country thinking that will keep them safe, but since we're already in the country..." She let the statement dangle as she took down the broad board that served as a counter.

"Could they go to another country?"

"They could if they had relatives there."

That had to be the secret, having someone in place waiting for you. They slipped back into the woods with Eleanor calling farewells to a passing trio of women who gave her a head nod at best.

"Why do you even bother with them? It's obvious they don't like you." Meara watched the women move up the street with a stiff gait and their heads close together.

"They might pretend to ignore me, but Emmeline is one of my best customers. She just doesn't want to be seen talking to me. For some people, it's all about appearances. She wants to appear to be superior to me."

Meara almost asked why, and then she remembered. This was how Eleanor survived. The war made finances tighter for all households. Money for anything a person couldn't make or find on their own came dear. The fact that the woods weren't teeming with housewives anxious to supplement their meals with berries, nuts, or whatever herb they could find bore testament to superstition associated with area.

The birdcalls lessened as they neared the dark section. On the last trip, they skirted around this section on their return to the cottage. Even though it was a small section of woods, it felt oppressive. Even the sunlight hardly penetrated the thick canopy of leaves. Eleanor's gait picked up as she led the way. All Meara could do was follow her hostess while observing the thick glossy underbrush. No delicate flowers bloomed along the path as they did in the rest of the forest. No animals stirred the bushes or branches.

A sense of urgency caused her to move faster, even bumping into Eleanor, who grunted, but didn't speak. Instead, she gave her a sharp look before picking up her own pace. The sisters would have pointed out her dread about something lurking deep within the forest as the reason they never went outside the convent walls. Dangerous things happened due to the depravity of mankind. Normally, she'd disagree if only in her mind, but these few acres of dismal twilight forest might make her reconsider.

Up ahead a beam of light shone on the path and a bird trilled. They were almost there. As soon as Eleanor stepped into the sunlight, she laughed and withdrew something from her pocket. "Thank goodness I came prepared." A sharp end poked out of her closed fist.

"What is it?" If it were a knife, the tiny blade wouldn't have protected them from anything. Meara moved closer to examine the object Eleanor seemed to regard as magical. Her fisted hand opened to reveal a slightly bent rusty nail. "A nail?"

"Yes." The woman's head bobbed enthusiastically in agreement. "I was lucky to even find a nail without pulling the cottage apart."

"What does that have to do with a nail?" Another oddity that made no sense to her. Too bad the outside world didn't come with a type of guidebook for people like her.

"The dark faeries play tricks on travelers. Often, they make things appear to be something they're not. The nail keeps them away. For some reason, they fear it. It's almost like jail bars to them. It makes them powerless."

"My father was a friend of the faeries. You even told me that the faeries looked out for me."

"Aye. I did, and they do. Not all faeries are the same. For whatever reason, there are those who'd play tricks on humans. In that regard, I choose to protect myself."

A chill touched Meara's neck. So much information to take in and most of it seemed contradictory. "What's the worst thing a dark faery could do?"

The woman started walking down the path, leaving Meara to jog to catch up. After a while, when they were far away from the dark area, Eleanor finally spoke. "There's been tales of women going off into the woods and never returning."

It explained why the village girls and matrons avoided the woods, but it didn't do much for her peace of mind. Something evil hid in the woods, but an instinctual feeling told her it wasn't faeries, dark or otherwise.

Chapter Thirteen

T HE WIND PICKED up, pushing them down the path as if
hurrying them on their way. Eleanor stumbled forward,
grabbing at the nearby saplings. A raven almost touched her as it
flew past, shrieking its protest to the wind.

Her sudden revelation about the evil in the woods caused Meara
to look behind her, expecting some hideous monster to burst out of
the ground and belch fire in her direction. The branches creaked and
waved above her as a startled deer galloped for cover. Whatever was
out there, the wildlife feared it.

The roar of the wind and the hiss of something vicious she
couldn't quite place filled her ears, along with the thundering of her
heart. The already dim passage darkened even more as clouds
huddled together, blotting out the meager sunlight. Eleanor turned
and shouted something. Her mouth moved, but her words vanished
before they reached Meara. The woman held up her arm, gesturing
forward.

They were already moving in that direction, and there was no
way Meara would even consider taking a step back the way they had
come. It didn't matter if it took an hour to circumvent the area to
make it to the market. An hour she'd gladly take both ways. Her
arms chilled and pebbled due to the temperature drop while her
muscles ached, clutching the heavy basket. All she wanted to do was
get home and away from the unknown force behind them.

Something grabbed her foot, scratching it. Intense coldness
wrapped around her ankle causing her to jerk her leg up and stomp

down madly while reaching for her mother's locket with her free hand. The sensation released along with a discontented growl.

The tiny cottage came into view at the same time a cold raindrop slid down her neck. The wind roared as an ice pellet as hard as a stone hit her nose. A handful of airborne particles hit her, while one cracked a jar in the basket she carried.

Her companion grabbed her arm, pointing in the direction of the cottage. "Run!"

Arms locked, the two of them ran to the cottage. Inside, Eleanor's unsteady steps carried her to the kitchen where she picked up a towel and held it out. Meara reached for the towel and wrapped it around her head after patting her face dry. Oscar twined in between their legs, commenting on their drenched state in an aggravated tone.

"I'll get a fire started and some tea going. That should put everything to rights. Strange weather."

Indeed, it was. Inside the cottage, away from the battering elements and the incipient fear welling up inside her, she could think. It felt more like a battle than weather. She'd observed an occasional hailstorm in her seventeen years, but nothing like this. Standing in a doorway watching a storm approach, rather than being a part of it, was a different matter.

A living essence existed as part of the storm, every bit as real as the rain and the hailstones. Not visible, but substantial, it had pushed them down the path. The idea confounded her since the entity within the storm could have been either malevolent or beneficial. Her hand went to the base of her neck and massaged it as she contemplated the intentions of whatever power stirred up the storm. Any one of the stones could have hurt or possibly killed either one of them. Perhaps only luck had saved them. Then again, perhaps the stones weren't for them at all, but a way to hurry them on their way while keeping the evil that lingered near at a distance.

"Tea's almost done."

"I can tell you this will be the best cup of tea I'll ever drink, even if it's mostly water."

Two worn mugs thumped on the table as Eleanor readied the tea. "I know what you mean. I had my doubts back in the woods. Then the storm came, which worried me even more."

The steaming water joined the dried leaves creating an uplifting fragrance. "Peppermint. It smells so good."

"It's a favorite of mine. It soothes the nerves. I think we both could use some soothing."

Meara's fingers wrapped around the warm mug as she inhaled the scent. "I know what you mean, but I had a thought. Maybe it was more of a feeling."

The woman watched her over the rim of her cup as she enjoyed a long sip of her tea before speaking. "Do tell."

Her sudden impression—that somehow, she knew was true—Meara was too reluctant to share. What if she just sounded stupid? "I, ah, wondered if that strange storm was a form of protection as opposed to simply being the weather."

"Ah," Eleanor put her cup down and placed a finger on her nose. "I too felt something similar. Did you notice the size of the hail stones?"

"Big as I've ever seen. If either one of us had been hit, it would have knocked us off our feet." She hadn't thought about it too much as she rushed inside, but now she wondered. Dozens of hailstones littered the ground. One would have created a new hole in the roof. Her eyes scanned the dark ceiling looking for an expanse of sky. All was as it was before, no new holes.

"It was almost as if the stones were guided." The woman cocked her head, her forehead drawn up.

"One did strike and break a jar."

Eleanor shrugged. "A little thing really. It's a blessing you didn't drop the entire basket. Besides, it might be my penance for gathering up all the rose hips. I've been a bit of a glutton."

"Tell me why you think the stones didn't hit us or at least not the big ones?"

A sly look crossed her companion's face as she pointed her index finger in Meara's direction. "You first. I'd be more interested in your opinion. Could be you have more of the *fey* about you than you truly know."

She expected it to come to this. "Back when we were in the dark section, I felt an evilness gathering itself as if to pounce on us. That's when the wind started. At first, I thought whatever malevolence hid there caused it. Then I noticed the wind was propelling us out of the area and the wildlife, too. When the hail started, I didn't think about it too much since I was trying to reach shelter. Now that you pointed out we were never hurt by the hailstones, I have to wonder if they were for whatever was behind us."

"Woo." Eleanor shuddered, wrapping her arms around her. "I had similar thoughts, but hearing you say it aloud brings back the terror I felt for a heartbeat. I pushed it back telling myself it couldn't be. Maybe I didn't want it to be."

"You've lived here how many years? And never noticed what lived in the woods?" The image of Eleanor strolling nonchalantly through the dark energy on her way to market every week boggled her. How did the woman do it?

"Six, no, maybe it's been seven years. It's hard to remember. Can't say I always walked through the haunted section. Usually I avoided it. The darkness felt heavier and stronger than before."

"The sisters warned me there was evil outside the walls. Not too sure if I believed them when I found so much beauty in the forest." The endless services, the singing of psalms, and downcast eyes and closed minds seemed almost preferable to this unknown world of contradictory actions and unexpected attacks. She steepled her finger together as she exhaled, knowing her path had already been chosen for her by the accidental release of a bomb over the convent.

"You weren't safe inside the walls. No matter how thick or high they are. For all their outward piety, the women hid more than a few evil and hypocritical thoughts. The buttery sprites wreak havoc on that sort." Eleanor nodded with conviction as she pushed up from the table. "I think a bit of bread and butter would go with the tea. Butter for the buttery sprites." She chuckled at her wordplay as she opened the breadbox.

"Buttery sprites? None of the sisters ever mentioned such a thing."

A plate of thick bread slices and a crock of butter crowded the tea tray along with a butter knife. Eleanor balanced the tray against her belly as she placed the items on the table. "Check the cracked jar of rose hips, and we'll see if there's any jelly worth having."

Meara reached down and poked through the basket, not expecting anything more than sticky glass fragments.

Eleanor continued her conversation about the buttery sprites. "My grandmother told me about the sprites. They felt free to take any food not marked with a cross, especially butter. Not sure if they were spirits, demons, or faeries. No one has ever seen them. They have a powerful sense of right and wrong, which makes me think they aren't demons."

She gave a short laugh before continuing. "They declared vengeance on anyone who would cheat someone. They are especially irksome to cheating abbots and priests. Back long ago, the people had to pay a tithe to the church. Some abbots used this as a method to grow rich on the backs of the people."

An urge to defend the absent woman rose in her. Even though the woman could be stern, and often unlikable, she was as close to a mother as Meara ever had. "You don't know that anything was stolen. It could all have been freely given to benefit the convent." Her fingers carefully plucked the jars out of the basket to find the cracked one. She ignored her hostess' disdainful snort since Eleanor's feelings about Mother Superior was already known.

"I can't find any cracked or broken jars."

The two of them held the jars up to the lantern, twirling them to search for any spidery lines.

"Nothing but, I heard a crack and felt the basket bounce against my hip as if it had been struck."

"It could have been something else."

The memory of the cold tentacles wrapping around her ankle wasn't something she wanted to recall. "I suppose. In the end, the weather protected us. Do you think my father sent the hail storm?"

"It's a nice thought." She shook her head sadly. "If the man could not even save himself with a look away spell, I doubt he'd be orchestrating the weather beyond the grave."

Truly, she did not think her father could, but the idea brought comfort with it. Wouldn't it be grand to have someone looking after her in this thoroughly confusing place, especially if she ended up going to Ireland on her own? "Who orchestrated it then?"

"I'd like to say it wasn't orchestrated. That would mean I wouldn't have to think on all the other matters such as the evil growing stronger and its area increasing." She stared at the fire, lengthening the silence. After a while, she turned her gaze back at Meara. "I remember talk about faeries who could control the weather at will. Don't remember their exact names, but they live by water. There's a stream flowing through the forest. I might consider them as our rescuers and will gladly light a candle to honor them."

The theory resonated with Meara, a sort of rightness that sang to her and lulled her into a sense of complacency. The water faeries would be tall, slender, with long streaming hair clothed in flowing garments. They protected those they loved with a fierceness and loyalty unknown to humans. In her mental impression, one of the faeries smiled at her, leaned down and kissed her head. "That sounds about right. Why would they do battle on our behalf?"

"That's a tough one. Could be the hatred in people's hearts with the war and all that has coalesced and taken form."

A big sodden lumbering mess oozing pus and blood replaced her picture of the ethereal faeries. "That sounds horrible!" She preferred the water spirits who looked at her indulgently with large, almond shaped all-knowing eyes.

"It is." Eleanor agreed. "Let's talk of brighter things such as making you a new dress for the dance. I have one in a green material that will match your eyes and complement your hair."

If evil lurked outside the cottage, the common-sense thing would be to hide away inside as opposed to traipse through the woods again. Her fingers massaged the bunched muscles in her neck as she considered the practicality of never going outside. "A dress would be nice."

They spent the rest of the night measuring and cutting. The finished product was even grander than the dress she already had. She slipped the emerald cloth over her head for the final fitting. Eleanor walked a slow circle around her, frowning.

The woman's downward turned lips confused her. "What's wrong? I think it looks wonderful."

"The dress looks better on you than it ever did on me. Go look in the mirror and see for yourself."

Meara dashed to the mirror, anxious to see the effect of this new creation. The color of the dress played up her creamy skin and spring grass green eyes. Her tumbled curls glowed as a fiery backdrop.

Eleanor stepped up behind her and lifted her hair, twisting it one way, then another. "I think you could wear your hair up or at least in a braid. I could tuck in a few daisies for ornamentation. A crown of daisies would suit you better, but you're already pretty enough to draw the boys' eyes, which won't make Adelaide happy."

"I don't want to draw the boys' eyes. Well, at least not any here." Her shoulders drooped as she considered where Braeden might be this very night.

"Doesn't matter if you want them to look or not. They still do. It also means they might not spend time adoring Adelaide as they usually do."

The words danced on her already sensitized nerves. Wasn't it enough that they had to battle the evil in the woods without dealing with the meanness contained in one slight female? "Why does it matter to Adelaide? She thinks none of the village boys are good enough for her."

"It shouldn't matter. It only matters in the aspect that everything must be about her. Every eye must be on her. Every girl must envy her, while every male of marriageable age must have his heart set on her. She can only marry one of them, but she'd like to think that everyone wanted to marry her if only in their dreams."

No wonder Adelaide directed so much hate her way. She doubted the girl had been bested in anything until she showed up. An unknown stealing her thunder by simply existing. She didn't consider herself a great beauty even though Braeden called her beautiful. At best, she served as a novelty. If she stayed long enough, the appeal would probably diminish. "It must be a hard life."

"What?" The mirror reflected Eleanor's astonished face. "The richest girl in town who gets whatever she wants has a hard life?"

She wrinkled her nose at her own reflection, knowing it would be hard to explain what she meant. "Obviously, her father's money and power couldn't guarantee Braeden's love."

"True enough. I doubt there's anyone in town who likes her, except for her father."

Meara spun away from the mirror, not wanting to be accused of vanity, which would make her no better than Adelaide. "Grayson likes her. Braeden told me. His brother is more than willing to take his place."

Eleanor stepped back, giving Meara more room. "Pshaw. A pretty face always turns young men. Can't say they do their thinking with their brains. He'll find out what a viper she is once they wed."

"Perhaps Grayson's love will turn Adelaide up sweet."

Eleanor flattened her hand over her heart. "Ah, girl, there's so much goodness in you, willing to believe the best of others when they've proven themselves so unworthy. I'll give you the benefit of the doubt on this. As for Grayson, the *Labors of Hercules* will prove easy as opposed to taming that buggar."

THAT NIGHT SHE went to sleep hoping to dream of the last day she had spent with Braeden. They had such a brief time together it made sense to relive every moment. Howling winds inhabited her dreams, along with the cold chill of maliciousness, wrapping its bony hand around her wrist, pulling her back into the darkness. Sheer will had her digging in her heels and reaching for the nearest tree. An irritated growl accompanied the coldness, signaling whatever it was resented her refusal to cooperate. The bark splintered under her grip as the entity continued to jerk her wrist, trying to loosen her grip.

Why is this happening to me? Whenever she stepped outside, her heart sang as she took in the trees and wildlife. Her tranquility emanated from nature.

A shimmering representation of her father appeared beside her. Her grip tightened, deciding her parent's appearance meant imminent rescue. "Hold tight. I can offer no physical assistance, only advice. This quandary is yours to solve. Evil doesn't care if you merit it or not. You're one of the innocents and possibly the only one able to stand against it. It's only natural in the aspect that it is composed of centuries of hate and violence. Sometimes it can inhabit the unsuspecting human."

This was not what she wanted to hear. "What should I do?"

"Leave immediately."

The unexpected words almost had her releasing her grip to turn and gaze at her father more fully. As if sensing her intentions, a vicious backward pull had her grappling for the tree again. The slender sapling would eventually break, leaving her as fodder for the creature.

Her head swung from side to side looking for assistance. Her father's form grew fainter, but his words lingered in the air. "Go now."

The tugging continued at her shoulder rocking her back and forth. How could she hope to withstand it? A voice called her name.

"Meara, Meara! Wake up. You're having a bad dream."

Would the creature say such a thing to trick her? Possibly. Her grip tightened as she locked her jaw, determined to hold on for dear life. The tugging stopped, proving her decision right. The shock of freezing water had her blinking and gasping. Her eyelids shot open taking in the dim room and a shadowy form leaning over her. The hairs stood up on her arms as she cringed, trying to make herself as small as possible, wishing she could vanish into the ground.

"It's me, Eleanor. What has you so scared?"

The voice sounded familiar but didn't her father warn her that the creature could inhabit people? Eleanor had told her that goblins and faeries could shape shift, but there was always something not right, which gave them away.

The fire-lit silhouette resembled her hostess, but it was time to learn much more. Would they retain the same memories or feelings? "How are your children faring?"

The woman stumbled backward a few steps. Her shoulders sagged, and her splayed hand landed on her chest. "Why would you ask me such a question when you know my children died?"

Ah, she answered that right. Still wanting to feel sure of the identity of whatever or whoever stood so close, she posed another question, one that a random guess could not answer. "What was the name of your son's cat?"

"Meara, what's wrong with you? Perhaps you've taken a chill and have a fever, which causes you to babble nonsense?" The hand dropped from her chest as she stepped closer. "Let me feel your forehead."

The muscles in her body bunched and readied themselves for flight as the woman neared. Through gritted teeth, she pushed out her demand in a raspy voice that trembled more than she liked. "Answer the question!"

"Goodness, something has taken hold of you. My son had a dog, not a cat. His name was Rex. That dog was loyal as the day was long. I told you this already." She shook her head slowly.

Her held breath whooshed out as she dropped back against the thin pallet. It was the right answer, which meant it was Eleanor. What if it wasn't? A tingle of fear prodded her, causing her heart to trip a beat. What other test was there?

At best, she could play along and see how the woman reacted. "I had a dream."

"I suspected it was more of a nightmare since you were screaming." Eleanor crossed her arms, and her face folded into concern.

"True." She knew better than to deny the obvious. "My father came to me and told me it was time to leave."

Her hostess remained silent, chafing her arms. Wouldn't the entity urge her to stay? The better to consume, possess, or whatever it did. Eleanor sighed after a while. "I've wondered that myself. It certainly would be handy if your uncle showed up. It bears some thinking. Do you think you can go back to sleep or are you up for the night?"

"I'm up." She rolled to her feet, wondering if she could ever trust herself to sleep again. "Looks like I need to start planning out my life."

Chapter Fourteen

T HE CUP OF tea and toast that passed for breakfast occurred in total silence, with each participant lost in her own thoughts. Oscar broke the peace by meowing notice of his lack of sustenance. The feline head-butted Meara before moving on to his owner.

"I hear you, big fellow. I've saved the fish skin and a bit of bread soaked in water." The woman lifted a towel that covered the cat's meal and squatted to present the bowl. "Hear ya go."

Meara watched it all as if from a distance. The everyday actions had little to do with her. Her hand entangled in the locket chain around her neck, moving down the metal strand until her thumb encountered the smooth oval. Her father told her to leave as if it were a simple thing. Without any knowledge, even basic geography of the countryside and money, it didn't seem to be a possibility.

"How will I get to Ireland?"

Her companion stopped petting Oscar and looked up. "I suspect when your uncle arrives that you'll go by boat."

She suspected as much. "What if he doesn't arrive? He could believe I'm dead and return home or off to whatever expedition he had planned." Meara hoped the man hadn't given up trying to find her. Surely, someone in the village could have told him no young women were in the impromptu cemetery. If Braeden had been his only source, then he hadn't been told much.

Why hadn't she mentioned to Braeden about being that devil child his mother had condemned? If he truly loved her, it would have been a perfect chance for him to demonstrate his affection, but she hadn't chanced it. Love resembled a delicate morning glory blossom that only opens to the early ray of the sun, but closes when the heat becomes too intense. Since it was the first time anyone had ever declared affection for her, she wanted to hold onto it. If she hadn't been so frightened of destroying the budding attraction, she would have blurted out the truth. At least that way her uncle would know she lived. If Braeden had taken his mother's attitude and considered her an ill omen, he might have refused to help her relative.

"That's true," Eleanor commented, as she stood and shook one leg, then the other, to relieve the cramping that came with squatting.

Meara's brows arched at the declaration. Why did Eleanor think Braeden would turn against her because of his mother? Hadn't she spoken on the man's behalf? What was the last thing Meara said aloud? Nothing about Braeden. Meara kept that information to herself, especially since Eleanor already made her opinion known on the subject. Why reveal her innermost fears about Braeden not coming back or loving her? Her hostess would confirm them in her practical manner, saying something about a girl shouldn't fall for the first boy she meets.

The slight purr of the happy feline dispelled some of the anguish that had taken a chokehold on her throat, enabling her to speak. "What's true?"

Eleanor cocked her head and shot her a questioning glance. "What you said about your uncle heading back to Ireland if he thought you were dead."

That's what the conversation was. Even though her uncle may have abandoned her as dead, it eased her mind that Braeden hadn't been the topic of discussion. "Oh, yes." Her lips stretched up in what she hoped was a smile.

"Eleanor, how did you travel as a lone woman?"

"It wasn't that hard with the trains. My friend rode up with one of the farmers to meet my train. Most people will give you a lift in you're heading in the same direction."

It all sounded rather simple to her. "All I have to do is catch a train heading for Ireland." Already she could envision herself with a bag in hand, nodding to her fellow travelers as she boarded the train. "What's a train?"

"You have so much to learn. It has a big engine that runs on steam and pulls a series of train cars behind it. Some of the cars have cargo in them such as livestock, lumber, or coal. The other cars are for passengers. It is an ingenious way to get people from one end of the country to the other. Faster than walking and more dependable than cars. The train I took here from the old home took about four hours or more. It did make several stops."

It all seemed so easy now that she put her mind to it. The need to find her family existed in the back of her mind along with the need to seek vengeance or at least justice for her father. Every morning she woke up and realized there was so much to learn and do that it all threatened to overwhelm her. She certainly didn't dwell on traveling when she hadn't even mastered the art of conversing with people without bringing up her past.

"I could hop a train, then a boat, and possibly another train in Ireland." Meara held up a finger for each step of the journey.

"Don't go making it sound so simple. It isn't. I've never been on a boat before. I don't know specifically how to get one. Haven't been to Ireland, either. They may not even have trains, which would make your trip a lot longer and harder if you did it on foot, especially being an innocent girl. You'll be taken by some hooligan or other riff-raff."

Before she could even ask about hooligans, Eleanor clicked her tongue as she cleared the table, mumbling about the foolhardiness of the young. Meara helped, wiping the crumbs into her hand to throw out to the birds.

"So, my intrepid traveler, what will you do for money?"

The lack of money loomed as her greatest obstacle. Her hand

reached up for the necklace in what had become an almost automatic response. "I could sell my locket."

"I'd not ask that of you. The locket would only bring you a few pence."

Meara knew Eleanor must have been talking about money and from her dismissive tone, a pence must not be that much, even if she had more than one. There were berries, nuts, and honey she could try to harvest. It would take time, and those she sold to would be more likely to pay her in firewood, flour, or even a live chicken. She had a feeling that wouldn't buy her a train ticket.

The metallic clang of the purloined box hitting the wood table drew her attention. Eleanor pushed up the top that gave out a protesting squeak. "There has to be something in here we can sell." Her hand emerged trailing a long string of pearls. "Possibly this and another necklace of moderate value."

A glistening strand of green stones held together with complicated gold filigree tempted her. Meara held up the handsome necklace. "How about this?"

"It would fetch a decent price, but neither one of us looks like we would come by that expensive emerald necklace in a normal fashion. We'd end up with the constables calling on us. As it is, we'll be pushing our luck. I know a pawnbroker I've used before. He won't be too surprised to see me. I might need to find a new pawnbroker in the city, instead of the village. We'll go into town with one of the farmers who attends the city market. I'll ask around and see who'll take us."

The thought simultaneously excited and scared her. It was one step closer to leaving. It would also be leaving all she knew behind. How could Braeden come back to her when she was no longer here waiting as she promised? Her stomach twisted as she considered the pull of her roots and the attraction of new love. Maybe Braeden wouldn't come back for her. Maybe he wouldn't come back at all. Her eyes grew cloudy with unshed tears as she attempted to blink them away. She could grow old waiting for him as the war lingered on. Sister Gabriella spoke about the hundred-year war where grandfather, father, and grandson all took a turn in fighting an unwinnable war.

For all she knew, war could have been part of everyday life the entire time she'd been in the convent. "Do you think this war will go on for long?" A fast ending would make her decision to leave or stay that much easier.

"That's one for the fortune tellers. It depends on so many things, such as how determined the Germans are. Will the Yanks help us out? I heard a call went out, but they remained strangely neutral. Back in the day, when they were just a colony, they had plenty of fight in them. Now, not so much or at least nothing for their mother country."

Meara didn't care for the Yanks if they would not help England fend off the German invaders. "Are there many Yanks? Would it help if they joined the fight?"

"Depends on who you talk to. I heard their country is ten times larger than ours, which means they have many more fighting age men." Eleanor balled her fist and brandished it as she spoke. Red rushed up her neck and mottled her face. "True, they might not have the same feeling a Brit might have at repelling the invaders, but surely they must realize they could be next."

Her hostess felt strongly about the war. All Meara knew was that it could take away the one man who loved her. It already had. Braeden's words about it being the only honorable way he could get out of marrying Adelaide rang true, but it didn't stop her from wishing a man didn't have to brave death to escape the spoiled brat's machinations. She felt her own hands balling up with anger as her eyes narrowed. Someone should teach Adelaide a lesson.

"Ah, you feel the same." Eleanor gave her a knowing glance. "People should come when you ask them for help. Instead of pretending they never heard a knock at the door."

"Yes," she answered, knowing it was her first deliberate lie. It was easier than explaining she had no feelings about the Yanks' refusal to answer the knock unless it had a negative impact on Braeden. She expected a burning fire deep inside her or even a blackening of her fingertips identifying her as a liar. Her nail beds appeared a little ragged, but that came from harvesting fruits and herbs. There was some purplish stain on her fingers. It had started. Her gaze focused on her fingers waiting for the discoloration to move up her arms.

"Scrub your hands with the lye soap, and it should remove most of the berry stain. If it doesn't, the next day is wash day and that will do it."

Blackberry juice had discolored her hands. How could she have forgotten? A sharp clap interrupted her reverie on the nature of a lie and its aftereffects.

"Lots to do with the dance tonight. It will be the perfect place for me to find us a ride to the city."

The dance had somehow slipped her mind. The possibility of seeing the dark-haired girl who spoke to her intrigued her. Would she be her friend or merely a spy for Adelaide? She'd have to guard her words. Then there was the appeal of wearing the new green dress with its full bell-like skirt. Excitement coursed through her veins as she thought of spinning like a top making the skirt balloon out. That might not be the way of dancing, though.

"Eleanor, could you teach me how to dance?"

The woman picked up a table chair and moved it against the wall. "Help me move the table, we'll need some room."

They opened up a square that measured about ten by ten. Meara soon found herself laughing as Eleanor named off the dances that could be at this evening's entertainment.

"Surely, no one named a dance Lord Byron's Maggot?"

"They did. That's not the worst of the names, either. Of course, 'round here, there'll be many circle dances so all can join in, from small children to their grandparents. You form a circle, hold hands, skip one way, then the other, and go in with hands held high." She grabbed Meara's hand and held it up high as she skipped a few steps. "Then you skip back and repeat everything to the music ends. There isn't much to it. I'm sure once you see it performed you'll get it."

"Show me skipping again."

Meara watched as Eleanor galloped around the room using a rocking step. "I think I did something like that when I was younger, trying to imitate our cart horse." She fisted her hands on her hips and cantered around the room, allowing her right foot to lead.

"That's good, but switch feet as if walking, act like it's a happy, energetic stroll. I can't believe you don't know how to skip. Follow me." Eleanor skipped to the door, threw it open, and continued outside into the sunlight.

Meara followed, bouncing on the balls of her feet, only hesitating when she reached the door for a brief second. Eleanor gamboled about the garden with a huge smile. The birds sang, and a handful of daisies bloomed near the path. The air carried a fresh washed green fragrance. How could anything be wrong and smell that good? In the time it took to blink, she made her decision and skipped outside.

"It's fun. No wonder people like it."

A few minutes of skipping had them both laughing. Eleanor slowed to a halt. "That's about it for the country dances. Most of them are a version of the same. Don't be bashful. A person will have to learn sometime. I wager there will be many a boy who'd be willing to teach you the more complicated steps to a jig or a reel."

Her head swung in refusal, causing Eleanor to purse her lips.

"It's only a dance. No one is asking you to marry. Often, at the events, women dance with other women when they can't get the men to dance. Could be that nice Rosemary will talk you through the steps."

The idea of Rosemary coaching her through the moves sounded much less intimidating. "I could do that."

"No worries about any of those new dances such as The Castle Walk or the Maxixe. I saw those when I went up to London. Down here when it comes to the waltz most do the Alexandrina Waltz with crossed arms in front to keep couples the appropriate distance apart. There might be a fox trot, which looks a bit like couples holding hands and kicking up their heels, but I doubt it, considering it's more a city dance. You don't have to dance every dance, either. It will be good for you to mingle with people your own age."

The thought of associating with people her age alarmed her. She barely had enough words to converse with one single person. "What will I say?"

"You know your story as my cousin. If you choose to invent brothers or family pets, please clue me in later so I won't ruin your story. Remember Annalise, your sister, because Adelaide will. Mostly, you listen and smile. Everyone loves it when someone truly pays attention to them."

Eleanor grinned at her own statement. Meara wasn't sure if it meant what she had said was important or funny. If all she had to do was listen, smile, and occasionally skip, then everything would turn out well.

When it came time to go, Eleanor dressed in her finery, holding a lantern aloft. "We'll need this to find our way home."

They'd be walking home in the dark. She wanted to protest such an undertaking but didn't want to sound ungrateful, especially since so much of the afternoon was spent learning to dance.

Her hostess's eyes started at her hair, slid over her dress down to her work boots. "My goodness, you're a bit like Cinderella. There's no glass slippers, but maybe we can do something. Go get the slippers you scrounged from the convent."

The soft slippers only attribute was the ability to move quietly. She handed the filthy slippers over.

Eleanor dusted them off a bit. "I think I saw something in the box that might pretty these shoes up." She pried open the box, pawed through the contents, and held up a glittery pair of earbobs. "A few swipes of the needle and thread will attach them."

True to her word, the sparkling flowers improved the plain slippers.

"Of course, you won't put them on until we arrive at the dance. We'll gather up the food and go."

They left with a word to the sleeping Oscar to behave himself. One shutter remained unlatched and partially opened if the cat felt the need to leave. Neither one of them mentioned taking the short cut as they meandered down the long path. The sounds of revelry reached them before they had even stepped out onto the street. Families, courting couples holding hands, and children dashed past them toward a large barn that had an oversized Union Jack decorating the front.

Eleanor placed one hand behind her face to shield her words. "With the war on, any show of frivolity and fun has to be deemed patriotic in some manner. It might be labeled keeping the home fires burning or morale boosting. It's just a party, no matter what the name. Often, you don't even need an excuse to have one."

A few older women held up their hands, beckoning to her companion. Suddenly, Meara felt like the parent with her friend anxious to be off with her cronies. Before she could say anything, chattering voices of girls interrupted them. A girl detached herself from the group and joined Meara.

"It's me, Rosemary. I'm so glad you decided to come." She tucked her arm through Meara's and guided her down the street while maintaining a steady patter. "We certainly need some new blood in this town. Everything is the same except for Grant and Braeden leaving."

"Oh?" She tried to sound vaguely surprised but wondered if the mention of someone leaving would be the appropriate time to smile.

"Of course, you wouldn't know. Braeden was Adelaide's supposed sweetheart, but I think someone forgot to tell him. She's been hanging out for a couple of years, expecting to marry. Now that the man joined up, she's telling everyone she threw him over, and his enlistment was due to heartbreak." Rosemary shot her a knowing glance as her lips tugged to one side. "If it were true, then I'd think it's cruel of her bragging about it. I suspect the man joined to get away from her." Her laughter rang out in the night air.

The sound of a fiddle grew stronger as they approached the oversized barn. Meara, uncertain of what her response should be, laughed too. Rosemary had no clue how close to the truth she was.

The surge of mingled voices, music, and clapping had Meara halting short of the door. She should say something before they entered. It wasn't fair that Rosemary would offer friendship so easily and she gave nothing back. "I have a confession to make."

Rosemary's dark eyebrows lifted. "I hope it's juicy."

"Well, ah, I don't know too much about being juicy. I can't dance. Eleanor spent most of the day teaching me."

Rosemary dropped her arm, took a step back, and placed her hands on her hips. She gave her a once over starting at her hair down to her boots. "I imagine in that outfit most boys won't care if you can dance or not, especially in those boots. None of them would want their toes trod on by gal in heavy boots."

She pulled up her dress a little to peer at her boots "Oh, I'd forgotten I had them on. I have slippers for dancing." She jiggled the drawstring bag hanging from her arm.

"Good. I imagine with Miss Eleanor, a city gal, teaching you to dance that you'll know more than most of us."

She shook her head and smiled, her fall back response, which suited the gregarious Rosemary, who continued to talk as if never interrupted and at the same time, lowering her voice. "I can't wait until Adelaide sets her eyes on you."

Personally, Meara wished to avoid the mercurial female since she could never determine what she might do, especially now.

"As for me, my dark hair is common, especially so close to Wales and all. Adelaide prides herself on her blond hair even though there are more than enough females of marriageable age with the same colored locks. If a man felt a pressing need to woo a woman with light hair, he'd be better off to court Elizabeth, Molly, or Jane than the razor-tongued Adelaide."

"So, there are only four yellow haired girls left in the village?" Meara forgot her instructions to smile and listen when faced with the prospect of knowing about the other women.

Rosemary led her through the open barn doors and angled her head at several couples on the floor. "Madeline, Constance, and Mary already have been spoken for." It was easy to pick out the three blonde heads in the dancing group. Their beaus had their heads angled toward theirs in an attentive fashion. It was easy to imagine the men staring at their betrotheds in a besotted fashion. At least, she hoped they did.

They both sat on one of the benches lining the wall as Meara unlaced her boots. She pulled out the slippers from the drawstring bag and gazed at them. A simple ornamentation had changed the basic footwear into something special.

Rosemary reached out to touch the sparkly flower. "How nice. I imagine you'll cause envy in more than one heart tonight."

Meara's hands landed on her cheeks as her mouth sagged open. The ridiculousness of the sentiment had her snapping her teeth together. "I won't cause any envy." She almost added that it was one of the deadly sins, but managed to stop herself. The limited exposure she had to the outside world was people neither talked much about sins nor appeared overly concerned about them.

Her companion's sparkling laughter and twinkling eyes confused her.

"Meara, here I thought I was the country mouse, but you're more mouse than me. You can't stop people's feelings. A person could meet you, and you never said a word. Still, the same individual could decide to hate you, love you, or look past you based only on who they thought you were."

"Did you do that?" It puzzled her that Rosemary wanted to be her friend.

Her friend's gaze wandered around the room until it landed on a couple near the dais where a fiddle player, a drummer, and a piper played. "Look over there where the band is."

"You don't see Adelaide crying over Braeden. Oh no, she's making up to the second Douglas brother. With the eldest gone and possibly never coming back, Grayson Douglas is the top bachelor in town." Rosemary spoke the words almost in a growl.

Clearly, she had something against the town's self-appointed princess. "Why do you dislike Adelaide?"

Her new friend's head swiveled fast, and she found herself on the receiving end of an intense glare. "You stay here long enough, you'll hate her too. Heaven help you if you come between her and something she wants. I did."

The anger and hurt glistening in Rosemary's eyes sparked compassion. "What?" Once again, she opened her mouth before thoroughly considering her words. Eleanor thought it would be easy for her to listen and smile. It might be for someone else, but so far, she had failed at it. She pushed her scuffed boots under the bench, and then pulled her dancing slippers on as her friend talked.

"Braeden wasn't always Adelaide's first pick as a beau. Her father had taken her to the city to a round of parties since his daughter felt she was better suited to live there. While she might have been the big fish in a small pond here, in the city, she was just another fish, not even a desirable one. She returned with no ring on her finger and a bitter attitude. At the time, Braeden had been courting me. We'd gone to a dance. He walked me home. A couple of times he came over to my family's farm to help, then stayed for dinner. It wasn't a big deal, but people knew we were courting, that was until Adelaide decided to meddle."

An invisible hand squeezed her heart when Rosemary mentioned that Braeden had courted her. The vivacious, dark-haired beauty would attract any man. The bigger question was why more men weren't interested in her. Rosemary should be dancing with a beau as opposed to keeping her company. "How did she meddle?"

"It's been a few years ago, but the pain and stigma remain. Everyone knows my father likes his drink. He gets drunk often when he does drink. Most folks accept it's the way he his. He's not the only one in this village with a liking for liquor. Still, a rumor started about the time Adelaide returned that I liked the bottle, too. As a female drunkard, my babies would be simpletons, a passel of village idiots. Shortly after the rumor started, Braeden quit visiting. He saw me once and tried to apologize, saying it was a family matter and he had no choice." She shook her head and managed a trembling smile.

Did she still love him? If she did, then Meara would be no better than Adelaide, stealing away the man Rosemary loved. "Are you sure it was her?"

"I'm sure. She has her circle of sycophants who go along with her. One day, I caught one near our farm, scared her good. She confessed that Adelaide had them start the rumors so it couldn't be traced back to her. Somehow, she managed to fool her devoted father." Rosemary shrugged. "It doesn't matter now. The damage is done. No man will have me for not being sure if I'll hit the bottle and give him idiot children."

"What a shame!" She reached for the girl's hand and gave it a squeeze. She understood from what Eleanor told her there was little opportunity for women. Most of the country girls expected to marry and be mothers. The limited opportunities to be nurses, clerks, or secretaries existed in the cities, not small towns. "Did you ever consider going elsewhere?"

The lively music segued into a slower song as a young man strolled closer, casting them both a nervous smile. Her friend nodded at the approaching male. "Here comes Jimmy Audley, the first to ask you to dance. Don't let him hold you too close. Keep daylight between the two of you."

Rosemary needed to get away where vicious gossip hadn't painted her in an unflattering light. Meara needed to get away, too. "Have you ever thought of leaving, going somewhere different?"

A throat clearing announced Jimmy preparing to ask one of them a question. Rosemary ignored the young man and hoisted an eyebrow at Meara. "Like where?"

"Ireland." It was her end destination. She didn't feel any fear revealing it. From how Eleanor talked, it wouldn't be a short trip and few would have any inclination to pursue her.

"That's a far piece, and you'd get there how? I might fancy myself an Irishman. At least, I know they wouldn't mind a woman who drinks since they do so much themselves."

Jimmy coughed loudly, choking on whatever he was going to say. He cleared his throat again and nodded at Rosemary. "Could you introduce me to your friend?"

"Of course. Jimmy, this is Meara, who's staying with her cousin Eleanor for a while. Meara, Jimmy."

She nodded at the slender young man wringing his hands in front of her. "Hello."

His lips tilted up as he bobbed his head. "I was wondering if you might like to dance to whatever is left of the song."

"I would." She dropped her glance to her feet before looking back up into Jimmy's flushed face. "I'm not much of a dancer."

He held out his hand to her. She grasped his slightly damp hand. The tingle she felt when holding Braeden's hand didn't exist with Jimmy. All she felt was slippery sweat, which would make it hard to hold onto his hands while dancing.

"Don't worry about your dancing skills. It might be better if you looked out for your toes. Mine are sorely lacking, but I do try, which is more than some of the village bachelors do." He angled his head toward the young men leaning against one wall, talking and watching their slow process across the dance floor.

He held their joined hands out high at a rigid angle before placing his free hand on her waist. Should he be doing this? She looked around at the other couples and saw they had their arms arranged in a similar fashion.

"Meara, as the woman all you have to do is follow my lead. If I step forward, you step backward. I guide you across the dance floor as if you were a ship."

A giggle escaped as she imagined how many girls would enjoy being compared to a ship. A doe, a flower, a starry night, even a summer's day would be flattering, but not a ship. "Lead away."

They made several slow turns as the song wound down to an end. Maybe dancing wasn't that hard.

AS THE NIGHT wore on, she pulled Rosemary into the circle dance, although usually a different village bachelor held her other hand. The names ran together with multiple Williams, Roberts, and Davids. The songs were lively and partners plentiful, but her concern was with Rosemary, who often sat on the bench alone. Occasionally, another girl sat down beside her, but usually never stayed long.

Out of the side of her eye, she kept track of Adelaide and Grayson. Adelaide, she wanted to avoid at all costs, while she needed to talk to Grayson. Braeden promised his brother would serve as a go-between for the two of them. Perhaps he'd already received a letter, although it had been little more than a week since Braeden left.

Older couples and families straggled out, leaving mainly the young people and a few older chaperones. Meara glanced around for both Rosemary and Eleanor. Her hostess sat between two middle-aged matrons chatting away while Rosemary stood against the wall with one hand balled by her side while a male held her other hand and leaned close. Whatever was being said did not please her new friend. Perhaps she should interrupt. That's probably what friends did.

Her determined stride would have taken her straight to Rosemary's side, but Grayson neatly inserted himself in front her before she could reach her friend.

"I believe this is my dance." He held out his arm and waited for her to place her hand on it.

He hadn't asked, just appeared as if they had an understanding. They did. One that revolved around him relaying information from his brother. Over his shoulder, she could see Rosemary mouthing words and pointing to her left. Grayson spun her in a series of fast turns that also foiled her sense of direction. Where should she be looking?

"Can I walk you home tonight? We need to talk."

Why couldn't they talk now? Her eyes traveled over the intent faces watching them dance. Not a good place, each person seemed more interested than the last. Some offered broad grins, usually the men, while some of the women gave her speculative stares. A blonde woman bedecked in a fancy party dress stared at her as if she could strangle Meara with her bare hands. *Adelaide.* That must have been what Rosemary was pointing at.

"You can walk us home, but you might need to dance first with Adelaide."

Grayson peered over her shoulder. "I see what you mean. My brother would not thank me for bringing the wrath of Adelaide down on you."

Instead of answering verbally, she settled for a small nod, and then the dance was over. Grayson gave her a nod before heading over to claim Adelaide. Rosemary met her, having extracted herself from her clinging vine suitor. She grabbed Meara's hands and pulled her out of the barn into the cool evening air. There were several couples outside with their heads close together.

"Let's walk." Rosemary indicated the couples with her hand. "I would hate to ruin someone's wooing."

They walked a few steps before Rosemary whistled, startling

Meara. "I knew when I saw you that you'd stir up some sparks, but I had no idea. Adelaide's steamed that your name is on everyone's lips and her newly designated beau danced with you."

"Not for any wooing purposes. He was being nice."

"That may be. All Adelaide will see was time not devoted to her."

Meara's shoulders went up in a shrug. "What about that man holding your hand?"

"Ian." She spat on the ground. "He's not courting me. Since no one else is, he figures I'm good for a romp in the hay and nothing more. Ireland is sounding better to me all the time."

"I can see why. Say nothing. I need to make plans, but I'll let you know when I'm ready."

Eleanor had ventured outside the barn calling her name.

"I need to go. My cousin is looking for me."

She turned toward the barn, but Rosemary held onto her hand and whispered in her ear. "Work fast, Meara. You have an enemy in Adelaide. With Braeden gone, she's desperate. She'll do anything to ruin your reputation in the village." The woman dropped her hand, turned with an abrupt pivot, and walked off into the night.

Chapter Fifteen

"THERE YOU ARE." Eleanor's voice carried, causing Meara to turn.

"Are you ready to go?" Her voice didn't portray any of the trembling she felt at Rosemary's ominous warning. If she told anyone else, he or she would call Rosemary the odd duck and ignore whatever she said. She glanced back at the dark woods behind her with a type of affection. Few people would enter the woods at night. Adelaide would not be one of the bold ones.

The lit lantern in Eleanor's hand cast a small circle of light around her barely three feet in any direction. While it was better than walking in the dark, their time would be slow. A basket hung on the woman's other arm. "I got your boots. You'll want to put them on before we leave."

Normally, yes, but her eyes stayed on the open door of the barn. Silhouetted figures stood in the opening. She couldn't tell who was who. Apprehension danced up her spine. Even now, Adelaide could be staring at her, planning something. If she were as truly desperate as Rosemary indicated, then she needed to hurry. Plan her departure and get out of town fast.

Meara grabbed the basket with her boots in it. "Let's go now. It won't be the first time I walked through the woods in these slippers." Her lengthening strides took her outside the circle of light, but she could still hear her companion's grumbling.

"I don't know why you're in such a hurry to be gone. A person would think you'd be tired with all the dancing you did."

Her muscles ached, but the possible scenarios her mind manufactured kept her moving. Her pace kept her out of the light and in danger of stumbling across a tree root. Necessity made her stop and wait for Eleanor to catch up. The moist earth scent competed with the sharp green smell of the undergrowth. A pungent ammonia note informed her that an animal had passed not too long ago. She closed her eyes to try to isolate the different aromas while waiting for Eleanor.

The breaking of twigs and rustling of leaves had her eyes opening in alarm. There should be no reason for Eleanor to run unless Adelaide had decided to wreak vengeance on the woman. She dropped to the ground, feeling for a tree branch or rock in the dimness. Another branch snap had her stiffening. If she could see nothing, that meant whoever was behind her couldn't either. Her heart skipped a beat as she crouched in the dark.

A masculine voice called out. "Meara. Where are you? I know you can't be that far ahead. I just passed Eleanor on the path."

Grayson, of course. He'd mentioned walking her home. Her fingers loosened on the branch she held and let it drop.

"Grayson." Her voice trembled as she whispered his name.

"I said I'd walk you home."

The words sounded overly loud in the dark forest. A flurry of wings and some chattering indicated she wasn't the only one who thought so. "Don't talk so loud."

"Why?" Grayson's hand reached out and swept over her head. "Where are you?"

"On the ground, squatting." It didn't seem prudent to mention she was preparing for an assault from his newest love interest. The man could easily be led by a pretty face, false compliments, and pouting lips. It would be better to say nothing. Anything she told him in confidence could reach Adelaide.

Her fingers reached out and encountered the rough texture of a shagbark tree. The tree balanced her as she stood up in the dark. In the distance, she could see the warm glow of the lantern. Grayson needed to go. She shifted her feet, rocking on one foot, then the other. He could have news about Braeden, but she didn't want him here. Adelaide's cloying perfume wafted off him.

Eleanor's whistling interrupted the night and signaled her approach. Grayson glanced back at the approaching woman. "I thought you'd want to know about Braeden."

"I do." *More than anything. Talk now, because I may be gone on the morrow.* She inhaled deeply, calming herself enough to say," Do you know anything?"

He shook his head. "My brother isn't much of a writer. He told me to take care of you."

The words cheered her, although they were general enough. The males on the outside of the walls believed women were incapable of taking care of themselves. It would be normal to ask his brother to look after her. The better question would be what did *look after* entail.

Eleanor and her light had reached them. The oil lantern threw shadows on Grayson's face, making him look sinister, but that could be her fear playing tricks on her. "Thanks, Grayson." She waved, hoping he'd take the hint. "I know you want to get home now. Morning comes early."

"Meara Cleary, watch your manners." Eleanor smiled at Grayson. "We have the escort of a handsome Douglas brother, which should make us the envy of all the single girls." She punctuated her statement with a giggle.

Perhaps men weren't the only one led by a pleasing face. She angled her head, trying to convey a message without speaking. For it to work, it would involve actual eye contact, which she didn't have. Grayson held out his bent arm, and Eleanor placed her hand in it as if readying themselves to walk to the dance floor.

Meara had no choice but to fall behind, close enough to hear, but unable to exchange any significant looks. The conversation started out about crops, weather, and upcoming marriages. Tired, she had a challenging time putting one foot in front of the other, when she heard Grayson ask a strange question, then another.

"Where were you when the convent caught fire?"

It was an odd change that raised the short hairs on the back of her neck. She expected the woman to insist she was sleeping. Most of the good villagers would have been snug in their bed.

"You mean bombed. The convent was bombed, then a fire started."

An indrawn breath meant this was news to Grayson. She hadn't even mentioned it to his brother. If she had, it would have led to other questions, such as how did she know.

"Why would you say that?" His question sounded curious, not exactly dismissive.

The woman giggled, making Meara cringe. Apparently, her hostess had more than her share of the hard cider served at the dance.

"Say what?"

"About the convent being bombed by the Germans."

"I never said anything about Germans." Her tone leaned toward belligerent.

This wasn't going well at all. Meara had never seen her friend tipsy before, but she'd witnessed Sister Augustine after she imbibed too much of the sacramental wine. She, unfortunately, had told too many of the sisters what she thought of them. The convent had felt like a silent order for a few weeks. The last thing she needed was for Eleanor to do likewise.

"Who else would bomb the English countryside?" Impatience colored his words.

It was hard to tell if he was upset at Eleanor's less than sober state or suspected her of backtracking. For all she knew, Grayson's presence indicated a threat, an unexpected one. If he walked them all the way home, then he'd know where she lived, even though he might already know from strolling or hunting in the area.

"Aren't you going into the city tomorrow? You'll need a good night's sleep. We appreciate your company, but we know the way back." Her plan was to get him gone before coming too close to the cottage. It wouldn't take a genius to figure out where they lived from watching for smoke or listening for noise if they came close enough.

"Grayson, Meara's right. You need to hurry home." Eleanor finally seemed to understand the threat the man posed.

A branch broke nearby, causing Meara's breath to stop as she considered what it could be. It could be anything from a badger to a fox, although she suspected a fox wouldn't step that hard. Grayson was the first to break the quiet.

"As I remember, you two are going with me."

Only hours ago, she thought the idea a godsend. Now it felt more like a trap. Everyone would know where she was.

Eleanor gave a girlish giggle and gave Grayson a playful push. "You're so right. You must be the smarter brother."

"I think so." His voice warmed with the assertion.

His reply made her roll her eyes. Braeden had proven himself the smarter brother by leaving. The nearby leaf rustling chilled her blood. Since Eleanor told her bears and wolves no longer existed in the woods, she didn't fear them. No, her thoughts rested on a more dangerous predator.

Just when she was sure Grayson would walk them to the door, he changed his mind. "You're right. I need to be getting back."

Eleanor dropped his arm and held up the lantern. "How will you see?"

He pulled a metal cylinder out of his pocket. "I have my torch." A thumb press powered it on.

The two of them listened to his soft footfalls and watched the bobbing light. Meara glanced at her companion. "He had a light all the time. Didn't mention it. Didn't offer it. He came up on me in the dark, too."

His behavior baffled her. Eleanor held the light up to her face, while putting a finger to her lips, then turned it off. The sounds in the woods grew louder as the two of them stood and waited. A muttered curse, then a sound of footsteps going the other way.

"She'll have to hurry to catch up with Grayson. When did you know she was following?"

Meara reached out for her friend's hand, and they shuffled slowly in the dark. "Do you have any matches?"

"No, I used my last one at the dance to light the lantern. Even so, I wouldn't light it if I had one, especially with us being followed. It's better if we don't talk."

Unknown threats lingered in the darker areas on the path. Meara shrunk away from bushes' outstretched branches. After they touched her and their identification was certain, she allowed herself to breathe. Stones, broken branches, and raised tree roots took every opportunity to trip them. Since neither of them stumbled at the same time, they could prevent the other from kissing the ground. They finally reached the cottage where Oscar met them with a plaintive cry.

Eleanor threw the latch and opened the door to the dark interior. "We should make sure all the shutters are closed before we light the lantern."

A spill of moonlight illuminated most of the windows making it easy to find and latch the shutters. With each one she closed, the room grew darker until finally, she could see nothing. The sizzle of a struck match preceded the bloom of light, while the sulfur stink rode the air.

Eleanor turned in a tight circle holding the lantern aloft. "I was afraid of this."

"Of what?" Meara peered into the shadowy corners trying to see what hid there. "I don't see anything."

"It's more of a feeling. Someone has been here. They were careful not to make a mess, perhaps to make us think everything is as it was."

The overfed cat had greeted them. "We had to close all the shutters."

Eleanor gave her a meaningful look as if her statement meant something, and Meara remembered. They closed all the shutters before they left, leaving only one open for Oscar to leave when he wanted.

"If someone was here, what did they want?"

"Hard to say. Could be an opportunist thief. Someone who came across an empty cottage. It had to have been after we left since they opened the shutters to let in daylight."

It sounded like an unplanned visit or a poorly planned one. "The jewel box!" Its contents represented her way out of here. Meara darted to the fireplace where the metal box rested beside a basket of kindling. She slid her thumbnail in the crease between the lid and the bottom and pried it open. The lightweight feel told the story before she could get it lid up.

The metal hinges groaned as the lid released to reveal an empty box. "Everything is gone!"

"Maybe not." Eleanor gave her a wink. "As a woman alone, I have to be more cunning than the average robber. Where would a robber least likely look?"

Since the cottage only contained one room, there weren't that many places you couldn't see at a glance. "The fireplace?"

"A good bet if the fire isn't burning, but that's not it." Eleanor picked up the lantern and walked to the door. "I'll go check and make sure I'm still smarter than the average criminal."

Meara's heartbeat slowed as she followed Eleanor to the door. Had she buried the valuables outside somewhere? Wouldn't a fresh mound of dirt be obvious? The lantern headed for the outhouse. Of course, who would want to visit the odorous shed?

The lantern light blinked out indicating a closed door. Seconds later, Eleanor exited the outhouse carrying a bag at arm's length.

"Looks like it's all here, but it's wet. Our burglar chose to use the facilities. Bring me the box and we'll empty the jewels and coins into it and not bring this nasty bag inside."

Meara darted back into the cottage to retrieve the box. She carried the heavy object on her hip. "We'll need to wash everything too."

"True." Eleanor waited until the open box was on the ground before pouring the jewelry into it. She tossed the bag aside. "Might as well wash it inside."

MEARA HELD UP a string of pearls. "These were going to the pawnbroker's in the morning. I think they'd benefit from a bit of polishing, if only to get the soap off."

"I'm not so sure about our morning trip."

Meara looked up from where she was kneeling near her pallet. A smooth rock she had found by the creek, a candle stub, and a needle was all she brought from the convent. Her sturdy novice's tunic she hoped to use on the pearls was gone. "My tunic is gone. Did you take it?"

"No." Eleanor swore long and vigorously. "I bet it was one of Adelaide's toadies. They only hang around her and do her bidding to protect themselves."

"Why would she want my tunic? What purpose could it serve?" The pearls dripped on her feet as her imagination took over, filling in the details of someone digging through her meager possessions. She didn't have any plans for the tunic, but it felt like a part of her had been nicked.

"Depends on who stole it. I believe they took it to prove you're not who you say you are. We need to hurry. The good news is everyone will expect us to show up at the Douglas farm in the morning for our truck ride into town." Eleanor knelt and pulled a knapsack from under her bed. We can't take any more than we can carry."

Meara watched her friend shove some underwear and a clean dress into the bag. "What are you doing? If it's about me, I'll leave."

"That you will. From what you told me about the bee incident, there's no stopping Adelaide. Now that you've been at the dance and set male hearts aflutter, she'll be twice as upset. It didn't help that Grayson walked us home."

"He walked you home more than me. Besides, I'm not so sure. What's so special about me. I'm not even sure why the boys asked me to dance."

"Ha. You're pretty and mysterious. That's more than enough." She put her hands on her hips and looked around the room. Her gaze rested on the fireplace mantle where the pictures sat.

Without needing to ask, Meara picked up the pictures and carried them over. Eleanor's tension was palpable. Still, fleeing in the night wasn't how she expected to leave. She had pictured a tearful goodbye exchanged in the sunlight.

"In my dream, my father urged me to leave. His urgency felt so real." Had that only been a day ago? "I didn't want to leave until I had heard from Braeden."

Eleanor disassembled the pictures, plucking the photos out of the frame and placing them in a book. "I know it's hard. If it's meant to be, then it will happen. He should care enough to find you. If he doesn't, then it was only infatuation. Love proves itself over time."

Her nose crinkled, thinking Eleanor had reduced their love to something similar to a head cold. Wait it out. Infatuation is bound to pass.

She carried the knapsack over to the dry sink where she loaded a cup, fork, and a plate into it. "Where was love when I needed help?"

"Ah, love." Eleanor stopped rummaging through the shelves to wrap Meara in a tight hug. "Love has been here all along. Your father coming and telling me to help you. The faeries shielding you from that nasty darkness in the forest and the evil Adelaide. I love you. Your presence had given me the push I needed to return to my world instead of hiding out in the woods. Love is all around you. Even Rosemary is extending herself to help us."

"What do you mean?"

"No time for an explanation. That will come when we are far from here."

Meara watched the woman rush about the room, grabbing items and stuffing them into the bag. "What do you want me to do?"

Eleanor paused in her stuffing, glancing around the room wildly. "There's another sack under my bed. Grab it. Put your extra dress and underwear in it. Put on your boots. Take the two canteens from the peg and fill them with water. Wrap up the loaf of bread I made, along with the smoked meat I stored on the shelf above the stove. A sharp knife and a jar of jelly should go into the bag, too."

Her footsteps thumped across the stone floor as she half ran to gather the items. Clothes, food, water, which showed Eleanor, had thought out the situation. The knife she wrapped in a towel to prevent it from cutting into anything and to prevent cutting her when she reached into the sack. She placed it on top since it could serve as a weapon. The canteen straps made an X across her chest against the background of her emerald dress.

When she'd donned the dress, she'd hoped and feared someone would ask her to dance. The lively music, the laughter, rapid-fire turns, and compliments on her hair to how her teeth shone in the light were better than her fantasy. Of course, when she imagined it, there was no escaping into the night at the end. At best, a few friends might have been her goal.

"I've done that. What else should I do?"

Eleanor cradled a small pinch pot her daughter had made. The woman was either saying goodbye to it or deciding if she should take the fragile item. Why should she lose everything of value due to her compassion? Meara grabbed a towel and plucked the item out of

Eleanor's hands.

"I've room in my bag." After she stowed the item safely beside the loaf of bread, she sat down to don her boots. The slippers she tucked into the bag.

Eleanor knelt beside the pallet, arranging the pillow and a wad of linens before pulling the covers up. The bed had a soft, rounded shape has if someone slumbered under the covers. She rocked back on her heels and regarded her work. "That should do it."

Before she could ask, she remembered all explanations would come later when they were safely away. Meara gazed at the cozy room that had become her home. Clothes and linens littered the floor. The flour tin rested on its side with the lid off and cat prints led away from the mess. In their rush to get ready, they had destroyed the tidiness of the home more than the robber did.

"Shouldn't we put things back to normal? We don't want people to suspect anything."

"Doesn't matter. I doubt if they'd taken any notice of what type of housekeeper I am. We need to go now." Her pack on her back, Eleanor swung her cloak over it.

Meara copied her actions and reached for the lantern.

"Leave it." The no-nonsense tone of her voice had Meara releasing the handle and stepping back from the lantern as if it had morphed into a deadly snake.

Eleanor scooped up Oscar on her way out. She half-turned and gave the woodland home a final look in the moonlight. She motioned for Meara to close the door, which she did.

They crept from the house as if they were the housebreakers. The moon and the stars shed scanty light, but not enough to see the ground at their feet, until a silent flank of lights floated near the ground, lighting the path.

"Thank goodness for your father and his faerie friendship."

The illumination brought reassurance with it. How could they not survive with their magical helpers? "If someone is following us or looking for us, won't they see the lights?"

"I'm not sure how faerie magic works. We might be the only ones able to see them. The faeries may be able to control who sees them."

Their pace picked up once they could see where they were going. This path would go past the convent. She hadn't ventured much farther than that in her wanderings. A loud whoosh sounded in the distance behind her. Eleanor jerked as if punched, then slowly turned. Wood smoke drifted into the air along with the crackling of a hungry fire.

Flames shot up from where the cottage would have been. Her breath caught in her throat as Meara considered that less than a half of hour ago, they were inside the house readying themselves to flee. She didn't know who or what caused the cottage to catch fire so fast or burn so brightly. If hate could be used as a fuel, a cartload must have been poured onto the simple house without a care for those inside. Thank goodness Eleanor had grabbed Oscar.

Instead of tears or an angry tirade, Eleanor turned back to the path and increased her pace, forcing Meara to do likewise. The sharp lines of the building ruins came into sight, silhouetted against the dark sky. Most of the convent remained except for a portion of the roof the fire destroyed. Eleanor followed the perimeter of the wall that encased the convent. The undergrowth butted up against the walls, making it a fight to pass.

Mother Superior didn't believe in cutting back the growth, viewing it as a second wall. A stomped down area indicated Meara hadn't been the only one to take a stroll. Had Mother Superior known some of the nuns were taking trips to the outside?

The snort of a restless horse and a stomp of a shod hoof on flagstones froze her in the process of taking a step. Had they come so far only to be snuffed out like a bug?

Chapter Sixteen

THE WARM, BOBBING lights that had kept her company blinked out of existence. A bad sign if the faeries had fled the scene. Did they leave or choose to remain invisible? Eleanor moved ahead as if she had no fears, which meant she hadn't heard the horse. A lunge put Meara close enough to Eleanor to hiss, "There's someone in the courtyard."

Instead of stopping her friend's progress as she expected, Eleanor continued, holding the wiggling cat against her chest as she sidled along the fence wall. Oscar let out a plaintive meow at his handling.

"Sorry fellow, I couldn't let you down. You'd chase away our escort. I couldn't have that."

Cats and faeries didn't mix. Something else Meara should remember. Even though Eleanor felt confident that whoever was waiting in the courtyard meant no harm, Meara had her doubts. She sprinted around the woman to peek into the courtyard. A farm wagon pulled by two large draft horses waited. A cloaked figure held the reins. The long sweep of a skirt indicated it must be a woman. The knowledge did not put her at ease at all. Were they not fleeing a woman now?

If it was Adelaide or one of her friends, how would they know their destination? Better yet, why hadn't they accepted the huddled forms under the sheets as Eleanor and Meara? The muscles tightened in her neck as she fought the impulse to escape back into the woods. Her back rested against the stone fence making herself as small as possible, grateful for the oversize weeds that provided cover.

The cloaked figure sat perfectly still giving no hint of what she must be feeling. Would someone go to this much trouble over the lack of affection from a man? Her upper teeth worried her bottom lip as she considered. Her experience gave her no basis to draw a conclusion. It might not be about who married whom. From what little she knew, marriages tended to be practical matters, especially if the selection was small. No, Adelaide could be reacting to diminished status and power. To her, it was probably the same as stripping her of her identity.

Eleanor pushed past her, causing Meara's fingers to flex against the wall. What was wrong with the woman? She reached to pull her back, but the woman was already out in the open, waving at the figure.

The cloaked figure turned and pushed the hood back. A tumble of black hair showed along with a smiling familiar face. *Rosemary?* Meara closed her eyes for a second. *It couldn't be.* When she opened them again, Rosemary took Eleanor's hand and pulled her into the wagon. This must be their escape plan that she knew nothing about. Her initial urge to burst out of hiding she suppressed as her hand rested over her heart. What if this were an elaborate scheme? Rosemary could be pretending to be her friend to lure her into confessing her feelings for Braeden or even her origins.

Her heart thundered loud in her ears as she considered the possibility. That would mean Eleanor would have to be in on the plan or at least fooled. The woman didn't strike her as anyone who could be tricked by Adelaide's shenanigans. The rude male at the dance who whispered lewd suggestions to Rosemary would be part of the scheme, too. While she accepted the mayor's daughter wielded her power like a cudgel, she doubted she could make everyone do her bidding.

"Meara, hurry," Rosemary called as she gestured in her direction. "Dawn isn't far off. Even though my father went to bed with a soaked head, he'll still get up in the morning and discover Samson and Goliath missing."

Her new friend's panicked voice convinced her she wasn't part of an elaborate plan to remove Meara from existence. She stumbled out of her hiding place and squeezed onto the seat with the other two. Rosemary clucked to the horses and pulled them into a tight circle, exiting the overgrown courtyard.

The fountain remained, but the moonlight revealed some cracks as if someone had tried to move it and failed. The bare branches of the rose bush remained.

The shod hoofs of the horses rang out as the wagon lumbered into motion. Her shoulders drooped as she took a final look at what was left of The Holy Rosary Convent with its blackened roof with a gaping hole, appearing shabby and strangely small. How could it have been her entire world? It would have remained so if the Germans hadn't mistaken it for something else. The thought had her tightening her cloak around her. Still, Uncle Simon would have rescued her and taken her back to her remaining relatives. It hadn't happened, which meant fate had different plans for her as opposed to a simple ending. Meara shivered as she contemplated the unknown future. What was so wrong with simple?

Eleanor's elbow poked Meara's rib cage. "See, I told you Rosemary would help."

"I'm helping myself more than anyone else. Eleanor spoke to me when you were dancing with Grayson. It was right after Ian made his disgusting proposition. I decided then I needed to get out of Hogstead since it would only be more of the same."

Meara understood and admired the woman's quick thinking. "What are your plans?"

"None. Except for getting out of town and not being arrested for theft by sundown."

"Arrested? Theft?" This didn't sound good. Here she thought the wagon was a form of escape, but it served as another target on her back. "Is it the horses?"

"Yes. The good news is my father's drunkenness will cause people to ignore him. I'm leaving the horses at his brother's house. People will assume he lent them to his brother and forgot about it."

"I can see the tale working, but what about you? Surely, a daughter matters more than a team of horses."

Rosemary gave a harsh laugh. "You'd be wrong. I left a note telling them I took off with a passing tinker who proposed marriage. Both he and my mother will be glad to see me gone since it's an embarrassment to have a spinster daughter at home. It makes them appear as if they did something wrong as opposed to Adelaide's vicious gossip. There'll be some talk for a while, then it will die down, and it will be as if I never existed."

The enormity of Rosemary's decision pressed on her. "You didn't do this for me? I have no mother or father, but if I did, I would be reluctant to leave them behind."

The wagon bounced as it hit a hole in the dark. "I'll light the lamps as soon as we get far enough away. I don't expect anyone to be following us, but I'm sure you didn't expect the cottage to go up in flames, either."

No, she hadn't. The memory of the hungry fire gobbling up the cottage sent a cold chill over her body. "What's to stop the forest from catching fire?"

Eleanor held onto Oscar, nestled in her lap, with one hand while reaching for Meara's other hand. "We've had several good rains recently. Anything that burns was meant to burn and season the ground. Don't go blaming yourself for another person's actions."

"It's still hard to think of the creatures scurrying for cover. I like to think the evil that existed in the dark part of the forest could be burned out. At least that way, something could come of it."

Rosemary didn't comment on her statement. Too busy peering into the dark for other possible hazards. The seldom-used road had more than a few that jangled their teeth and bones.

Eleanor clucked in her unique way. The action puzzled Meara

since she never knew if it meant agreement or disagreement.

"No, I'm afraid the treacherous actions of burning my house with the possibility of murdering us only feeds the monster. Truth, love, and kindness would defeat it. Unfortunately, there doesn't seem to be an excess of that around here."

Meara grimaced, not knowing how to reply. The wagon stopped as Rosemary pulled back on the reins. She leaned over Eleanor, handing the reins off to Meara.

"Hold tight. I'm lighting the lanterns, which will help us see better."

The worn straps felt smooth and slightly terrifying that slender leather could control two huge beasts. She pulled back hard making sure the animals didn't gallop off, leaving Rosemary behind. One horse shook his head while the other whinnied his disapproval.

"Not so tight," Rosemary called from the ground where she had one lantern lit. "My father may have a heavy hand with liquor, but he always had a light hand for the horses' mouths."

Her muscles relaxed and allowed a little slack in the reins. The fact she knew nothing about driving a team or even riding a horse was another missing chunk in her life that she intended to remedy. The wagon dipped as Rosemary stepped back up.

They bypassed the nearest town due to Rosemary's uncle not living there. It was probably for the best. If people thought to look for them, they'd look there. Eleanor's chin sunk to her chest. A slight snore indicated her slumbering state.

"Good thing she has the two of us to hold her up," Meara commented, thinking it was one benefit of crowding onto the narrow board seat.

"It is." Rosemary readily agreed. "It's also good she's leaving the area. I know you think she's leaving for you. Part of that might be true, but no doubt, she's leaving for herself, too. For a while now, there's been whispers about her living in the woods, making jellies that make women return to the pink of health. Some say she's a witch."

A coldness grabbed her belly and squeezed. Nuns weren't too superstitious, but they all universally feared witches, which explained the sprinkling of herbs to keep them away. "That's not true. She's no witch. If she were, then she'd have known everything that would have happened tonight."

The lantern light threw a shaft of illumination onto Rosemary's face and uplifted eyebrows. "How do you know she didn't? She was the one who asked me for help. Why would she ask me, probably the only person who had befriended you, to leave town? I hadn't told her about the rumors being spread about the flowers on your shoes since I didn't hear them until Grayson left, galloping after the two of you."

She had a point. Everyone knew witches were ugly, mean, and had a cat as a familiar. Oscar blinked his eyes and returned her stare. Oh no, it couldn't be. She rejected the notion as fast as it arrived. "What's this about the shoes?"

"Mary Lynn lost some earbobs like the trinkets on your shoes. She had them one day. The next they were gone. Most people know her husband, Luke, is a gambler. People assume he gambled them away. The men would tell you since he gave them to his wife that it was his right. Besides, he never acted too disturbed about the theft story. Odd nothing else was stolen."

The flowers had been earbobs, but they had come from the box, which would mean Mother Superior had accepted stolen goods. She swallowed and rubbed the back of her neck. "What do you think?"

"I know Gus runs a fair business of lending money on items. He takes them to the city and sells them for more. Some say he has a middle person who handles things for him. All I know is if you need money, ask Gus, but you had better have some collateral. I considered it once, but I didn't have anything to offer."

"Gus," she repeated the name, thinking he was the same person who took off with the sacramental items from the chapel. Her surprise almost had her confessing what she'd witnessed. She coughed to hide her change of mind. "Eleanor told me he'd take whatever wasn't nailed down."

"True." Rosemary pursed her lips. "Never heard of him breaking into anyone's house, though."

"Somehow, they'd connected Eleanor to the stolen flower jewelry on my shoes?"

Rosemary whipped the reins with vigor as they came to a paved section of road. She waited until the animals broke into a trot before answering. "That's what the constabulary does in all the detective novels. You could invite a stranger to stay at your house, and if he has stolen goods with him, that makes you an accessory."

"A what?"

"A person who helped him with his crime."

"That's not right. A person couldn't know all about a stranger's life. Then a person is penalized for being nice?"

Rosemary nodded. "I'm not arguing with you. It's the law of the land. The law of the village thrives on gossip. If someone thinks you did something, you're a suspect. If enough people declare you did something, you're guilty. It's a regular witch hunt."

No wonder Eleanor chose to keep her distance. "What do you think?"

"I think Luke sold his wife's jewelry. I suspected she knew it but decided to say it was stolen if anyone asked. I'm sure she thinks she's saving face."

"Yet, they would come after me, and possibly Eleanor, because of something they knew didn't happen." She fisted her hands as she considered the villagers. "Why would they do such a thing?"

"Jealousy. Most folks had no idea who you were before tonight. A few might have acknowledged that Eleanor had a young cousin visiting and that would have been the end of it since most knew that you'd return to wherever you came from, but not so much now."

"Why is that?" Meara knew there was no home in Cumbria to

return to, but no one else knew, except for Eleanor.

"You've riled up the bachelors of the town with your sweet manner, vivid red hair, and mystery. A few of them had been carrying on a dispirited courtship with a few local girls. Tonight, they were all vying for your attention while the girls of the town would gladly push you into a horse trough or worse."

Too concerned with making the right step, she hadn't peered past her partner's shoulder to see a discarded woman glaring at her. "So, you're telling me the local single women will be thrilled that Eleanor and I died a grisly death."

Her friend shrugged. "You make it sound so harsh. Since they didn't set the torch to the cottage, most will rationalize it as things happen. Even the ones who did will say the two of you had time to escape. In the end, they'll be glad you're gone."

Her hand pressed against her chest as she asked in a strained voice, "You're joking, right?"

"No. They'll be glad to see me go, too. Apparently, I'm a regular Delilah without doing the deed. Maybe their suitors won't marry me, but they think about me plenty, which makes me just as undesirable."

"I had no clue women could be so vicious."

Rosemary narrowed her eyes in Meara's direction. "I may be a small-town girl, but I don't think people are that different elsewhere. What was it like where you grew up?"

That was a hard one. "There wasn't a lot of men for women to fight over. In fact, most of the women had no interest in men or marriage." That was mostly true if she excluded Sister Gabriella.

Rosemary laughed. "That's a good joke. It helps to lighten the mood after so much dark talk. We're close now."

The darkness faded to gray as the birds called up the sun. Rosemary stopped the team and handed the reins to Meara to climb down. Eleanor woke with a jerk and blinked at her surroundings. Elms, oaks, and a copse of pines lined the road with a willow in the distance indicating water. The sound of other wagon wheels and the full-throated roar of a horseless carriage announced other travelers on the road.

Rosemary swung back into the wagon and took the reins. "I put out the lanterns and stowed them since most would wonder why three females were traveling at night. We're close to my uncle's, but I want to water the horses first."

After the animals waded into the nearby stream and drank their fill, they headed down a dirt path. Several cracks of the reins had the horses moving at a lively pace as dawn illuminated the forest. Meara gripped the edge of the seat to stay on, while Eleanor clutched Oscar. Rosemary stood wide-legged, bracing herself against the front bar of the wagon as she urged the horses on. Her dark hair streaming back over her shoulders made her look like a warrior princess, going off to battle.

The surrounding trees gave way to a rough-hewn fence post and railings. An occasional group of cows paused in their grazing to stare as they dashed past. The placid animals may have questioned their hurry. Meara wondered about it, too.

They pulled into a drive marked by a board with a name. Rosemary sawed back on the reins, slowing the team to a walk. "I'd hoped to tie them up front, but I'm worried my uncle might not see them right away. I'll drive them into the barn. That way he can't miss them."

Ten minutes later, after removing the horses' bits and settling a bale of hay in front of them, they left. They crept alongside the barn and ran for the shadows of the trees with Oscar meowing his complaints about such rough treatment. Meara's knapsack bounced against her back. How did Eleanor fare with a much heavier pack?

Buckshot, peppering a nearby tree, had them ducking and running. Eleanor lagged, gasping, holding onto the complaining feline. Once they'd passed the sign that denoted the farm, Rosemary signaled them to walk. Half bent over, she announced, "My uncle is quick to fire, but he's lazy. This is good for us since he won't follow."

Eleanor leaned against the signpost and loosened her grip enough that the cat wiggled free. The animal streaked in the direction of the farm. Meara pivoted and made a lunge after it.

Eleanor's words stopped her. "Don't bother. The train may not allow cats, especially ones not in a cage."

The large striped cat vanished into the underbrush. Rosemary pointed in the direction Oscar took. "Don't worry too much. My Aunt Linda has a love for cats. I'm sure your cat will become part of her collection."

Eleanor pushed off her perch. "I hope so. How far is it into town?"

Rosemary rolled up her eyes, before replying. "I'm not too sure. I always rode in a wagon or astride. I think it's two, maybe three, possibly five miles." She managed an apologetic smile.

Both Meara and Eleanor sighed as they shuffled in the direction of the road. While skipping alongside the resigned pair, Rosemary clutched the bundle she had brought with her. "We could sing, and that would make the distance seem less."

Eleanor settled a disbelieving look on the woman and continued to move forward with small, measured steps. They pushed themselves onward without a song. A wagon passed, stirring up the dust on the road and coating the three of them. A horseless carriage rattled by with a great deal of noise and smoke.

Meara rubbed the back of her neck and yawned. She knew better than to ask how much farther since her friend didn't really know. The adrenaline boost that came from running for her life had long since died away. Coupled with the lack of sleep, she could barely put one foot in front of the other. If Adelaide wanted to, she could run over her now without Meara having enough energy to jump away. A whine of harness leather, clucking, and the clip-clop of hooves signaled traffic coming. The three of them moved to the grassy shoulder. With any luck, it would be Adelaide come to mow them down as if they were tenpins.

Two mules pulled a shabby wagon driven by a woman wearing a dated sunbonnet, faded shirtwaist and skirt and men's boots. It wasn't Adelaide, which meant Meara had a few more hours to live at least.

"Rosemary Callahan! What are you doing walking alongside the road?" The woman aboard the wagon called out while giving both Eleanor and Meara an obvious stare down.

Her cupped hand served as a sun shield, allowing Rosemary to look up at the woman. "Well, ah, Mrs. Johnson. My friends and I are walking into town."

"You're headed in the right direction. The three of you look a bit worse for the wear. Would you like a ride?"

The issue about them not being recognized lost validity since Rosemary already had been. Then again, there would have to be some excuse for the team arriving at her uncle's house. Her friend turned and shot Meara a questioning glance, mouthing the words, "What should I do?"

The wagon creaked as Eleanor pulled herself up into the wagon bed content to sit beside a crate of live chickens. The decision made, Rosemary sat beside Mrs. Johnson, who quizzed her on her various relatives and recent events at Hogstead. Their discussion made Meara's stomach lurch. Wasn't the goal to go far enough away that no one knew them? How unlucky could they get to stumble across someone who knew Rosemary and used to be a Hogstead resident?

The trip went faster by mule than foot. Rosemary told elaborate stories, acting out various emotions including details of meals from the soup to the cheese. She even elaborated on dresses worn and songs sung. How she remembered such minutia amazed Meara, whose eyelids fluttered closed more than once. A jerk of the cart woke her. The sun beamed bright overhead, meaning that morning had vanished, unlike the three of them.

"Appreciate your help, Mrs. Johnson. This is fine."

Rosemary nudged Meara's shoulder and angled her head to Eleanor, who was petting one of the birds through the cage slats.

Mrs. Johnson swiveled her head and clicked her tongue. "There's nothing here. It's a bad section of town. Too close to the train station and often riff-raff hangs out there. What could you want here?"

A hand shaped sign lifted in the breeze. Behind it sat a tidy house with floral curtains and a single flowerpot on the stoop. Dark hair and exotic eyes peeked through a wedge of the window, retreating when Meara returned the gaze. "Isn't this the place you told me about, Rosemary?"

Meara pushed herself out of the bed and turned in the direction of the house as if that would convince Mrs. Johnson. A dull *glop* signaled Eleanor made it out of the wagon while Rosemary kept a tight smile and tried to wave on the helpful woman. "We're here now."

"The woman who lives in the house is a foreigner. Do your parents know where you're at?"

Under the eagle eye of her inquisitor, Rosemary wrung her hands while throwing an anxious glance at Meara. She'd have to rescue her. Not knowing what she'd say, she grabbed Rosemary's arm, nodded at the woman, before pulling her friend down the path. Eleanor was almost at the front door.

Mrs. Johnson snapped a whip over the horses before yelling, "You might ask her for a love spell! As old as you are, you need every bit of help possible!"

What type of house was it? It didn't matter since they were going towards it, only pretending long enough for Mrs. Johnson to leave, then would double back to the train station.

The door swung open before they even knocked. A dark-eyed woman garbed in a vividly printed skirt and an off the shoulder blouse stood in the doorway, balancing a toddler on one hip. "I knew you would come. I expected you sooner."

Eleanor stopped, crossed her arms, and swayed side to side. The woman's matter of fact statement baffled Meara. How could she know they were coming if they hadn't even known themselves? Rosemary stepped up beside her, their shoulders touching, which gave the semblance of unity and strength.

"How could you?" It may have been Rosemary's voice, but it felt like the sentiments of all of them.

"It's my profession. I see into the future." The woman stepped back a little, leaving space for them to enter.

Eleanor pointed her index finger and announced in a stern voice. "I don't believe you."

The woman sighed. "Eleanor, Eleanor, you of all people should believe me. Didn't I tell you your future that fateful day, so many years ago?"

The older woman stumbled backward as if hit and tumbled sideways into the grass in a dead faint.

Chapter Seventeen

MEARA KNELT BY Eleanor, chafing her friend's hand. Rosemary squatted on the other side while glaring up at the woman in the doorway. "You caused this!"

The woman shrugged her shoulders. "You could think that, but her realization of all that I told her before has come to pass. That's what did it."

A groan and a fluttering of eyelids drew their attention to Eleanor, who pushed up into a sitting position. She blinked and groaned again. "It is you, Destiny."

Rosemary mouthed the name.

Destiny. It was unlike any name Meara had heard before. Sister Clarence once told her that in earlier times people would give children names for a characteristic they wanted for their child. A male child could be named Orval or Fergus, meaning strength. Hard to imagine anyone naming a child Destiny, which didn't seem to have a clear meaning since your destiny could change.

The woman in the door nodded in her direction. "My birth name is Melisandre, but I felt Destiny suited me better, considering my work."

Eleanor struggled back to her feet with Rosemary pulling on one arm and Meara the other. Destiny stepped out of the house, jostling the baby on her hip. When they drew closer, the child grinned at them, a picture of innocence. The mother inspected each of their faces with a thoroughness that had them rubbing away non-existent smudges and smoothing down flyaway tendrils.

"Looks to me as if the three of you could use some tea. You have a long journey ahead of you."

Eleanor moaned and shuddered at the pronouncement.

Destiny held up one finger and slowly waved it back and forth. "Not you, the girls have a long journey. Your part in this tale is almost done, not quite, but close."

"So you say, but as I remember you left out a great deal in your last prediction."

The woman laughed, which resembled the soft tinkling of a fountain. If ever a laugh were magical, it had to be hers. Meara's eyes stayed with the woman as she sauntered to the door. The colorful clothes, her exotic coloring, even her cryptic speaking made her totally out of her realm of experience. When you got right down to it, most things were a novelty since she'd witnessed so little. Destiny's cottage wasn't close to any other homes. It squatted on the outskirts of town.

Eleanor followed the woman without hesitation, grumbling about needing a good cuppa. Rosemary moved close to whisper. "I wouldn't be opposed to her serving some actual food with the tea."

Destiny reached the open doorway, turned, and beckoned them in with her free hand. *The devil takes many forms.* Those words were quoted at her whenever she asked why they never left the convent walls. She naturally assumed that most of the sisters had issues recognizing the devil, which is why they stayed within the safety of the walls. She stared after the woman searching for a feeling of dread or danger. Curiosity to see or hear what the woman would do next propelled her inside.

The cream-colored walls were bare except for a picture of a tree with outspreading branches and an involved root system. The wooden floor bore a colorful rug while a couple of straight back chairs waited against the walls. In the middle of the room, underneath a chandelier light composed of hanging glass fruit, sat a round table with a lace tablecloth. A china teapot with a faded rose design sat with four teacups and saucers surrounding it.

As surprising as the four cups were, it had nothing on the rest of the table. Scones dotted with berries, muffins glistening with sugar, and sliced brown bread loaded down one side. A plate piled high with rashers of crisp bacon competed with black currant jam, lemon curd, and clotted cream for the third side.

The trio breathed a reverent sigh as Destiny put down the child who toddled around the room with glee. Only the very young can take delight in what would be considered a mundane thing.

Destiny motioned to a closed door. "I have inside facilities if you ladies would like to use them."

Without answering, Eleanor moved fast to the door and threw it open. Meara and Rosemary peered around her. A large white tub took up most of the room, along with a sink, and a strange white seat that caused Eleanor to shriek with delight. "Indoor plumbing, how I missed you!"

Rosemary turned on the faucets at the sink. Water streamed into the sink bowl. She splashed water on her face, then neck before reaching for a bar of soap. After lathering and rinsing, she patted herself down with a fluffy white towel hanging nearby.

"Ah, heaven. I'd be willing to marry a man who had a room like this."

Eleanor's smile trembled a little. "I used to have one. How I miss it."

Rosemary's mouth dropped open. "Why would you leave such a thing?"

"At the time, I thought I deserved to leave since I was unable to nurse my own family properly."

The story she'd heard before and the guilt Meara suspected. "What about now?"

Eleanor steepled her fingers together. "I'm ready to move into the 20th century. With that in mind, the two of you need to leave."

They turned, anxious to get back to the feast. Meara held up her grimy hands. "I never had a chance to wash them."

"Come along," Destiny urged her into the kitchen where another miraculous sink waited. As she scrubbed her nails, her hostess chattered. "I also made baked beans and fried up some herring. Kept them on the stove to keep them warm."

A kettle whistle swung her into action. She turned off the small fire under the kettle with a twist of the knob before wrapping a towel around the handle.

"I hope you ladies are ready to eat," Destiny announced as she entered the room with the hot water. Meara hurried around her to pluck the lid off the teapot. A plume of steamy water hit the tea leaves, releasing their fragrance. It didn't take too much urging for the three of them to pick up plates and load them down.

Destiny drifted off to see to her child as something fell in another room, followed by an ominous *oops*.

Mouth crowded with food, Rosemary managed to moan as she chewed. Eleanor's eyes sparkled as she held up her plate. "I haven't seen this much food in such a long time."

Everything on the table made Meara's stomach growl just looking at it. "It's a first for me. They never had any feasts at the convent, afraid it might fall under the sin of gluttony."

Rosemary choked beside her. Her fingers tightened on her empty plate. It hadn't been Meara's intention to mention the nunnery. She never even told Braeden for fear of this reaction. Her shoulders slumped as she backed away from her new friend.

Instead of turning a horror-filled face to her or at least a surprised one, sticky jam covered Rosemary's face as she held up a muffin. "You have to try these."

Maybe Rosemary hadn't heard. Eleanor listened, a questioning eyebrow lifting when she looked her way for an answer. Destiny breezed back into the room, talking.

"Robert's down for a nap, and the tea should be steeped now. You can have as much tea as you like, but please leave the tea leaves in your cup."

"I've cooked all morning preparing for your visit, and you eat nothing."

The woman perched her hands on her hips and gave Meara a censorious glance. "You think your friend would reject you because of your origins. If so, she's not your friend. Tell her, Rosemary."

"I knew you were different from everyone, which was one of the things I liked about you, that and the fact Adelaide didn't. I knew you had to have been hidden somewhere since you didn't know how to dance or that girls could be cutthroat. Why would I care? Obviously, my father is a known drunk, and I'm on the shelf. You could have chosen not to associate with me."

The thought puzzled her. "Why would I do that? You were the first girl who was friendly to me." Her feet carried her closer to the table and Rosemary.

"Try this." Her friend placed a muffin on her plate.

Eleanor used a serving spoon to ladled beans on her plate. "You'll need your strength after the night we've had."

The hot scent of egg custard wafted upward as Destiny plucked the serving dome off a plate revealing six perfectly golden-brown egg custards. "They were your mother's favorite."

As ludicrous as the claim appeared to be, Meara accepted it as she plucked one from the platter. Room was made around the table for each of them to put their plates and pull up a chair. The teacups were passed around, each filled by their hostess with the exact amount of sugar and cream each diner said they liked.

The strong, sweet tea with a dash of cream Meara held in her mouth, luxuriating in the richness of the liquid, almost reluctant to swallow. If this were gluttony, it's no wonder so many fell prey to the sin.

Destiny raised her cup. Her eyes caught Meara's. "What's a real sin is that you never enjoyed any feasts where the dishes outnumbered the people. No Christmas puddings, no holiday gatherings, no teacakes, not even a birthday cake. Often people embrace misery in the name of piety."

The strong box they found behind the crucifix harbored more than enough assets to fix the roof so that no one need sleep in a continually damp room. A bit of syrup for their morning porridge or even jam for their bread would have been nice. The fine tea set she spotted in the Mother Superior's office probably wasn't used for plain bread sandwiches. While the sisters suffered, Mother Superior never did without.

Her free hand resting in her lap fisted.

"Good." Destiny clapped her hands together. "I'm glad to see some fire. Your path is not an easy one."

Rosemary chimed in before Meara could. "What about me? Can you tell my future?"

"Be careful what you wish for," Eleanor added, shaking her head slowly. "I asked for the same such a long time ago. A friend threw a party and hired a fortuneteller, which we all thought would be wholesome fun. I was around your age, possibly younger. All I wanted, as did most of the girls, were fortunes of dashing men pledging to marry us and sweep us away to a life of luxury."

"What did she say?"

Eleanor cradled her face in her hand as she settled in for a good tale. Destiny stood and carried a few dishes to the kitchen. Meara debated about helping her, but she wanted to know about the fortune.

Aware of the eyes on her, Eleanor folded her hands, closed her eyes, and inhaled sharply, then released a long breath before speaking. "First, she told me how lucky I was, seeing that I would marry a man who actually loved me. He'd treat me well and be a good father to my children."

"Was he?" Rosemary, unfamiliar with her story, was anxious for the details.

"He was the best of men."

What a wonderful description. Would her mother, Sorcha, call her father the best of men? Somehow, she knew she would. "Surely that wasn't the end of your fortune?"

"No, it wasn't." Eleanor's lips trembled a little. "Destiny told me there would be a time of weeping, anguish, and anger at the world. Even at that time, I'd find my feet again, and more importantly, I'd rescue a child of legend. I'd be a part of the prophecy."

"What prophecy?" she asked before her back straightened in a jerk.

The house shuddered, and metal screeched on metal, followed by a long piercing whistle. Had the evil in the forest had somehow followed her?

Rosemary wrinkled her nose and mouthed the word, "Train."

The idea of a huge force hurtling her across the country while admitting ear piercing screeching did nothing to reassure her.

Eleanor blinked and narrowed her eyes in Destiny's direction. "You never told me what legend."

The exotic beauty pushed back her chair and straightened her legs. Her eyes twinkled as she returned Eleanor's stare. "I'd told you more than you wanted to know already."

"True. You could have warned me about the epidemic." She winced, glanced down at her hands, and picked at her cuticles. "It would have helped."

"How?" Destiny laced her fingers together, turned her palms outward and stretched. "Would you have still married your husband knowing he'd die one day?"

"I…" Eleanor paused, looking confused. "I don't know. At first, I would say I would, knowing we would have several wonderful years together, but that's the old Eleanor talking. As a young girl, I'd never really had anything too bad happen to me. My parents indulged me, although at the time I didn't think so. If you had told me Donald would die and would give me children that would die too, then I wouldn't have married him"

The lounging woman straightened up in her chair, one arm against the table as she leaned toward Eleanor. "If you hadn't married him, then you would never have had any happiness in another marriage. Most men of that time thought of wives like buying livestock. A healthy wife provides children and serves her purpose admirably. Most men do not love their goat or cow, but Donald adored you. He considered himself fortunate to be married to you."

"He did."

A loud gulp and a swipe at her eyes with a napkin reflected the woman's emotional disintegration. Why was this woman hammering away at her rescuer's fragile emotions? "Stop it!" She jumped to her feet. "There's no reason to be cruel to her."

"I'm fine, Meara. Really. The tears are those of gratitude. I spent so much time in Hogstead being resentful of what I didn't have and almost no time being thankful for what I did have. I couldn't move on to the rest of my life until I learned that. Time helped, but you helped more. As much as I might have grumbled about getting out of bed to find you, it made me feel important, needed. It also made me think about leaving. I went somewhere where no one knew me. It's time I return to where I belong."

"It is." Destiny nodded. She hooked her finger into the handle of the cup, turning it slowly in its saucer. "Perhaps we should read the tea leaves."

In a high thin voice, Meara asked. "What about the prophecy?"

"It's important. It might help you understand your path better." She gestured for them to come closer. "It's a tale best whispered between those who need to know." A cloud drifted over the sun, darkening the room for a second before moving on.

Even though it was a natural occurrence, Meara felt like someone or something had caught up to her.

Destiny reached into her pocket and brought out some quartz points. "Put one on each window sill and at the doors. Don't worry about Robert's room. I always keep that well protected. When you're done, we'll be ready for the story."

Meara raced through the small house, certain they were talking while she was gone. The task could be a way to remove her from the room so they could discuss her. The crystal columns heated her hand. If that meant protection, then they had it. She slapped one down by each window and door, eight in all. Rosemary was talking when she entered the room.

"I don't understand how I could be part of a plan when I decided only last night to leave my hometown."

The possibility puzzled Meara as well; she slowed her pace to a stroll, hoping she'd hear the answer.

"We all believe we control our fate, but the cloth for it was woven a millennium ago."

"Are you saying we have no choice in the matter?"

Rosemary's question could have been her own. She crept closer, crossing her arms, eager for the response.

"Indeed you do, however, it doesn't change your path or your life purpose." Destiny arched her eyebrows and nodded her head as if that settled the matter.

It hadn't for Meara. The woman may have spoken, but she might as well have kept her mouth shut for all the sense she made. Rosemary pushed against the table, scooting her chair back. "You say I have free will, then you tell me I have this plan that was thought out for me before I was born. My impulsive decision resulted from a jerk named Ian. It made me see I had no real future in Hogstead. What if I drove Eleanor and Meara to the train station and was back before dawn?"

"You could have." Destiny acknowledged with a slight tilt of her chin. "Come in," she waved at Meara. "Take a seat, we'll move on to you eventually."

Not wanting to distract attention from Rosemary, she slid into the vacant chair without saying anything.

Their hostess continued her pronouncement. She held up her index finger. "You would have been miserable if you'd stayed." The middle finger joined the first. "Eventually, you'd leave. If not yesterday, perhaps in a couple of months when Ian finally convinces his friends you were little more than a round-heeled woman."

An indrawn gasp, followed by a closed fist thump to the table that set the dishes to chattering, gave voice to Rosemary's feelings on the matter.

"Hold your ire." Destiny commanded in a high voice that threatened laughter. "The dishes are old, but they're all I have at the present. I'd like to keep them. The good news is that won't happen now that you're gone."

Her friend slumped back in her chair, exhausted by the could-have-beens. Meara edged to the end of the seat, anxious to hear her part in the story. Their hostess tossed back a hank of her long black hair before picking up her cup, a delay that allowed her to study the woman.

Destiny's dark eyebrows drew attention to her expressive eyes. Her high cheekbones, strong chin, and a prominent nose signaled more than her dusky coloring that she wasn't a local. Eleanor had met her years ago when she was young, which would mean they should be near the same age, yet the woman bore no obvious wrinkles or stooped posture associated with age. The sharply etched features and confident manner didn't belong to a young woman, either. There was also the child, which may or may not be hers.

"Are you done trying to figure me out?"

A flush heated Meara's neck. She hadn't meant to be obvious. "I am."

"Good." Destiny brought her palms together and gazed over their heads. Meara turned to see what had caught her attention. The picture of the trees with the exposed roots was the only thing in that direction, but her stare had become unfocused. Her voice changed as she spoke. The light, musical, playful tone had deepened to a more resonant timber.

"Long ago, before people swarmed the face of the planet spreading hate and destruction, there lived a different race. They were loving, happy beings who lived in harmony with nature and all its living creatures."

"What did they look like?" The question popped out before Meara thought it through.

Destiny blinked but continued in the same fashion. "Some say they were children of the Celtic Goddess, Danu. Others whispered they were children of Eve that she hid from God. In his anger, he made the children invisible, so Eve could never see them. Still, others concluded the gentle people who worked the land were fallen angels, too tricky and willful to remain among the heavenly hosts. Whoever or whatever they were, they were here first. People called them *The Fair Folk* because they were beautiful to look upon, both male and female."

This sounded nothing like the creation story she'd been taught, but something inside of her unfurled, like a flower blossom reacting to the heat of the sun. She knew enough not to interrupt. A slight nod signaled she needed to hear more. The entire trio leaned forward with avid expressions as if hearing a secret.

"Eventually, the Celtic tribes crossed into the areas held by The Fair Folk. As hard as it might be to believe now with our country at war, there was a time when humans were peaceful. This was such a time. The tribes and the Fair Folk became fast friends. The Folk taught them the secrets of growing plants and befriending wildlife. It was said not only could a Folk befriend an animal, but also could shapeshift into one at will. They shared this knowledge. It wasn't too surprising that some of the men chose wives from the Fair Folks since they were pleasing to look at. Their handsomeness came from their true hearts. They had no evil intentions. Children born of these unions had characteristics of both parents. Often the child could commune with nature, even read thoughts, or divine the future.

That may have been when the trouble started."

As beautiful and lyrical a tale that it was, Meara couldn't understand where she fitted in. Her hips shifted restlessly on the chair. Her mind shaped the question. *What trouble?*

Destiny leaned back in her chair, wincing a little. She held up a hand as if warding off something. "You needn't yell. I was getting to that part."

Meara shrugged her shoulders. How could she have known her thoughts sounded like yelling?

Destiny picked up her cup and took a small sip before starting again. "The people and The Folk had lived together peacefully for years. Some say it was centuries. They often had feasts with dancing that went on long into the night. The Fair Folk loved their music. Eventually greed destroyed this idyllic existence. Some say a Fey child born of a man and a Fair Folk woman caused the mishap due to a tendency to read minds. Although most Fair Folk have the ability, they have manners not to go snooping through people's thoughts without an invitation. This child, whom I suspect was a boy, was proud of his ability and eager to show off. At first, he would tell the tribesmen of those who coveted a man's home, wife, or piece of land. Once this ugliness was exposed, the accused felt free to act upon it. Soon the people were stealing, lying, and cheating one another. Often fights broke out that the Fair Folk tried to settle without luck. It is useless to talk to a man in a rage. Sometimes, they'd even attack the peacemaker. Eventually, the Folk grew fewer and fewer. Spotting one became a rare occurrence."

Destiny stopped her narrative and glanced at her folded hands. Rosemary broke the silence.

"Where did they go?"

"No one knows. The Irish believe they went back into the Earth since they were creatures of nature. All the hills and mounds you see in Ireland are believed to be the home of the Fair Folk. They even call them *Aes Sidhe*. *Sidhe* means mounds with *Aes* translated as people of. Now the leaders were sad to see this great union destroyed. Despite all the stories you hear about faeries causing mischief, they weren't like that. They don't care for the name *Faeries,* either, with its unfavorable connections to those German tales." The storyteller wrinkled her nose as if she found the tales offensive too.

"What about faeries tipping over milk?" Meara asked, having heard the excuse when a sister brought in a half pail of milk as opposed to the expected full one.

Eleanor joined the discussion. "When something goes missing, it must have been stolen by a wee person."

Rosemary fingered a strand of her hair. "My mother plaits her hair every night so faeries won't knot it."

Destiny reached for the teapot and poured tepid tea into her cup, then drank. After placing her cup in the saucer, she gave each questioner a long look. Meara squirmed, knowing it was a puzzle she was being asked to solve. Her instinct would be to close her mind. Instead, she sat up straight, her hands in her lap and accepted the question. *What could be another answer for incidents blamed on The Folk?*

She opened her mind. Once freed of suspicions and old sayings, the answers were obvious. "The sister who brought in a half bucket tended to be lazy and it takes time to milk a cow. As for the hair, anyone who rolls around a great deal as they sleep is bound to create tangles. As for misplacing things, often you put something in the wrong place. Then there is always the possibility it was stolen."

"Excellent. I'm glad you're using your mind instead of relying on other people's beliefs. I think there are so many ugly stories about The Folk playing tricks on humans. These tales probably sprang up because people missed them and resented their departure. Soon, they forgot the magic that made their gardens grow well and put fish on their hooks. Life became a struggle they never blamed on themselves but blamed on beings so pure in heart they couldn't bear to be around evil."

The well-told story answered many questions, but not the one that burned in her. "What does this have to do with me and my purpose in life?

Chapter Eighteen

T HE LOCKET HUNG heavy on Meara's neck. Her fingers tugged at the chain, pulling it away from her body. Normally, the only thing she had left of her parents gave her comfort, but today it felt like a burden.

"You're feeling your purpose, little one."

Her fingers stilled on the necklace long enough to glance at Destiny who appeared smug with a sly smile and knowing eyes. "It's the necklace. It feels heavy all of the sudden."

"Can I see it?"

Meara corralled her hair with one hand and carefully pulled the necklace over her head, making sure the chain didn't get tangled in her wayward curls. She held out the necklace to Destiny who pointed to the tablecloth. Instead of picking it up, her hands hovered over it. Emotions chased over her face before she finally released a gusty exhale.

"Objects hold energy. They have memories. Each person who touches the object leaves something behind. This is why I chose not to touch the necklace. I do not want to muddy its connection to you. There's much love contained within it."

The thought of her parents adoring one another pleased her. "My mother loved my father dearly. She left country and family for him."

Destiny bit her lips as her hands continued to hover over the locket. "I think there's something else here. Let me see what it is."

The dull locket lay against the tablecloth looking hardly different from when she rubbed the jewelry cleaning solution off. What if she accidentally rubbed away the memories or the love?

"Aha, I got it. Your father was an unusual man."

Even though she knew little about men and their ways, she knew her peaceful father didn't fit in with the boisterous crowd. It was no wonder the people took an immediate dislike to him when he inherited his cousin's farm. Her short experience in the world proved people tended to dislike anything different.

"There's a protection charm mingled with a look-away spell. This kept your mother safe. It also protected the locket."

"How so?" Even though she could have done little as an unborn babe, she'd felt sad for her mother who most likely witnessed her husband's death as she fled for her life.

"Your mother reaching the convent wasn't miraculous. It was magical. So much could have happened but didn't. She was meant to make it and give birth to you. In doing so, she released the next envoy into the world. Perhaps our last chance to reach The Folk before they blink out of existence altogether."

Envoy? Her? She was missing something. Her cupped fingers went up to her chest to indicate herself. "Why me? Why not send someone else more capable? Why will The Folk vanish? If they've lived this long, aren't they eternal?"

Rosemary put both elbows on the table. "How do I figure into this?"

Destiny cocked her head as if listening to something. Her chair tumbled to the ground as she stood abruptly. She placed her ear on the doorframe before announcing, "The train is coming. The one you need to be on. I'll make you a basket. Do you have money for passage?"

Eleanor held up her knapsack. "I'd hope to sell something at the pawnbroker."

Destiny shook the sack. "Old Wally wouldn't give you much. I'll take the pearls and pay for your passage. Once you arrive at Eleanor's old town, it will be safe to sell the others. Keep the emerald necklace. You'll need it to pay the gypsies for safe passage to Ireland."

Rosemary echoed the woman. "Emerald necklace? Gypsies? Ireland?"

The pearl necklace ended up beside the teapot as Destiny responded to the child's cries. Rosemary darted off to make use of the facilities, while Meara stood poleaxed, unsure of what an envoy was and how she'd reach The Folk and ensure their continued survival. Every day, something new, complex, and often frightening faced her.

"Let's go!" Destiny threw the door open. A sleepy child peeked over one shoulder as the woman led the way in long ground-eating strides. "No reason for the engineer to stay any longer than it takes to restock the train. If we buy tickets, he has to wait for you."

Meara closed the door to the house, unsure if she should lock it. Rosemary loped beside Destiny, while Eleanor struggled to keep up. Clearly winded, she asked, "Won't there be another train if we miss this one?"

This caused Destiny to stop and regard Eleanor with wide eyes. "This is the last possible one." Then she broke into a trot, causing the babe to bump up and down against her shoulder. The child laughed from to the motion.

Meara didn't feel like laughing. She wasn't sure what she felt as she galloped behind Destiny. The sound of Eleanor's breathing became more and more distant. Her hand brushed Rosemary's shoulder.

"Eleanor can't make it. We need to slow down."

Both Meara and Rosemary slowed, which earned a censorious look from Destiny. "Too many people died so you could leave. I can hide Eleanor since she carries no magical taint. Those that are after you sense your movements. They'll take many forms. Be alert. I put the jewels you need to barter in your bag. Remember the emeralds are for the gypsies."

Destiny took off in a sprint after her ominous speech. Meara had no choice but to run after her. They reached the ticket office the same time the train pulled in. The white-haired ticket agent nodded at them.

"You barely made it. How can I help you ladies?" His lips stretched wide in a smile, showing yellow teeth and an empty spot where one used to be.

"Two tickets to Swansea."

The agent named the price and money was exchanged. Tickets in hand, Destiny herded them in the direction of the coach cars. In the distance, she could see Eleanor sitting in the grass with her hand held up. Meara knew it was goodbye. A bittersweet one for someone she'd only known briefly but had done so much for her. She'd taught her how to think for herself.

A few interested faces looked out the coach car window. Destiny drew them to a stop and huddled them together to whisper her final instructions. "I've not had time to give you details to my satisfaction, but there are many along the way who will help you. As you know, your father was in good with The Fair Folk. They gave an emblem of their devotion to him."

Meara's hand went up to her necklace that warmed under her fingers.

"It's not the necklace. Something is buried on the farm he'd inherited. Right now, you must make your way to the Cleary family where you'll find many allies. Rosemary, your job is to be the guardian. At no time leave Meara alone or unprotected."

"How can I protect her?"

Destiny ignored the question as she hissed the rest of the instructions. "At Swansea, there will be a small craft called The Humble Maiden. They'll take you across. In Ireland, you'll meet a band of gypsies. Make sure it is Red Monesha's caravan. I'd trust no other. Keep going. Never stop. The world is depending on you."

The soft hand of the child reached out and rested against her cheek. Meara smiled at the child who echoed Destiny's words in a childish drawl. "On you."

A long, shrill whistle broke the moment. The conductor walked by while yelling. "All aboard that's going aboard!"

They sprinted to the open car door as Destiny yelled after them. "Heed the necklace. It recognizes the closeness of evil."

A woman near the front of the train grumbled. "Goodness! That woman sounds like one of the Old Testament prophets. I guess that's what you get in these backwoods places."

The man next to her cut his eyes in their direction before murmuring, "Hush, dear."

Two empty seats near the back served as their destination. Rosemary dropped to the padded seat with a sigh. Meara joined her and twisted to look out the window at the departing countryside. Destiny was in the process of helping Eleanor stand while the child stood transfixed, waving at the train. She knew with a certainty that he could see her.

Her fingers wrapped around her locket, searching for some type of reassurance as she pushed out into a world she knew nothing about. The necklace grew cooler and lighter as the train gained speed. Odd, it was probably her imagination. A few surrounding passengers conversed in hushed tones while others slept or read. A foursome of men played cards. Rosemary glared at each one in turn.

The angry, determined demeanor was something new for her friend. She'd demonstrated outrage, but this dogged expression with the tight jaw and heated eyes was something else altogether. "What are you doing?"

"I'm protecting you. It's my job to determine who is a threat. Right now, I think it's that elderly lady across the way."

Meara glanced at a diminutive woman dressed in black, knitting a blanket of sorts. As if she could feel her gaze, the woman looked up and gave them both a sweet smile, which she returned.

"Definitely not."

Rosemary puffed up similar to a Bantam rooster, sure someone was infringing on her territory. "Didn't you read The Wizard of Oz?" At Meara's blank look, she continued. "Oh, I forgot. It probably wasn't recommended reading in the convent." She held up one hand in a dramatic gesture. "There was this annoying old lady who no one thought was more than an annoying old lady, but she was really a wicked witch." Rosemary folded her arms as if that ended the conversation.

"You ever wonder if accused people could be innocent? You yourself were blamed for stuff you never did."

"True." Rosemary grimaced, possibly thinking about those who chose to blacken her name. "It works the other way, too. Often people that get all the praise and compliments are undeserving."

It wasn't a stretch to know to whom Rosemary was referring. "Sometimes, they may deserve their good reputation."

Her friend gave her a narrow-eyed glance. "I assume you're thinking of Braeden."

The mention of his name had her wiggling in her seat. She had been, but was also aware Rosemary had dated Braeden briefly before Adelaide had settled on him.

"Braeden only had eyes for you. He may have thought he was clever, but why would he up and join the service when the war had been going on for more than a year? Did he suddenly get patriotic? No. I know he was trying to get out from under Adelaide's thumb."

Her friend's animated face displayed none of the rage Meara expected. She knew and still drove her to safety. Even now, she was on a voyage to who-knows-where with her. "Do you care if Braeden likes me?"

Rosemary intertwined their fingers. "Did you forget my rule? Anything that upsets Adelaide's plans makes me happy. Braeden is a fine fellow, but I knew we'd not make a match of it. Didn't mean I wanted him with Adelaide though. He tried to stop the rumors being spread about me, which only made it worse."

The idea that Braeden defended Rosemary suited the man.

"You're fine with me liking him then, though it's not like I'll ever see him again." A dull ache started in her chest and spread out as her nose took the inopportune time to run. Meara used her hand to shield her dripping nose. "Do you have a handkerchief?"

Her friend pulled her bag onto her lap. "I think so." She untied the drawstrings and pulled the opening wide. She yelped, then grabbed Meara's arm. "Look."

On top of the folded clothes rested a dark gun, next to a sheathed knife. "Oh, my goodness! Destiny wasn't kidding."

"I wonder if it's loaded?"

A few people slept in the car while the rest ignored them. They wouldn't be so calm if they knew a possibly loaded weapon sat inches from them. Meara stared at the harbinger of death, wondering how someone could point this weapon at someone else and pull the trigger, knowing the outcome. Even now, Braeden would be trained to do that very thing. It made her tremble. Would he come back the same person? She doubted it. Eleanor's reminder that war changed people didn't go unheeded. She meant the soldiers, but the crimson stain touched everyone, from battlefield nurses to children left without a father.

The sun shone outside the windows as the train clacked against the rails. A tractor worked one field while the remaining fields stood fallow. One of the card players put down his hand and peered out the window. "A lot of fields unplowed with England's sons off to war."

The man across from him gave him a dark look while the one beside him replied. "Not enough workers, which means not enough food."

The man had a point, but all she saw was four able-bodied men that weren't fighting on a foreign shore. Did that make them smarter than Braeden or just self-serving?

A rib nudge brought her attention back to Rosemary, who was waving a clean kerchief. "Clean up. I checked to make sure it was unloaded since loaded would just be stupid."

The cloth covered her nose as she tried to talk, sounding as if she were in a tunnel. "You're right."

"You have a clue how you're going to save the world?" Rosemary asked, managing to keep her face expressionless as if she just asked about picking berries.

Her eyes cut to her friend's, who had a definite sheen of curiosity. The woman thought she knew something more than she did. The two of them had sat and listened to the same story about half-fey kids who sowed dissension in the perfect world. During the recounting of the story, she had felt a wave of recognition. No one would have told her that story before. She doubted few people knew it. Perhaps her mother or father had mentioned it as she grew under her mother's heart.

"I'm clueless. I hope when I reach my uncle's, he'll know what to do." Someone had to know more than she did. The locket lying against her skin warmed. What were the exact words about heeding the locket? Wasn't Destiny going to read the tea leaves? Their abrupt departure had upset that possibility.

A large boom sounded in the distance, causing a few of the women in the car to yelp in distress. The men crowded the windows as the train continued to chug along. Meara angled her body, trying for a clear triangle of space no one had blocked. A plume of black smoke wafted up as the men speculated on the cause.

"Could have been the tractor."

"Sounded like an explosion."

"Couldn't have been a bomb."

"Why not?"

"Those lousy Jerries wouldn't dare." The man who spoke stood straighter as if that gave his words a certainty the others didn't have.

Meara wanted to tell him that the Jerries dared a lot, but she didn't. She shuffled back to her seat and shrugged her shoulders when Rosemary asked what happened. For an envoy, she had to be the most ill-informed one.

After throwing out every theory they could think of, including Britain bombing their own fields to keep the enemy from having them, the men took a seat, still grumbling, taking the incident personally.

A skirt covered leg pressed against hers. Rosemary scooted the rest of her body close. Her hot breath on Meara's ear made her wince but she held still as her friend whispered. "You don't think it was someone after you?"

Her arms wrapped around her torso as she considered. "No, it couldn't be."

"Why not? Do you even know what the evil looks like that I'm supposed to be protecting you from?"

"Remember, Destiny told us to be on alert, that evil could take any form." They both stared at the woman across from them, halfway through knitting a blanket.

"That's not helpful. Did you feel anything?"

Had she felt the presence of evil? Good question, though not necessarily one she could answer. When those men had captured her, she felt terror but was it evil? Whatever the lights were, they helped her when she needed it. On her most recent visit to the convent, she'd felt as if she were being watched, but that could have been Gus. Her heart nearly beat out of her chest when she heard Adelaide threatening to mess up her face. Could the woman be the face of evil?

"I'm not sure. There were times my locket grew warm, and I sensed someone was following us, especially in the dark stretch of woods."

"No one goes there with good reason. Talk is the dark elves will lead you astray." Rosemary shivered, emphasizing her claim. Before Meara could refute her words, Rosemary held up her hand, palm out. "I know. I know I shouldn't go blaming things on elves, faeries, and trolls. Still, I believe there is something evil out there."

Meara didn't know what to call it, but she had definitely been near evil, even if she hadn't been in the presence of it. "I'd have to agree, but I have no name for it."

The conductor came through, checking people's tickets and waving away people's inquiries about the boom. "This is the country. If sunlight hits manure just right, it will explode."

A few nodded and appeared content with his explanation as easily as accepting a description of the war as an endless land grab. No, it was much more. It served as the furnace that fed the evil, which lay dormant in every person until aroused with the right fears.

The rocking motion had her head nodding, and her eyes closed.

The sound of gunfire rattled off to her right. Meara tumbled into a foxhole where a soldier with a powder-blackened face laid face up, eyes open. The red spot on his chest grew larger, reminding her of a rain puddle, if puddles were composed of blood. She backed up, distancing herself from the body until she bumped into the dirt wall. She had to get out. How had the soldier ended up in here? A short homemade ladder was at the other end, close to the man's head. All she had to do was skirt around him and scamper up the ladder right into the crossfire.

Her legs felt weak as she edged around the body. Black spots danced in front of her eyes. It could be debris from the shelling. Almost there. She mentally calculated how many steps it would take to get away from this dead or dying man. Six, maybe five if she made them big steps. Her back against the wall, she moved her right foot a few inches, then followed with the rest of her body.

Her breath came out in short pants that were surely audible, making her easy to trace. Every attempt to breathe through her nose failed. Her panting breaths matched her pounding heart. Another step. Her eyes fixed on the ladder as her means of escape.

A hand tightened around her ankle. Her heart tripped as she forced herself to look down. The soldier's eyes were on her, and the fierce grip indicated he wasn't quite dead.

"You're not going to leave me to die? Are you, Meara?"

He knew her name. The familiar voice plucked her memory. It had been only days since she'd heard his voice.

Her knees shaking, she managed to kneel in the tight quarters. Her hand smoothed his grimy hair back. "I wouldn't leave you."

"Ha!" He forced out a laugh that made his blood spew out in a gush. She had to stop the bleeding. Using her hands, she pressed against the wound, hoping to staunch the blood flow, but it oozed out beneath her hand, warm, sticky, and metallic smelling. The man she loved was dying, and she couldn't prevent it. A sharp pain pierced her back, causing her to bow forward over Braeden. Her head was close enough to hear him whisper. "You're not the first envoy I've defeated."

Chapter Nineteen

A VIOLENT TREMBLING racked Meara's body. She hugged her arms around her torso trying to still the shakes and the voice inside her head that continued to whisper her guilt. Meara resisted it, unwilling to accept she'd been responsible for Braeden's bloody death or had been fooled by whatever faceless enemy she'd been sent to fight. It was the equivalent of putting an elderly toothless dog in a dogfight.

"Meara, wake up. You're having a bad dream." Rosemary's voice, along with another whipcord shake that rattled her teeth, forced her to open her eyes.

Her friend looked concerned, but then another face came into view. The friendly elderly woman, only she wasn't smiling this time.

"Shame on you for frightening all the good people on this train with your screams and mumblings of war. They already have enough to worry about. What do you have to say for yourself?"

A thorough scolding had her uttering her own apologies. "I'm so sorry. I have a fiancé in the army and sometimes my thoughts take me where I don't choose to go."

Her confession eliminated some of the stern lines in her lecturer's face. She patted Meara's hand. "All right, deary. I wish all the best to you and your brave lad."

Meara pushed up into a seated position. All the heads immediately averted, returning to their papers, magazines, and crossword puzzles. None of them would willingly admit they'd been watching a woman twitch in terror as she slumbered. Nor did they act overly concerned that something blew up yards from the train. Maybe this is how evil made inroads. It made the bad appear ordinary or not that threatening.

People rationalized their actions no matter how heinous. It made her wonder what story Mother Superior told herself as she dropped a new trinket into the strong box. Whatever it was, it relieved her mind of any guilt. There were so many better choices for an avenging heroine than her. Even Rosemary had more gumption and guile.

Meara regarded her friend with a lifted eyebrow. "The fates or whatever decided on me for this mission could have chosen better. You handle a team well, and you bluffed Mrs. Johnson admirably. You'd be the better choice" It could be her job wasn't to be a go-between, but rather to find the one legend spoke of.

"Nice try." Rosemary knocked her shoulder against Meara's. "Besides, it might be a bloodline thing. Having a drunk and a whiner as parents doesn't qualify me for much, except holding a straight face while lying outrageously."

"Perhaps. I have the feeling your lying skills may come in handy. I'm not too sure if I have ever lied successfully." She tried to recall deliberately misleading anyone. Her lie to Eleanor was more a sin of omission.

"Ah," Rosemary closed one eye and cocked her head. "What about the story of you coming from Cumbria?"

"That wasn't my lie. Eleanor made it up. She told me people would like me better if I had a connection to the village. That doesn't count as a lie. Did you believe me?" The idea she could portray a different character, even a cousin from another county, made her feel lighter.

Her friend wrinkled her nose at her explanation. "Not really. You never complained about your family. Most girls would. You seldom talked about the local boys or even a fellow back home. A girl your age would have, especially to other girls. Let me see if I can think of anything else."

The prospect that there were more things wrong with her cousin impersonation chased away her light feeling. Disappointment settled down around her shoulders, like a horse collar, pushing her back into the seat. "I don't know how I'm going to do what I need to do. How should I act?"

"The way I see it, you're the real deal being who you are. Be yourself. We'll make it to your uncle's place. Perhaps nothing eventful will happen, such as people or evil entities trying to wipe you out. When we get there, you might have a handsome male cousin around my age." Her eyebrows went up and down in a comic fashion. "I'd appreciate it if you say I'm younger than I look."

"Six?" Meara found herself smiling at her friend, already calculating the possibility of husband material.

"No, although sixteen might work."

Unwilling to tell her friend her sharp eyes and ready wit wouldn't belong to a girl of sixteen summers, she smiled, not committing herself to anything. The conductor entered the car and announced in a booming voice, "Next stop, Swansea."

Her hands tightened on her bag, unsure what they'd do once they disembarked. The roar of automobile engines and the curses of teamsters urging their draft horses onward floated through an open window a fellow passenger had lowered to smoke his cigar. The sound of a barking dog mingled with a woman laughing. Swansea sounded much larger than Hogstead.

How would they manage? Two country girls with a bag of jewels and a gun did not make a good combination. Meara hung back, not anxious to get off the train. Not knowing what to do next caused her to rock side to side on her feet, mimicking the motion of the train. The people shuffled on the train while a few remained seated, deep into their reading or conversation, uninterested in the stop.

"We're here. Adventure awaits. I can't wait to get to Ireland and find me an Irish husband. I've heard they have the gift of gab, unlike the average reticent Englishman."

Standing on the platform, surveying the station, Meara wished she could be as confident as her friend. The acrid coal smoke scented the air while the soot clung to everything, making the clean architectural lines of the station grimy. Vendors wove through the crowd hawking coffee, sausages, and sweets. Taxis, both the horseless and horse-driven kind, lined the street fronting the station. Her friend descended the steps as if she were the queen, smiling and nodding at people. Perhaps the gun had something to do with her confidence.

A short, bald man with spectacles hurried forward. He glanced at a paper in his hand. "Do I have the pleasure of addressing Meara Cleary?"

Rosemary shook her head and waited for Meara to descend. The man threw her a tight smile and stepped back in a jerky fashion. His hand went up to his collar and tugged at it. His behavior, while odd, wasn't threatening.

"Did Uncle Simon send you?" The man nodded his head with great vigor and put out his hand. "Name's Samuel Taylor. I'm here to take you to your loving uncle."

Meara grasped his hand, which was strangely cool and damp, creating an unpleasant sensation. "Ah, thank you. I assume you have a vehicle close by."

Rosemary waded into the conversation with a confident mien. "You'll take us to our boat to Ireland?"

Instead of a prompt yes, the man gestured to the direction he wanted her to walk. Meara walked beside the man while trying to catch Rosemary's eye. Too bad her friend couldn't read thoughts the way Destiny could. If she could, she'd ask how she felt about this stranger.

Even though Destiny mentioned which boat to take and gypsies meeting her in Ireland, she never mentioned a nervous bald man. That fact and that the man knew her name made her slow her steps.

A shiny, burgundy automobile trimmed out in brass appeared to be their destination. Mr. Taylor opened the door and indicated that Rosemary should climb in first. When Meara tried to follow, he closed the door. "You'll sit in the front since you're my guest of honor."

The way he said *guest of honor* didn't sound anything like the nervous man who met them at the train station. She shot a worried glance at her friend, who trilled, "What fun. I've always wanted to ride in a car. I can't wait to tell my friends."

Meara caught the message in the words. She slid into the front seat and smiled at the man that planned to drive away with them and do who-knows-what. It would be good to know what game he was playing. "I appreciate the ride. How did you know what train we were on?"

His eyes darted side to side, probably realizing he'd been caught. The car coughed to life, and he steered it into traffic. With the top folded back, it was hard to carry on a conversation, which made it easy to ignore uncomfortable questions. The car putted down the street, where some buildings were three, even four stories tall. The signs stood at crazy angles pointing to various sites making it hard to know which way to turn.

People swarmed everywhere. Elegant ladies strolled with their parasols, accompanied by their husbands with their mutton chop sideburns and canes. A cat streaked in front of them, followed by a dog causing Mr. Taylor to slam on the brakes.

An animal lover, which meant he couldn't be all bad. Her hand covered the locket, which felt heavy. Didn't Destiny mention a look away spell? If the man had some nefarious purpose in mind, shouldn't the necklace protect her? Meara swiveled her head, watching the parade of people on both sides of the street, the man might not want to draw attention to themselves. A few turns later, the traffic was less heavy. Rosemary leaned forward and yelled. "I'm so looking forward to seeing the sea. Can you take me by the sea?"

The man grimaced, but turned left toward the sea. Currently, he was pretending to please them, but his willingness to do so would end soon. Even though she couldn't read Rosemary's thoughts she understood her intentions. Once they got close to the sea and wherever the Humble Maiden was, they'd abandon the car and its driver. Although she wasn't exactly sure how they'd accomplish such a task.

A stretch of dark blue crowned the horizon with white sails crowding the harbor. The strident call of the gulls drew her eyes upward. When Destiny had mentioned helpers would assist, she assumed it would be people. What if she meant otherwise?

Stevedores unloading boats shouted as fishermen prepared to set sail. Bells rang, small motors chortled as they propelled the boats seaward, and sails caught the wind with a crisp crack. The Humble Maid had to be around here somewhere. Meara drew her right hand up to the side of her face, trying to signal Rosemary without looking like she was.

"This is such a beautiful place. How about we stop and walk for a bit?" Meara forced cheer into her voice, hoping to mask her nervousness. She wanted to walk, which was no lie.

Taylor's lips firmed as he stared straight ahead. "No, we have places to go. Don't want to keep my boss waiting." His foot depressed the accelerator, pushing up the speed. A few of the dockworkers abandoned the crates they carried and jumped out of the way.

This wasn't working out at all. Meara had expected the man to calmly agree with her and stop the car, allowing her and her friend to escape as they strolled by a likely building or constable station. No, she hadn't thought it out at all. The scenery whipped by so fast that it made it hard to plan. They could jump out of the car, which would probably involve getting hurt. The important thing was to do it together.

A quick cut of the eyes toward the back revealed Rosemary

clutching the gun with two hands. The motion of the car caused the barrel to move wildly. It would be more likely she'd shoot Meara with her fluctuating aim.

Rosemary leaned forward, ramming the nose of the gun into Taylor's neck. "Stop now. I want to get out."

The man slowed slightly but didn't react in the way they needed. He remained calm, although there was enough of a snarl in his voice. "Put away what gewgaw you're pressing into my neck. I peg you both for innocent country lasses without the least bit of guile. Even if you had a gun, you wouldn't pull the trigger."

Meara knew she couldn't, but what about Rosemary? Her friend's jaw was tight, and her eyes narrowed as she kept the gun end embedded in Taylor's neck. The scarcity of boats signaled they were leaving the harbor and their only way to Ireland behind. Something had to be done now. Rosemary shook her head and mouthed *no bullets*. No help. She withdrew the gun and flopped back against the seat.

Taylor laughed. "Good. You two are helpless out here. Not sure why you decided to make such an idiotic journey. What are you trying to do?"

"Rid the world of evil and continue the stewardship of the earth with The Folk." It sounded stupid and impossible when she said it aloud.

"You two aren't smart enough to leave the house. Typical females. Next thing you'll tell me is you can talk to the animals." Taylor laughed long at his comment.

What the man intended as an insult suddenly gave her an idea. Her eyelids fluttered shut as she concentrated. *"Friend birds, hear me now. Help me, if you will, escape this man driving the car."*

She kept her eyes closed as the cries of the gulls intensified and came closer.

"Damn birds!" Taylor growled the words as he stomped on the brake. "I'll have to put up the top."

It was the opening they needed. Meara gestured to Rosemary, who'd already stowed the gun and was in a crouched position. A blood-curdling cry sounded beside her. The gulls swarmed the man's face, targeting the eyes. Blood streamed down his neck, soaking his shirt. Meara hesitated, wondering if she should help, when a harsh voice sounded in her head. "*You asked for help. Take it.*"

Rosemary waited beside the car. "Hurry. We need to get out of here. We'll be blamed. Everyone knows birds don't attack people for no reason."

The car door handles confused her. What should open the door didn't. Taylor's screams along with gulls noisy gulping made it hard to concentrate. Rosemary grabbed her arm and pulled her over the vehicle's side as opposed to using the door.

She grabbed her friend's hand and the two of them ran back the way they came. What had taken mere seconds to drive now stretched on forever as they pounded down the paved road. The impact shot up their legs, stressed their joints, and occasionally knocked their teeth together. After a few minutes, they stumbled to a walk. They both wheezed horribly while Rosemary clutched her side, bending at the waist. Meara blew out a long breath and then giggled as she wrapped her arms tightly around herself. The knapsack banged against her back with the action but it didn't hurt. Nothing bothered her after escaping possible death.

"We made it!"

Rosemary looked up from her position with her hands braced on her knees. "I bet we ran a mile, maybe two."

They turned in tandem to see how far they'd come. The shiny car was still visible along with the flock of gulls. No sign of the man or what was left of him. Their footsteps carried them closer to the water. The death of another human being made the mission much more real than she liked.

Small anchored sailing crafts bobbed near the shore. A bearded man waved at them from the deck of an aging craft. "Hullo."

Rosemary and Meara stopped, exchanging glances, before Meara held up a hand. Would it be more suspicious not to reply to a greeting? She didn't know. A slimmer, beardless man threw a leg in the water and walked toward them. The water dampened the man's pants only to the knee, proving the water's depth.

When he was almost four feet from them, he doffed his hat, revealing a cascade of hair. The man was actually a female. The woman smiled in their direction. "We've been waiting for you."

Rosemary was the first to respond. "Waiting for us?" She pointed back to herself as if there might be some confusion.

"Yes." The woman's balance shifted as she picked her way through the rocky part before reaching them. "My da and I crew The Humble Maid."

Her accent made her speech much more lyrical than what Meara was accustomed to hearing. It would be the way hummingbirds sounded to each other if they spoke.

"Oh." Meara's heart gave a leap. Things were starting to fall into place after the terrorizing ride with Taylor. Then there was the revelation she could communicate with animals. Maybe not animals, maybe just birds. Only time would tell.

"We were here at the right time waiting, and then the automobile roared by." She held her hand out for Rosemary's knapsack that she refused to yield. Meara looped hers around her back, not wanting to take the chance of dropping their fare for the gypsies into the water.

The cold seawater splashing around her legs washed away the taint of Taylor and his nefarious plans. She knew better than to think the demise of Taylor meant all threats had vanished. In time, they'd increase sevenfold.

Her shoulders relaxed as they waded to the boat. The sun's rays glimmered on the gentle waves. Near her knees, she could see small fish. The small grouping would open with every step, and then flow back around her. The phenomenon so intrigued her, she had no clue she'd reached the boat until a weathered hand reached out to help her aboard.

"Welcome aboard The Humble Maid."

She took the proffered hand, but glanced down at the fish. Closing her eyes briefly, she constructed a message of gratitude she hoped fish understood. One leaped in the air as she stepped into the boat. It may have been the sunlight reflecting off the creature, but she could have sworn it winked.

"Making friends, I see." The man chortled and pointed out bench seats for them. "My name's Ardan, and you've met my daughter, Shona."

The daughter nodded at them as she pushed her hair back under her cap. Ardan cranked up the anchor, talking as he worked. "I knew it was you when you zoomed by. Felt your distress."

Shona must have noticed her gaping mouth. "My da has a bit of the fey in him. He knows things others don't. He feels things from long away. You must understand since you have more than a touch yourself."

Meara blinked in the bright sun. Did she hear, right? Could be the musical accent played havoc with words. "Not me. There's nothing fey about me. Boring. Just ask Rosemary."

Her friend looked up at her name. "Fey or not, she did steal the top bachelor from the reigning beauty. Not sure what you call that, but it's as close to magic as I've ever been."

It hadn't been stealing. Braeden had smiled at her and engaged her in conversation. She, on the other hand, did nothing. Well, she did smile back, talk, and walked with him in the woods. "No magic, no spells, I swear."

Shona moved around the boat, tightening rigging and ducking under the sails until she reached the rudder. Ardan sat down beside Meara and offered her a drink from a jug. "It's just water."

Meara took a drink and handed it to Rosemary.

Ardan arched an eyebrow. "Could you tell me how you called

down the gulls?"

Her friend, who was still drinking, choked and held the jug away from her. She coughed, managed to clear her throat before squeaking, "What?"

The man beside her sounded interested as if he believed.

"I thought about it in my mind. I didn't tell them what to do. Long before I had sent a message, I believed they were purposely following us."

"Could be. The gulls are one of the smarter ones, almost as clever as crows." He nodded as if agreeing with himself.

The fact the man regarding her talking to birds as seriously as others would the weather, grain prices, or the war surprised her. Here she sat in a simple boat with strangers sailing to a country she'd never seen, but that exerted a powerful pull on her. She couldn't explain her mission since she didn't know exactly what it was, but that didn't stop it from needing to be done.

Rosemary conversed with Shona, their voices lifted on the breeze. "Do you think there are many men in Ireland in search of a wife?"

"There's more than a few. Some joined up to fight in the war. Still others are involved in the conflict in our own country. You could call it a war of sorts. Still, with your Black Irish looks you should be able to interest one or two. The accent will hurt you since the Irish have no love for the English."

Ardan, overhearing the same conversation held up a finger. "Correction, an Irishman has no love for an Englishman, but he always has time for a pretty girl no matter who her forbearers are."

His answer made Rosemary beam. All seemed right in the world as the waves moved them closer to her mother's homeland. What would she do when she arrived in Ireland? Obviously, there were gypsies she'd meet who could possibly get her all the way to Galway.

"You do have trains in Ireland?"

The man slapped his leg. "It's not the backward place the English think it is. I imagine our train system is as good or superior to the Brits'."

"Odd. I'm not sure why we're not going by train then to my uncle's home." It would be a quicker and easier route, though the train depot probably wouldn't accept jewelry in payment.

The man's eyes drifted back to shore where the car was little more than a dark dot. "You tend to meet unsavory types at the train station. It also makes you easy to follow."

Her lips twisted to one side as she considered the possibility of someone at the station alerting a mysterious boss at the end of their impending arrival. With the Germans pressing their borders, their workforce diminished, and the economy suffering, it didn't make sense why one girl on a quest to connect with her heritage would matter so much.

The swell of the waves carried the boat up high only to dash away, allowing the craft to crash into the flat water. The spray flew back, saturating her face and clothes. Shona laughed in glee as she exclaimed, "It's a fine thing to be on a sailing boat on a good day!"

The waves continued their game of pitching up the boat and tossing it down as if it were a ball. The shore disappeared behind them as the ocean stretched wide before them, stretching endlessly away. Could a person sail over the edge? She had heard mention the world was round, though. Her eyes stayed on the horizon, waiting for the slightest curve to show.

After the sun had already reached its zenith and was heading for the west, Shona climbed the main mast to a small wooden platform that served as a perch. "I can see Ireland from here."

Even though Meara strained both her neck and eyes all she could see was water. The rocking motion made her slightly nauseous, although she'd not admit it.

Ardan handed a peppermint sprig to both Rosemary and herself. "Chew on this. It will ease your belly. It's a must for new sailors like yourself. I should have thought of this before. Didn't until the two of you turned that unusual shade of green."

The leaves did settle her stomach. When she turned to thank him, the man's eyes were fixed on the western horizon where dark clouds stacked up in an ominous tower. "I'd not like to think you came this far only to be lost at sea."

A chill that had nothing to do with sea spray coated her skin.

Ardan continued to talk, but she wasn't sure if the speaking was to her or to himself. "Others have tried, but none has gotten as far as you. I have high hopes, especially with your ability to call the birds."

He cupped his hands around his mouth as the winds picked up. "Reef the sails. I'll drop anchor so we don't drift off course in the storm." The two of them worked in silence as Meara contemplated the sudden storm that had come out of nowhere.

Shona thrust a stiff folded sheet at her and another one at Rosemary. "It's a tarp. Wrap it around you. Secure anything you don't want washed overboard. Can either of you swim?"

The question did little to inspire confidence. She shook her head no, while Rosemary gripped the tarp at her neck so hard her knuckles showed white.

Sister Gabriella confessed to knowing how to swim since her father had taught her. He considered it important since his own sister had stumbled into a pond and drowned. A self-respecting English woman wouldn't know how to swim since it involved disrobing to enter the water with little to almost no clothing.

Fat raindrops fell. The first ones came slowly. The soft droplets wet her hair and kissed her face. If this was a storm, then she welcomed it. With her head back, eyes closed, her face turned upward to the rain, which felt like a benediction. A few times at the convent, a visiting priest or a bishop would come. At the end of his homily, he would hold up his hands and bless the congregation. It made her feel special that someone found her worthy of blessing. The rain similarly blessed her.

Although this connection felt different, deeper. It felt like the spirits of the ocean reached up for her while the clouds and the sky reached down to kiss her face.

"*Never worry, never fear, we are with you.*"

The concept gave her a confidence that appeared to be lacking in the faces around her. "It's going to be all right. I know it is."

Still, she reached under the tarp to tighten the straps of her knapsack. A slight thrill danced across her skin as the rain pelted them with an intensity that felt like pebbles hitting her face. She drew the tarp up over her head to block the stinging water bullets.

An enormous wave threw the boat up and capsized it in the air. Meara flew past the mast and into the raging sea. The boat crashed into the water, barely missing her. A broken spar bumped up against her. She wrapped her arms tightly around it as she searched for the others. The storm clouds blotted out the sun, making twilight dim. The waves crashed into her face, making it hard to see.

She thought she heard her name, but wasn't sure. A white face stood out near the hull of the boat. A woman was clinging to it, calling her name. The sound of her name reminded her briefly that it meant sea. She could be one with the sea.

Shona's muscular arm gestured for her to come closer. If only it were that simple. Her wet dress weighed her down while the waves consistently pushed them apart. She kicked out in frustration that she had come so far to die.

The spar drifted a little closer to the boat.

"*Why punish me, Ocean? What have I ever done to you?*"

A few angry kicks pushed her closer. Was she swimming? A strong wave pushed her back almost making her weep. Something underneath the water propelled her forward. Her breath stilled as she refused to think what could be pushing her. Whatever it was, it was big.

The creature kept pushing her onward until she reached the boat. Shona gripped her hand. "You're going to have to trust me."

Hadn't she and some sea creature made an effort to return? That demonstrated trust. What else did she want?

"Let go of the spar. I'll take care of you."

It didn't appear a smart plan to let go of the only thing keeping her afloat. Still, no evil emanated from Shona, unlike Taylor. What were her options here? Didn't she have an epiphany that she'd survive? Shona had a good grip on her hand as she loosened the spar, which the waves immediately took. A hand on her head pushed her deeper. Why had she listened? Her dream told her not to trust anyone.

She opened her eyes underwater, seeing nothing but darkness. The saltiness of the water irritated, but it was the least of her problems. An edge of something rubbed against her back. By the time she realized it, the object vanished. If she grabbed it, she could have used it on Shona. Where was the traitor she had foolishly trusted? Her lungs ached as she kept her mouth shut, reminding herself not to breathe. A tight grip on her hair hauled her up into a dark place out of the water.

"Breathe now." A slap on her back caused her to exhale hard. Meara greedily sucked in air as Shona propelled them forward until her head bounced off something.

"Oh good, you've found the seat. Grab on to it. I need to check on Da and your friend."

With a watery splash, Shona slid underwater, leaving her in the dark. The sound of hard rain sounded, soothing in the upside-down hull. She could see nothing and had no clue what happened to Rosemary. Meara should be out there looking for her friend, instead of hanging out inside the boat, gasping as if she were a beached fish. First thing she'd do is learn to swim. Anyone named after the ocean should probably know how to swim. A splash and a gurgle meant she had visitors. Human, she hoped, and preferably Rosemary and the crew.

"Got her."

Legs bumped up against her. The trailing skirts let her know it was Rosemary. She put one arm around her friend, pulling her close. "You're going to have to hold onto the seat."

Her friend breathed hard, but didn't speak. Meara wrapped her fingers around the wrist and slung it over the seat. "Hold on." At first, no response, which wasn't good. Meara's strength couldn't hold two people up. Finally, Rosemary's hands flexed, and she grabbed onto the wood.

"Thank you." Meara clung to the upside-down bench seat, winded and bewildered. Did she thank the spirits of the sea for her survival? The Folk? Did the Folk live under the waves?

A harsh coughing filled the small area. "Da, are you good?"

A rough chuckle that dwindled into a cough served as an answer. "As good as I'll ever be. I suspect the ocean will eventually take an old sea-dog like myself but not today."

After assuring that everyone was accounted for, Shona reminded them not to talk to save air. The rain slowed to a soft patter, then to not at all. The storm had passed and they were miraculously still alive.

"It's time. I'll go out and see if we drifted." Shona dove into the water, leaving the three of them. What if they had drifted farther into the ocean? Before the storm, they were almost at Ireland. Who knows where they might be?

Shona's wet head popped up beside her. "Good news. We may have lost the anchor, but the storm worked in our favor, pushing us to the shores of the emerald isle. Come and see."

It would involve sticking her head back into the water, not an idea she relished, but this time she knew Shona wasn't trying to kill her. She allowed Shona to take her hand, guiding her to the edge of the boat.

"Duck."

She did and popped up into the fading sunset and the view of bonfires on the beach. Meara almost asked why Shona hadn't told her to duck before, but the question faded as her eyes ate up the rocky hills topped with grass so green it almost glowed in the fading light. A few sheep *baaed* their protest as a sheepdog herded them home. Tears swam in her eyes as she devoured the view. Her mother had left this. It must have been an amazing love.

Her toes touched the shifting sand under the water. Meara turned to look at the capsized boat, surprised at how close to land they'd drifted. Rosemary and Ardan splashed through the water.

Her friend's voice carried. "I'm coming. Stay there. I'll keep you safe. I may have lost the gun, though."

Meara halted, pulling Shona to a stop. "My friend takes her duties seriously. The least we can do is wait."

The four of them linked arms and waded through the surf. Several colorful wagons circled a large fire, while smaller fires dotted the beach.

"They're here." A shout went up and people spilled out of the wagons, some ran toward her while others picked up instruments and played.

A woman with wild red hair, not too unlike her own, wove around women in vivid skirts, some carrying babies, and men with flowing mustaches and elaborate vests. "Welcome, welcome to the second part of your journey. We were told you would be coming in farther down the coast." Her hand flattened over her heart. "Monesha knows better than to listen to words. I listened to my heart instead and waited here. It's time."

She held out her hand to Meara who took it.

TO BE CONTINUED

Faerie Lights: Smolder

Available October 2017

Smolder

Rayna Noire

Chapter One

Ireland 1915

THE BONFIRES ON the beach picked out the colors on the gypsy wagons causing them to glitter in the setting sun. The craggy hills provided a backdrop in the lengthening twilight and created solid arms that embraced the crescent shaped beach. The deep roar of the waves swept through Meara as if her breath and heartbeat. As she stumbled from the water, Shona's strong arm wrapped around her shoulders and Rosemary's arm encircled her waist prevented her from going head first into the surf. Ardan lifted a weary hand to the people on the beach and shouted, "We made it. At the end, I was sure the sea had decided to take us for her own."

"They're here." A shout went up and people spilled out of the wagons. Some ran toward her while others picked up instruments and played.

A woman with wild curling hair glowing red in the twilight walked to them with a smile while gesturing for the others to follow. This must be Red Monesha that Destiny, the fortune teller, had mentioned would take her the next step of her journey. A hand of uncertainty squeezed her chest as she wondered if she had lost the pearls in the sea that would serve as her payment for the ride. The weight of the pearls swung underneath her shirt reassuring and puzzling her since she hadn't remembered looping them around her neck.

Meara unlooped her payment from her neck and put them in the redhead's hand that she held open discreetly at hip level, almost buried in her skirt.

Her smile brightened as her fingers closed over the necklace. "Welcome, welcome, to the second part of your journey. We were told you would be coming in farther down the coast." Her hand flattened over her heart. "Monesha knows better than to listen to the words. I listened to my heart instead and waited here. It's time."

She held out her hand to Meara who took it.

A few dark-haired men, barefoot and pant legs rolled up, waded into the surf to help the others to the fire.

The ordeal of fleeing the convent, along with being kidnapped and subsequently almost drowning caused Meara to collapse by the fire. The welcome heat warmed her while stiffening her ocean-soaked clothing as it dried. A large-eyed toddler peeked from behind her mother's skirt to stare.

It didn't take a mirror to know she must be a sight, something spat out of the sea. Her lips tipped up not wanting to scare the curious girl. The child grinned back, causing the adults to laugh in response.

The mother ruffled her daughter's hair, resulting in a small heart pang for Meara. If her mother had lived, would she'd been the type to drop an affectionate hand to her child's head?

"*She would and most likely a kiss, too.*" The voice echoed in her head. Somehow, her father made it to the far shores of Ireland, too.

"You're here."

She must have said the words aloud because everyone standing near in the firelight stared at her. She gestured to the avid faces that watched her. "I, ah, meant all of you."

No one responded, but voices from outside the circle of those surrounding her carried.

Ardan spoke to the red-haired woman. "No, I saw it with my own eyes. She called the birds with her mind. I saw them flock together, then swoop down and attack."

"If nature does her bidding, this is a sign of great power. She could be one of the chosen."

It felt like that the intensity of the gazes sharpened as she squirmed on the log, wondering if she could be the person they wanted her to be. There had to be a mistake. Did no one realize she'd been convent raised and had no information about the world. How could she possibly be of service?

A few high voices carried over the chatter.

"I don't see what's so special about her."

"I was making good money in the city before Monesha decided we had to leave in a hurry."

Someone hushed the voices, but not before Meara realized not everyone was happy about their detour. Normally, this would worry her, but right now sitting took all her concentration.

The gulls dipped in the falling light, making a final raucous cry before settling down to the beach. The wave-generated breeze caused her to chafe her arms. A flurry of hands dropped blankets and shawls still warm from their bodies around her shoulders.

Rosemary, who sat across from her, managed a short nod. Was her friend regretting her decision to chaperone her to Ireland?

In the disappearing light and flickering flames, her friend managed a strained smile. "So, this is Ireland." Rosemary glanced around at the various faces. "Everyone here is so friendly and nice to look at."

Her last comment caused the group to nudge each other and chuckle. One man whistled long while another hooted.

Meara let out a long breath, grateful for a friend who could lighten the mood. Rosemary continued to talk. "I don't know much about Ireland. What's best about it?"

Several voices shouted enthusiastic replies.

"The food."

"No, the music."

"The poetry and the magic of the tales."

"Ha, that's a good one, and you tell a mighty tale, too."

Perhaps a story, might put off whatever great and miraculous thing she was supposed to do. Never mind, she didn't know how to accomplish it or even what it was.

Meara pointed to the bearded man who boasted about the tales. "Could you tell us one? It would be welcome, especially after the trip we had."

"I could." The man inserted his thumbs under his suspenders and puffed out his chest, but glanced in the direction of the talking couple. "Might as well since Red Monesha is still deep in conversation with your friend. Well, now, ready yourselves."

A few hooted and whistled, while someone shouted, "Make it a good one, Rom."

The self-proclaimed story teller's name must be Rom. Meara glanced around to see if there were any other bearded men. Some, but not too many, and the others had grey beards, while Rom didn't.

He held up one hand gesturing to the group then flattened his palm and moved in a horizontal fashion. "Once very…"

"Long ago," the crowd chimed in.

Instead of being upset, Rom grinned, indicating this was a familiar routine. "…there was unrest in the land. Many called themselves king and their land were their kingdoms, but there was talk that one king united over all would help the isle prevent any greedy raiders from stealing from the sons of Ireland."

"Still unrest," a voice in the dark grumbled.

A grunt followed indicating the original speaker may have received a good nudge for the comment. "Be still."

A woman brought offered steaming bowls of stew to Meara, Rosemary, and Shona. Meara murmured her appreciation and dug into her fragrant stew thick with potatoes and onions.

Rom viewed his audience, dropping his hand and turning. Once assured all eyes were back on him, he started again. "The kings all voted who would be their one ruler. Once the vote had happened, they all took a knee and swore their loyalty, all except Lir. He turned his back on the group, packed up, and headed home."

"Ooh," a nearby woman exclaimed, "there's going to be trouble. Men don't take that insult lying down."

"You're right, Briana. Those who swore their allegiance wanted to go after Lir, bring him back for killing, but the newly elected king forbade it. He knew he'd need Lir's help to govern the land. He'd rather have the man on his side. The best way to do that was—"

"With a woman." Several people shouted, obviously familiar with the story. A few laughed while one man shouted, "Run while you can, Lir."

Meara glanced away from the fire and could still see the silhouettes of Ardan and Red Monesha against the setting sun. The couple glanced back and moved farther away, making it impossible to hear them. The waving hands indicated whatever they were talking about elicited strong emotions. She hoped it wasn't her. All she wanted was to make it to her uncle's people.

Rom's expressive voice drew her back into the tale. "The king knew Lir had no wife or heirs, so he picked out three beautiful sisters of high estate and sent them to be Lir's bride. He picked Eva and married her. They had two children and then twins. Eva dies giving birth to the last. Grief overwhelmed the man, making him take no notice of everyday life." Rom held his hand, pausing his tale.

"Go on!" Shona shouted the command almost in Meara's ear.

"Aye, I will. Some say the king was worried about him and sent him another sister to wed, but I think it happened somewhat differently. The sister, Aoife, was jealous of Eva. After all, she married noble man, who adored her and gave her children, while Aoife remained unmarried in her father's home. One day, Aoife appeared to look after her sister's children. She explains how much she loves the wee ones, although before this she had not been around to visit.

"Aoife always looked her best and made her manner as sweet as honey, but still that did not tempt Lir. Finally, she resorted to a

Druidic wand she stole from her father's house and caused Lir to agree to wed."

A Druidic wand? This was the first Meara had heard of such a thing. If her father had one, why hadn't he held off those who stormed his land?

"Bewitched, he married the tricky sister, and all was well for a while."

Meara leaned forward as Rosemary asked with an avid expression, "What happened next?"

Rom spun around to face Rosemary. He held up a finger to his lips and whispered loud enough for most to hear. "It's a secret, but I might be persuaded to tell more if you graced me with a smile."

A wide grin pulled Rosemary's cheeks tight.

He splayed his hand against his chest and announced, "Ah the lass wants to hear more. I must obey."

The crowd chuckled, while one man added, "You were going to go on all along. Be done with it. Put us out of our suspense."

"Very good, then." He bent, placing his hands on his knees to put himself at child level. "Lir loved his children. Perhaps more because they reminded him of his departed wife, Eva. Each day, he'd draw them on his lap and hug and kiss them. At first, Aoife considered this the act of a good father, but eventually she grew jealous. All his love he lavished on the children. As for the spell, it got her married, but really nothing more. A nefarious evil bubbled up in her heart. Something so vile and black, she dares not tell it to anyone."

A flurry of whispering sounded as Rom paused for breath. Meara found herself caught up in the tale. Stories like this had never been told at the convent, and the tales she'd heard since had not been as skillfully rendered as this one. "What evil?"

All the eyes that had been on Rom were on her. It wasn't a situation she wanted. "Please continue," she urged. Her voice sounded thready and weak.

"The children were all wonderful swimmers. Some say they turned into fish when they hit the water. They had no issue going to the river with their stepmother. She led each of them to the shore and prodded them with the Druidic wand, turning them into swans one by one. The last child pleaded with her stepmother to at least leave them with their voices so they could talk to one another."

Meara looked around at the heads nodding. No one looked shocked or surprised as he told the ending, perhaps there was more. "Is that it? What did the father do?"

"He looked for his children everywhere, but couldn't find them. Finally, one swan went to her father and explained what happened. The spell couldn't be lifted, and the father visited his children faithfully. Six hundred years had passed before the swans were blessed by a monk releasing them from their spell."

The group gave a collective sigh and muttered something about the dangers of women scorned.

A chill swept over her. What if Druids were evil? Perhaps, her father had the ability to turn children into swans. If that were so, shouldn't he had been able to turn his attackers into livestock? Maybe the story he'd told her of being killed was just a tale, not real at all. Despite the several jackets and shawls piled on top of her, a shiver started at her feet and worked its way up to her ears, chasing away the warmth. Had she'd been tricked somehow. Had the bearded man talking to her in her dreams been an illusion?

The hatred Adelaide directed her way after Braeden took an interest in her felt very real. Maybe she would have been forced to leave town anyhow, especially with Adelaide's father being mayor.

Rosemary voice sounded above the others. "I don't understand. Druids aren't bad. As far as I know, they aren't running around turning children into swans or bewitching men."

"Aye, you're right." A high clear voice called out from the back of the crowd. The crowd parted and allowed a tiny, white-haired woman through. She walked with the help of an ornate staff, and the firelight played across her wizened face. Her dark eyes reflected the light as she moved forward, stopping in front of Rosemary. "You do well to question such a shabby ending. Once the priests came, they changed our stories to suit their own purposes. Even took our beloved Brigit and made her into a sanctified saint in clean robes."

She shook her head emphatically and continued her explanation. "That's not our Brigit. She's happiest with her sleeves pushed up and laboring over the forge." She held one finger. "That's the first Brigit. Sometimes people consider Brigit to be three sisters who are the same age and face. Others consider Brigit to have three distinct aspects. The smithy is only one."

Rosemary spoke. "What are the other Brigits known for?"

The wizened woman smiled at the query and held up two fingers. "The second one is well known to all Irish wives and daughters. She is queen of the hearth and helps with midwifery and healing."

Feeling a bit emboldened by her friend's actions, Meara called out, "What about the third?"

Before the revered crone could answer, Rom did. "Ah, she is beloved of bards, actors, poets, writers, and singers since she provided inspiration." He gave a little bow, earning some light clapping for his efforts, but the white-haired woman was not a fan. She gave him a narrow-eyed look that had him stumbling backward. "Many pardons, Grandmother Biddy. Please go on."

The woman gave a sharp nod and continued. "As for the Druids, they ended up in the story because the Jesuit Brothers wanted to be rid of them and all the old ways. It served their purpose to change some tales, which worked well since only the brothers could write. The way I heard the story, the children were restored to their normal selves by a faery."

A faery that sounded right. Meara's shoulders relaxed some, but her teeth still chattered, causing the old crone to stare in her direction. The side that had faced the fire grew tight and uncomfortable as it dried. Her back, especially her backside, was still wet and chilled despite the coverings.

"The gel is freezing. Have you fluff for brains letting her sit here in her wet clothes? Go get her changed." She nodded in Rosemary and Shona's direction, too.

A couple of older women along with a young woman close to her age, stood and hurried toward her. The three of them herded Rosemary, Shona, and Meara as if sheep toward one of the colorful wagons.

One gave an anxious glance back in the direction of the fire and muttered low enough for Meara to overhear. "Grandmother was right. When Monesha hears of this, she'll be displeased since she doesn't embrace the old ways."

The remark made Meara wonder who really ran the group. They were greeted by a woman named Red Monesha. The crone who many called Grandmother Biddy wielded her own power, which wasn't too surprising since respect was usually given to the elderly due to their years. Now, Monesha might be angry? This was so confusing.

They reached the wagon painted with purple and red flowers with curly vines and closed red shutters and bright yellow stairs. One of the older women, motioned to the young woman. "Jane, you go ahead and light the lantern. Find something," she tapped Meara's shoulder, "appropriate for her to wear."

While the idea of clean, dry clothes appealed, Meara didn't care for the thought of depriving someone else of their wardrobe. At the convent, she only had one clean shift. "Don't go to too much trouble. Anything would be fine. All I need to do is wash out what I have on and let it dry, then I'll return your clothes to you."

The younger woman slung back her long straight hair as she turned to face Meara. "I am honored to have you wear my clothes. Just think, when I'm old like Grandmother Biddy, I can tell tales around the fire about how I leant my clothes to…" She cocked her head and pursed her lips before asking, "What is your name?"

"Meara," she answered softly, unsure if she should attach a last name. Her father's name, which she could have claimed remained unknown to her. All she knew for sure was his first name had been Fulmen, which meant lightning. Her mother, Sorcha, had declared to her brother, Simon, that Fulmen stole her heart just as fast as lightning struck. Still, she could lay hold of her mother's maiden name. It could serve her well since she was trying to find the family. She cleared her throat and repeated her name, a little louder. "Meara Cleary."

"Meara, of the sea, which seems fitting considering the sea brought you to us." The young woman crinkled her nosed and opened the arched door to the wagon. She stopped in the middle of ducking through the low opening. "I forgot to mention my own name. Jane of the Fox clan."

Shona and Rosemary were guided to a different wagon, just as gaily decorated, but the colors were different. Her friends entered their wagon and disappearing. For a heartbeat, desolation swept over Meara, making her knees weak, forcing her to put one hand against the wood frame to hold herself up.

The remaining woman rushed up and wrapped a supporting arm around her, urging her inside the wagon. "Sweet Brigit. What fools we've been to overlook your condition. We'll get you dressed and tucked in bed."

"That sounds wonderful." Even though she should have tried to stay awake, at least a little longer until Ardan came back and explained their situation, sleep offered a sweet respite from the out of control turn her life had taken. Maybe in the morning, a solution would present itself.

"As it should. Most of us sleep outside when the night isn't too severe."

She nodded, not sure if an answer was expected. Clean clothes and a blanket would serve well enough. The starlit sky could keep her company as she analyzed all the bizarre things that had happened so far. Just maybe, her father would enter her dreams and explain everything. "I understand."

A colorful skirt and blouse appeared in Jane's hand, which she held out to Meara. "This should do. There will be no sleeping outside for you. Gypsies are known for their hospitality. You get to sleep inside the wagon."

The older woman, who Meara assumed was Jane's mother, stood outside the wagon on the steps, but it didn't stop her from joining the conversation.

"It's best you stay inside for everyone's safety."

The ominous phrase hung in her head as Jane prepared her a pallet to sleep on. Best for everyone, which had to mean whatever the threat had been had followed her. The young Romany woman patted the bedding and grinned at her.

"Off to dreamland for you. Perhaps, you'll meet a tall, handsome man in your sleep."

The image of Braeden before he told her goodbye and left to fight the Germans came unbidden. She thought of her sweetheart plenty and their almost non-existent romance. A few kisses and a promise to wait for him was all there was. Her intentions had been to stay, but after Eleanor's isolated cottage was attacked and burned because the woman had befriended the orphaned Meara, it was clear she should leave.

With any luck, Braden's brother would explain, but she doubted it, since he too was under the pampered and vicious Adelaide's thumb. The wagon darkened as Jane turned down the light, and bid her goodnight. Meara echoed the sentiment as she closed her eyes and willed herself to think of happier things.

If you enjoyed this book, why not sample the entire Pagan Eyes series.

Leah Carpenter thought being the only witch in her local high school was hard. That was until she inexplicably found herself in the past, running from an angry mob, which turned out to be much harder. Lionel, the man in charge of the mob, holds a grudge against a girl he calls Arabella. He thinks she's Arabella.

Luckily, just about the time it looks as if she's done for she pops back into her century. This causes trouble at school, but at least she has an understanding family. What happens in the past can hurt her. The whiplashes covering her body are proof enough.

Her Nana believes she must right a wrong in the past to stay in the present and go out with her crush, Dylan. What she discovers in the past is an evil so pure that it makes her blood run cold. She might not ever make it back to geometry class or more importantly a possible date with Dylan.

Nora Carpenter is a trainee assistant physician, a part-time diner chef… and a witch. Hiding from the memory of a traumatic rape – fueled by prejudice over her eccentric reputation – she keeps to herself. Demanding work, study, and a cold shoulder to any guy that crosses her path, seem like her best defense until she starts having vivid dreams about a compelling, mysterious stranger with dark curls, sexy eyes, and a charming Irish lilt, her defenses seem to be breaking.

He says he is her soul mate – that he has conquered many centuries to contact her. Can this be real? Or is she going mad? Nora tries to fight the gentle seduction that threatens to thaw her icy façade. But when she's forced to come face to face with real evil she must call on all her magical resources, including her lover from another life, to save her.

Ethan finds himself trapped between the world he knows and the world that could be. A sadistic bully, an unsympathetic principal, and an unreachable love interest make high school difficult for Ethan. He feels like he's living a lie, trying to blend in at school to keep his head attached to his body.

Fear that he's not the son his father wants negates the support his Wiccan family offers. An impromptu trip into the future saves him from an enraged bully while instilling doubts about where he really belongs. Somehow, he must find a way to survive in his own world tossing aside his mask and doubts.

Stella's college life transforms from sweet to rancid when her boyfriend asks her to do the unthinkable. How did she end up holding her best friend's future in her hands? Anything she does will trigger the disastrous conclusion.

If that isn't bad enough add in a lunatic minister, a demi-goddess, and a walk through another dimension full of vindictive shrubbery and wildlife. It's a freshman year she may not survive.

Author Notes

Stop over at www.raynanoire.com to see what books are out, what contests are happening, and if I'll be making a personal appearance near you.

Make sure to sign up for the newsletter on the website too. It is a wonderful way to get free stuff included stories, swags, books, and Amazon gift cards.

Check out my blog www.raynanoire.weebly.com, which features a weekly Totem Animal Blog and Friday Book Reviews.

You can hang out with me at:

Facebook
facebook.com/AuthorRaynaNoire

Twitter
twitter.com/raynanoire